WILI

PAUL PI ... and was ec ... s in Bushey, ...ordshire and at Leicester University.

He has been a journalist since 1974, and has a special interest in South American politics. He writes mainly for *The Times*, and *Wild About Harry* is his first novel.

PAUL PICKERING

Wild About Harry

FONTANA/Collins

First published in Great Britain by
George Weidenfeld & Nicolson Limited 1985
First issued in Fontana Paperbacks 1986

Made and printed in Great Britain by
William Collins Sons & Co. Ltd, Glasgow

To Alice

I would like to thank Caroline Dawnay, Victoria Petrie-Hay and the many people who helped me in Paraguay and would prefer to remain anonymous.

P.P. London 1984

Prologue

His blood looked black in the fading light. Above him towered dusty red thunderclouds as the dark jungle hills glowed with a defiant wicked green. A white cattle egret turned gold for an instant as it flew above the valley, catching the rays of the retreating sun. In the distant west a river (or it could have been a lake as he had never been there) still managed to hang onto the day and shone like a polished pewter christening mug. But the trickle of blood was black against the vellum white of his skin and he felt like a dry and tiny fossil surrounded by the immense chattering primeval landscape. If you gazed at it too long that splendour could make you giddy.

Instead he reached down to snip a sucker from the base of the Peace rose he was pruning and pricked himself again. It's not my day, not my day at all, he thought and wiped his hand on rough khaki shorts above knees ghostly pale in the evening light. He stood up and put four bony fingers into the small of his back which had begun to hurt from bending and ferreting about and he reflected it had been one of those interminable days when he could not find enough to fill the time and England and home were constantly on his mind. In England you didn't have sunsets that looked as if the devil himself and all his angels were about to ride out of clouds infernally lit from within. There was something satanic about the landscape even when the sun was up and the sky enormous and blue and he hadn't felt at home there in more than twenty long years. Perhaps one never did in a place one is billeted, posted or otherwise deposited in the service of Her Majesty. He had wondered all day if anyone out there thousands of miles beyond the river still cared if he existed, or had they forgotten him entirely? For two winters he had been tensed for retirement, aching for release like a greyhound in the traps as the Birthday Honours List was announced on the World Service. I don't expect a knighthood; yes I bloody do. He snipped away the sucker and felt better.

He turned to a large pink standard rose, peering slightly but doing the job methodically and well, to the best of his ability, as he had always done with everything. Harry insisted on the best from others and reflected gloomily such devotion to duty instead of politics was probably why he was in the middle of nowhere on an almost precipitous hill above a tangle of jungle rivers pruning roses as out of place as himself. I have never been homesick before, he mused, not even at school, and put the small bundle of cuttings into a sack marked US Aid, No Hooks. He smiled at himself. I'm becoming a bit of an old woman. He stretched and threw his clippers into the well-intentioned American sack as he leant against a tree to admire what was left of the evening. It was hard now to make out the numbers on his wristwatch and the shrubberies of the garden were inky. Fireflies began to dance on a nearby stream.

There had been jaguars when he first came to Paraguay and for all he knew they were still prowling on silent pads in that black expanse of foliage which clung to the rolling hills. But they hadn't stood in the way of his rose garden. Harry loved his roses. He often wondered if it had been the very first thing he had perceived and he could imagine an intelligent yell echoing round a garden as he, fat and bald as a borough alderman, attempted to get free of the swaddling and grab at the flower. Harry's earliest actual memory was of his mother saying: "Oh he knows, look darling he knows," pretty in a straw hat with a ribbon hanging jauntily down behind as he presented her with a mangled specimen of her favourite bloom. His mother had been a beauty with curly brown hair tumbling down her back, a laughing woman running rings round a rather dull husband. He toiled in The Bank while she enjoyed the garden and her roses with Harry and, when Mr Copeland-Smith went overseas, with strange young men who adored her. At first he had a feeling of jealousy as Bertie or Clive put an arm around his mother's waist and hips snuggled together. But then he had discovered tennis balls and tadpoles and teasing the cook. Life is full of compensations and looking back on it after the initial hurt it had not bothered him a bit.

They had taken a year to pack, though he never saw most of his favourite things again, and toddled off to India, to live with his father and The Bank. His father had been insignificant at home but transported to that arid background he became prince of a rubber-stamp kingdom with an army of servants and clerks, implanting the idea in Harry that travel always meant bettering oneself. He loved the phrase "toddle off to India." It conjured up a picture of an infant John Bull scattering his toys across half the world until he finally got to the imperial sandpit. Henry and Maude Copeland-Smith, who never let her husband forget his grandfather had been a draper and hers a knight, lived in wordless enmity until one long hot summer killed her roses and made Maude look beyond her garden wall.

His father was a weak man who would swelter in dark suits on the hottest day and lecture endlessly about the virtues of patience. Mother's young men in blazers had given way to others in a drab fancy dress Harry later realized was military uniform; wobbly Adam's apples and bony white knees ruled at the time. He recalled sneaking into the bedroom and running off with one young subaltern's pistol and watching the man vacillate between bullying and coaxing as he tried to detect where Harry had hidden it and exactly what he had seen.

In the end a young man richer than the rest had reneged on a loan from his father and carried Mama off to Malaya. Harry had missed her terribly and she had sent for him, but his father would not allow it. Already there had been too much of a scandal he said and things had to get back to "normal", which inexplicably led to the sacking of three undergardeners. He had been packed off to school in England never to see any of them again, as it turned out, leaving nothing but a vague memory of a flower, her beloved roses, about which to be emotionally certain. India must be a lot better these days without those vicious white knees and random sackings.

He examined the severe short back and sides he had given the last bush. If only they called him home a discreet OBE would suffice. The full recognition of his services, his KBE, could come a little later. Harry Copeland-Smith was beginning to recognize a streak of bitterness in himself he did not really like but could do nothing about. The night air now was chilly and the sky rapidly darkened as if demon hordes from the red clouds had succeeded in causing the end of the world.

"I'll have that bloody knighthood," he muttered to the rose.

Chapter 1

Harry hurried down the path to the river, placing his sandalled feet more from familiarity than what he could actually see in the weak, yellow beam of the old black rubber army torch. He had been puzzled when, as the sun had gone down and the darkness crept over the garden, he noticed lanterns had been lit in the trees far down at the other side of the river near the armoury. Further upstream were the friendlier cooking fires of the Aché, but the lights by the armoury niggled him. He had given no orders for any such thing. Harry had been all set for a quiet whisky and a pipe before dinner but he knew he wouldn't rest until he found out what those lights meant. Sergeant Hindle was always springing things on him. Bloody hell, he cursed as night creatures scampered away from his footfall. His back hurt like blazes. Carefully he skirted the hill to the bottom of the garden, following the path which led through banks of thorn and jungle to the river. He was sure it was Hindle giving the men extra weapon training or some similar idiocy but he had to check; he was responsible. Things not part of his well-ordered routine irritated him and there was a chance it could be something more sinister. The guards would have sounded the alarm if there had been any intruders and shots would have been fired, but he thought it best to take a look all the same. His old Webley bumped in a holster slung over his shoulder while the clippers in the breast pocket of his shirt, painfully retrieved from the sack of cuttings, made him feel slightly ridiculous. Hindle was a damned pest.

On his left-hand side the land fell away, not quite sheer but very steeply to a fast deep stream. If I miss my bloody footing one night I'll be halfway to Buenos Aires before anyone knows what's happened to me, he thought as he sensed the power of the torrent in the darkness. I don't know how long they expect me to go on doing this sort of thing.

He wondered if his case had been misfiled. They were forever changing buildings and putting things on computer these days. All it needed was a mistake of one digit and he could be here for the next twenty years. Perhaps they thought he was seventeen or something. Not that he looked or felt old. Indeed a Canadian couple he had met in Encarnación, as they took a turn round the seedy town from the river steamer, had said he didn't look a day over forty. What tended to make him appear so young was a soft voice and seeming lack of assertiveness.

Harry stopped at the wooden bridge over the river and shone his torch at a rustle in the bushes; two small eyes blinked back. The sound of water filled the valley and he walked towards the lights upstream. They had a severe military pattern and must belong to Sergeant Hindle, who had been sent out to him seven years ago after his duties in the north of Ireland became ill starred. "Not manna from heaven Harry, I'm afraid," was how Chambers, the Rio Man, had put it. "Just another animal for your zoological gardens." Chambers had been right, as usual. Harry had politely loathed Hindle from the start. They could not bother to send him a bright young man to train up; that was considered too expensive nowadays. Instead he was sent Hindle, who although he claimed to have been to secondary school was not the proper stuff intelligence operations were made of. Hindle was what Harry would have called a "hard man" in the old days, a stick with which one beat the opposition, a scrapyard guard dog, a soldier who was classed as personnel not as "people". In the war and after it Harry had deeply regretted having to send brave sensitive young men into beastly situations, men who cried at night for weeks in their sleep before the monstrosity of what they had done or seen lost its shape and dissolved like sediment to the bottom of the soul until a word or a drink or two would let it loose again. The Hindles of the world did not have such limitations. "Go to sleep ya pansy," he had heard them yell when being kept awake by someone who had been on a raid the night before. Such men were quick to capitalize on what they regarded as weakness, terrified of being frightened themselves. Harry had seen Hindle's file. The man had never heard of Paraguay before, let alone knew where it was, but had been grudgingly thankful at first that he did not have to stand trial in an unfriendly Belfast courtroom due to "indiscretions" in South Armagh.

Ahead of him was another smaller bamboo bridge where a tributary joined the main river. Harry shone his torch at the water. Upstream lived his prisoner, their reason for being there, although lately he had begun to wonder who was imprisoning whom. One thing was certain: he would not have kept a dog in that tangled, guarded valley branching off the main one, and marvelled how the two souls up there survived. The stream seemed to suck a foul breeze out of that gap in the rocks as he drew opposite, a stench of putrid meat, a smell of death which made him shudder even though he knew it was only rotting vegetation and enormous growths of fungus. Harry did not like the place and it took him all his time not to show his feelings in front of Hindle who would have thought it funk. Hindle knew the secret of the valley but did not realize its importance; perhaps they hadn't sent anyone bright for security reasons. One telephone call could bring down governments.

The small canyon was the dampest place he had ever been. Water oozed out of the walls like a medieval dungeon and the slippery cliff faces were so overhung with trees and creepers that there was gloom even at midday, though the Aché ironically knew the place as the Valley of the Flowers; strange because no flowers grew there and Harry had sometimes wondered if it was perhaps a place of burial for some long forgotten tribe. The Aché muttered stories about demons, but then they said a particular type of blue demon lived under his house. He had a notion that the people who named the valley had become extinct by some change in farming or whatever, as might the Aché soon. Harry walked on. He could hear Hindle's voice.

"Where's the pin? Where's the pin?" Hindle pronounced the word "pen" and he was shouting. Harry guessed he had been trying to teach some of the younger Aché to strip the Self Loading Rifles, which began by taking a metal pin out of a hole near the top of the butt. Harry had discovered the Indians would only be taught individually and despised anyone who held them up to group scrutiny. They had obviously hidden the precious "pen". At least the mystery of the lights was now solved. Harry's armoury wasn't being ransacked by bandits; it was merely lit up to illuminate "jankers", imposed by the sergeant on the poor Aché for leading him a merry dance. He shook his head. It never did any good.

"We will stay here until we find the bloody pin," but not a flicker crossed the faces he could see. They could wait for decades if it suited them.

It always seemed to Harry as if he was forever approaching the Scotsman, not the other way round as rank dictated, trying to make up for some imagined gap of wealth or privilege that had produced the little monster in the first place. Harry was not tall but Hindle made him feel positively gangling and he noticed he had developed a stoop over the years which he blamed on the squat man he could now see under the lights. He stepped into the patch of white, like a heron from the cover of a reed bank, cautiously but conscious at the same time who owned the place. Who really does own the place? thought Harry.

The shuffling restless Aché, especially these particular Aché, had no real idea about work or property. They knew who their master was and that was Mr Harry or Mr Major, whatever they cared to call him. Hindle was not their master but Mr Major's servant and so on a par with them. They did not attempt to argue but quietly sabotaged his plans for them, which had been considerable and were now routine. Hindle had a word for this poker-faced warfare.

"Dumb insolence," said the sergeant. "That's what it is." He did not realize the Indians he dealt with were far from dumb but there again he never bothered to learn Guaraní, let alone the Aché tribal language. He did not even know much Spanish so how could he understand? "We will stay here until we find that pin. I'm warning you laddie, one more smirk and I will ruin your looks so even your mother won't recognize you." Impassive high-cheekboned faces stared out at him from under jet black fringes. They wore white cotton trousers and shirts which were dazzling in the hissing, blue-white light of army hurricane lamps. Harry noticed a mark on one man's arm and saw Hindle was brandishing his swagger stick. He took another pace forward further into the light and the sergeant, seeing him, made an involuntary movement as if to salute and then anger, or the fact Harry was not "properly dressed", caused the spasm in his right arm to subside and it flapped there for a moment. Hindle was correctly turned out right down to the soles of his shiny black boots and the badge of the Royal Green Jackets shone from the beret on his head.

"Having a party Sergeant? The place is lit up like Blackpool illuminations. Spot of trouble with the men?" He could not resist it. The square Scots face resting neckless on over-wide shoulders glared at him. These days Hindle did less and less to hide his anger.

"Come on Tatugi," said Harry in Guaraní to an individual more impish than the rest and stripped to the waist. His trousers were held up by an unblancoed British Army belt. It was imperative in such a sensitive area not to have a "uniform", which he could not seem to make Hindle understand, though some of the younger Aché pushed this to the limit. "Come on Tatugi. Give it back, there's a good boy."

Tatugi's eyes widened and seemed to shine with mischief in the icy light. For an instant the puckered face of Hindle with its close-set features looked towards him, searching the otherwise expressionless mask. Another boy shouted and pointed. Hindle looked down. The missing pin had magically materialized on the ground in front of the sergeant's spit and polished ammunition boots.

"Are you sure you didn't drop it Sergeant?" said Harry wanting to laugh. He knew the po-faced Aché were roaring inside, finding Hindle as exotic as a tribe of Hindles in a Glasgow pub would find them.

"Begging your pardon sir, what did you say to them?" The sergeant's words came breathlessly. "I have to teach these people Major . . . I will not be made a fool of. . . . "

But Harry was not to be intimidated. Hindle had his tantrums from time to time. "Don't make things difficult Sergeant. Dismiss the men, that's an order."

"I want to know what you said, I will. . . . "

Suddenly military, Harry turned to the Aché and dismissed them himself, again in Guaraní. They melted away into the blackness. He glared at Hindle who looked even more furious.

"Sergeant, unless you want to find yourself breaking rocks in a Ministry of Defence prison I suggest you refrain from hitting my Indians. Extra duty must be ordered by me and me alone, is that clear? All you will succeed in doing is destroying years of hard work. They wouldn't even eat when I brought them here. Aché won't do anything if you beat them, they just curl up and die. They give their obedience to us in return for food and protection and we need them. Is that clear?"

"Yes, sir, that's clear." The rift between himself and the sergeant grew even wider. He suddenly felt a desire to explain to the man how he bought the whole tribe lock, stock and barrel, in the town square of San Juan Nepomuceno on 7 March 1957 from a Portuguese trader called Jesús Da Silva. Harry had paid the undreamed-of price of one US dollar a head for the dirty, smelly, half-starved collection of humanity trussed like market chickens and with about the same life expectancy if no one wanted them. He had to look in each Indian's mouth, at the genitals and probe under the armpits for signs of plague or other diseases while Marmaluke slave catchers stood in the background, whips on the pommels of their saddles, their arms folded around Winchesters sticking out from under their ponchos. When the deal was struck they offered him a bottle of *caña*, not to drink but to disinfect his hands.

He had been allotted funds by the Foreign Office to hire plantation workers who could in turn provide security for his guests. To maintain a small force of British soldiers in the country would have been suicide if anyone had found out. It had been an electric realization when the deal was done in that dusty main square and he had wandered across to the *cantina* with Jesús, a dapper man who looked like everyone's idea of a favourite uncle, trying to come to terms with the fact that he, Major Harry Copeland-Smith, was a slave owner. So was the Queen's Government, who would have been horrified, he hoped, if they had known. But telling Hindle all this would be like talking to the floor.

The FO certainly knew about his slaves. It had proved to be the only answer in an area where smuggling was the booming industry and the politics were those of the early middle ages. The Paraguayan farmers would have robbed him blind if he had hired them and the Germans – for most of the colonists were German – were out of the question. The Paraguayan government had offered him soldiers, but that would have been like house arrest. He had had to train his own retainers and was now in many ways as indulgent to them as he would have been to a string of polo ponies. Yes, slave owning was the only real alternative and it still made him smile. In a way Hindle, because of his past crimes, was also part of Harry's "estate".

"Sorry I snapped, Sergeant. But try not to be too hard on them and they will do a lot more for you, there's a good chap. And no lights down here at night. You gave me quite a shock and it could confuse the boys on guard duty. I thought for a moment a local warlord was helping himself to our machine guns. You can clear up on your own I'm sure."

"Yes sir," said Hindle, glowering at the discarded rifles.

Rattling the man's chain certainly made Harry's own feel lighter.

His house was white and built on a classical pattern with columns under a Palladian arch in Georgian style, but from a French not an English design. The windows were far more delicate than anything from that period in England. Behind the façade, however, it was a typical planter's house, built of wood. He turned at the top of the hill, glancing back exhausted at the lights where Hindle still toiled. A drumming came from the Aché campfires. Their village of several hundred now rivalled the nearby Paraguayan settlement of Paradiso, and if anything his Indians were better off than the inhabitants of the crumbling little pueblo. Yet however envious those *campesinos* became they would never try to move against him as they knew he had powerful *Mbareté*, the Indian word for godfather or power; there were too many vested interests bound up in the secret he looked after in that damp canyon for there ever to be any serious trouble, though with the dreadful state of the roads it might be a week until help arrived.

"Come in señor, it is cold." It was his maid Maria and she had come out on the gravel drive with a glass in her hand. He could smell the whisky. She was a treasure, Maria; he often thought he would have cracked up long ago without her. Despite the orchids and the jungle, winter nights could seem cold and he took a quick gulp of spirit which warmed all the way down. "It's good?" said Maria. "Oh Harry, have you cut yourself? Come in, I will put a bandage on it. You should be more careful. You are always hurting yourself. Something could sting and bite you in the dark and who would look after me then?"

"It's nothing Maria, just the roses, the thorns of the roses, please don't fuss." They went inside. She chattered confidently in the English he had taught her.

Maria kissed him on the cheek. It was the gentle kiss of a lover not a mistress; not of someone who had a paid position in a household. He did not love Maria but was very fond of her, and had been ever since José Rodriguez, a smuggler in car parts of all things, had begged Harry to shelter him as half of Argentina were on his trail. They played cards all night and drank whisky Harry got through the embassy in Asunción, the capital. The game was baccarat and as Harry's eyes grew heavier the smuggler began to lose. Eventually past midnight he had bet all his pack animals and supplies on one hand.

When Harry had won José begged him to take Maria instead since he needed his mules more. Not wanting to have to keep a hungry smuggler for the rest of his life Harry let him go with a horse and two mules in the direction of Alto Paraná. Maria had been a lady's maid in Posadas until José had acquired her. But this time she was delighted with her new *jefe* and for weeks Harry, who had been something of an old bachelor except for the occasional trip to Asunción or Puerto Stroessner, was greeted by her grateful smile. She shared his bed from the start.

He slipped off his sandals and padded into the drawing room. Maria followed him. "Where have you been all this time? I was worried when I called out to you in the garden and you didn't answer."

"I've been down by the river, ticking off that damn fool Hindle for giving the boys extra duty. What's for dinner?"

She was concerned he had been blundering about in the dark, something that made him feel quite proud. He noticed she was wearing the WVS badge he had found in a drawer at the Asunción embassy and had given her as a present. She giggled at the way he looked at her and covered her mouth with her hand. He found her youth more attractive than her other attributes and felt flattered a girl of twenty-five seemed devoted to someone in his sixties. "But you are fine and strong," she would say. "You still have your hair and it's not grey, and all your teeth. You are not fat like that pig José Rodriguez and you smile at me like a young man. One day we will marry. It is in the stars." He doubted whether a tough piece of English brisket was preferable to her choice of Pampas tenderloin. But he liked his girl with moo-cow eyes all the same.

She poured him another drink and took his hand. Hers was calloused from hard work. He was never sure if her affection extended beyond cupboard love, beyond acceptance of him as a meal ticket and the dream of a home overseas: "I must see about your dinner," she said meekly and left him to his whisky. Maria was not beautiful although pretty perhaps for an Indian. Her liking for cakes and his nutty brown sherry was spoiling her figure but she was still one of the compensations of a shabby posting. If he had intended to spend the rest of his life here he would have married her, but her broad Indio face would not fit in with the neighbours of the large rambling house an aunt had left him near Cheltenham and which the Ministry of Defence let to tenants.

Harry often tried to imagine what England was like now, attempting to keep up with modern trends and fashions from dog-eared European magazines he was sent from Asunción. But now in his dreams the backgrounds and the imagery were of southern Paraguay and if he thought of home it was the country he had known before the war.

Maria was arguing with the servants. Harry plodded over to the silver drinks trolley to pour himself another tipple before dinner. He liked the room, which was unrestrainedly European, or rather colonial with Persian rugs and oil paintings including a study of the Paraguayan dictator Francisco Solano López and his mistress Elisa Lynch who once owned the house. Some said his ghost still haunted it but Harry didn't accept that; it was a happy house, by and large, despite his distasteful and increasingly marathon task, and if it was possessed by anyone it was by the spirit of the madcap Madame Lynch. He savoured his Glenmorangie malt whisky and sat down gingerly on the newspaper sniffing the air, an old dog waiting for his dinner. He was famished. There was a springtime quality about winter days which brought out the appetite; he hardly ate during the blistering summer. In the hall the clock chimed. Tomorrow's Sunday, he thought scraping the dried blood from his hand; better get Maria to have his best trousers pressed. Harry Copeland-Smith's was an ordered life, if at times a little strange.

Chapter 2

The minute but proud town of Paradiso, which still had the accoutrements of a mayor and town council though now it hardly had the population of a small village, was a mile and a half across the valley from Harry's house at the other side of the Aché settlement, which acted as a buffer to anyone who was curious enough to want to stray onto his land. True, he had entertained various mayors, a couple of priests who tended to be itinerants from the Verbo Divino Catholic sect and the odd – usually very odd – farmer, but Harry tried to make these meetings as formal and chilly as possible, at the same time recognizing that to cut himself off completely would put their backs up. It was a delicate balance, and going to Mass every Sunday was one of the points of etiquette he knew the residents of Paradiso would expect him to give in to. It had been decided that if he had isolated himself totally he could have easily become the demon of every folk-tale rumour they cared to invent. As it was, like the Aché, they respected him, even acknowledged him as a kind of local laird and when babies were christened in the ornate peach-stone church he was required to be the godfather, a part he acted out with all the dour reluctance of a Spanish grandee. The parents loved him for it and it was one reason he looked forward to Sundays.

"Mind the bloody bumps, Hindle," said Harry as another lurch to the right shifted his bacon and eggs.

The sergeant seemed to seek out all the muddy potholes, on

one occasion drenching the car in the red mud which was useless for crops and why the tangled jungle had never been seriously put under the plough. Hindle was sullen. He hated to have to drive into town, but above all he detested having to be Harry's personal chauffeur.

Four young Aché, who professed to be Christians, were neatly dressed in black trousers, white shirts, black ties and crimson ponchos in the back with Maria. They chattered eagerly.

"It's a disgrace," muttered Hindle as Harry braced himself against the dashboard.

"Just take it nice and steady will you. We don't want Father Gottfried to have to send out a funeral party, do we?" he said, wondering whether Hindle thought the roads were a disgrace or if it was a more philosophical comment aimed at God and Sunday. Hindle's jaw – a massive structure for a small man, making him look toadlike – was tightly clenched, always a sign he was angry.

"Everything all right, Ian?" he asked as the next crop of potholes hurled him the sergeant's way.

"What d'you mean, sir?"

"You don't look too pleased with creation this morning."

They narrowly missed a willowy stand of bamboo by a small swamp; Hindle had got out of the wrong side of bed.

"I'd hoped to take the lads for a bit of football this morning, sir. If I have to stay in town there won't be time when I get back as I've still got to show some of the new ones in D platoon the proper way to clean an SLR."

So what I said last night still rankles, thought Harry.

"They don't like football, Hindle. There's no use trying to make them like it. They'll play it but they won't like it. Football," he shouted into the back of the Land Rover and it drew a jeer and a groan. "You see, you're much better having a beer or two at the *cantina* with your German pals than wasting energy playing soccer. It does you good to get out some time."

"Football is good for morale," growled Hindle who, against all odds, had managed to clear a small pitch down near the river. The Aché tried their best to avoid it; being a soccer ace was not yet among the young Aché's dreams. Film stars were their gods.

Morale, said Harry to himself, not bothering to answer the younger man because he knew that Hindle only made sense of things in military terms, caring very little how the Aché felt, not even liking them but instead placing his trust in hammering weapon training into boys with the hope they would defend the house, the valley and the plantations against any attacker. He was the kind of man who regarded the world as deadly and dangerous and Harry had often thought that a bone would not look out of place through his pug nose. Hindle had his own bungalow by the main house with his own maid and preferred things that way, and it had intrigued Harry, on the times he had crept in there, to see a carefully kept family album of the clan Hindle, not coming from Glasgow as he made out but from the more genteel Edinburgh; not being of working-class extraction as the sergeant would have him believe and had convinced the person who wrote his file, but the son of shop-keepers, respectable folk who looked quizzically at the camera, probably wondering just how they came to be related to the hairy stunted pugilist who was pointing it at them. Hindle was so hairy that Harry had told him to take his gloves off when they had first met.

"I'm not wearing gloves, sir."

There was always a hunted look in Hindle's brown eyes beneath the mass of black hair he was constantly having to cut back which seemed as if one day it might join his bushy eyebrows, or rather eyebrow, mused Harry, as the black line joined across the bridge of his nose. Dressed in normal clothes the diminutive man would have looked like a dwarf. No wonder he joined the army.

They were now driving into the square of Paradiso. They pulled up by the petrol pump where two mules were drinking at the water trough which had been the forerunner of the petrol station only a few years previously. A cockerel on the side, balancing precariously, crowed a welcome. Harry recalled it was bad luck for cockerels to crow in the day-time, or was that owls? He went round the back of the Land Rover and helped Maria out.

The town had been mostly built of wood, and to the south were fields and marshlands that eventually joined the vast green sea of pampas. To the north were hills, his hills, still covered in forest which men had at times attempted to clear but it had grown back thicker, reinforced with springy impenetrable jungle thorn the would-be settlers brought with them in the seams of their trousers or in a cavity of a boot. These days men skirted round the hills and the tangles they had left and went in search of easier pickings. Harry often felt like an agricultural archaeologist when he pushed back the thorns a little way, to enlarge his garden or to build another hut for Hindle to play at administration in, and he found a coffee plant or cotton, or cocoa, breadfruit and even one time a cultivated rose which he had looked up and found was the wild descendant of a French confiture rose; it had made Harry's winter.

Hindle was standing in the centre of the square looking up at the small church surprisingly built in the baroque style and dating back to the Jesuits, it was said. It was a modest church by such standards, a box which had been decorated with swirling icing by a child who liked ascending S-shaped patterns; an ambitious child. At the top of these patterns was an arch in which hung a large brass bell. A man in red trousers and a green shirt, whom Harry recognized as the *cantina* owner's brother, had climbed a ladder with a hammer and was about to strike the bell as it could no longer be rung from inside. It was an extremely brave and unpopular chore since the front of the church was in such poor repair no one knew how long it would stand the vibrations of the bell or the weight of its reluctant ringer. Jóel Martinez put a finger in one ear and hit the bell with the hammer; it made a dull clanking sound and children laughed.

In the middle of the square was a small bronze statue of an Aryan woodman, axe over his shoulder, gazing purposefully towards the *cantina,* a large building of rotting mouldy wood which would certainly fall down before the church. The veranda was crammed with Paradiso's citizens, taking beer or *maté* or even at this early hour a glass of cane liquor. Figures seemed to melt into each other in the dark interior, as in a child's painting, and smiles crossed a few faces as they saw Harry. He gave them hope Paradiso was still a town.

But a town dying on its feet. The base of the Aryan statue was being eaten by a family of voracious snails and Harry's thorn thickets, spreading from the north, even grew on occasion through the ancient boardwalks, which in places were rotten as peat. The grocery store had taken to selling wares on the pavement outside since its owner, an old widow, had moved down from her room on the top floor because it was unsafe. A black vulture had taken up residence and small brown and white birds were busy burrowing their way into decaying wood after the insects which had undermined the structure. Paradiso did not have to put up with many of the disadvantages of livelier towns, like bands of drunken smugglers. The bases of these *Mbareté* were sometimes fortresses next to the river, often with an airstrip. Harry strode across the square in his best pressed linen suit and a wide-brimmed straw hat and took his place in his pew, as he always did. The priest nodded a welcome and the church began to fill up.

Harry had his own pew and Maria, being his servant and not his wife, sat in a pew behind him while the Aché, being Indios, stood at the back of the church. In some of the villages where the priests were old and the architecture straight from Bavaria with a green tulip of a church tower, Indians were not allowed in at all and no one would bother if an Indian was shot crossing a farmer's land. It was not that Paradiso was more tolerant but that the population was largely too old and apathetic to voice minor prejudices; you could tell it from the way they looked at his Aché.

The priest began to mumble the mass in Spanish, which would annoy the Germans. Harry enjoyed the incense and the hypnotic droning voice but fancied the poor wooden figure of the church's Black Madonna looked accusingly at him as he put the Host in his dry mouth. She was quite right; his Catholicism like everything else was on the orders of Whitehall. His piety was political.

The altar screen glowed with faded pictures and the place had a rabbit-hole cosiness. He was almost sorry to go out into the sunlight. The service was over and people were walking past him. He glanced round and Maria, wearing a lovely white dress which contrasted with her dark skin, smiled and then meekly looked down. It was a gesture he loved.

He stopped at the door and nodded at the fat German priest who was wearing a white straw hat against the weak sun and holding out his hand limply to be shaken by the people who passed. Harry had never met such an affected body of men as the priests of Paraguay, especially the Germans who turned a blind eye to the wicked things their boorish countrymen did all the way from Humaitá in the southern wetland to Pedro Juan Caballero in the north. The priest was trying to hide his interest in Harry and had obviously heard stories. Harry ignored him and strode on without speaking, an insult appreciated by the ladies picking over the manioca roots outside the tumbledown store. He waited for Maria.

"Why do you not like the priests?"

"I've never met a pretty one," he teased. She looked tired beneath her large brown eyes. Maria wore little make-up though constantly worried about the length of her eyelashes. In Europe she thought all the women had magnificent eyelashes and it was something she was quite capable of sulking about, which amazed him. The white dress was tied with a simple black leather belt, a thick belt which aptly contradicted the virginal whiteness of the cotton. All the muddy eyes lurking in the dark of the *cantina* were on her, but knew that she was the Major's woman, was faithful to him and would rather cut off both her hands than even return their glances. Hindle sipped a cold beer in a rocking chair at the corner of the *cantina*'s boardwalk but could not catch what had been said about the Major or Maria as he did not know the language. The rough men tried to include him in and once he had played a hand or two of poker and lost, not being able to rid himself of the suspicion he was being taken for a ride. It had been a disastrous poker game and he preferred loneliness to defeat, rocking backwards and forwards, a small man in a large chair, his mind on Harry and his eyes on Maria.

Suddenly there was a splitting sound and a crash and in a moment all the inhabitants of Paradiso were looking down at the vanquished figure of Hindle, covered in beer, who had fallen through the rotten boardwalk; thinking of Harry had made him rock the chair violently, throwing his strong back against the cane surrounds. But it had been too much for the floor. At first there was silence as the close-set brown eyes glared back at them like a badger in the two-foot hole, but then they laughed. In an instant Harry was pushing through the throng and giving Hindle a hand out.

"Well done, Ian. Now someone will have to do something about it, what? Can't leave you anywhere. I shall put in my report that I only left you in a bar while I was about my devotions in church and the next thing I know is that you have wrecked a *cantina*. I have a good mind to deduct the damage from your wages." He spoke the last sentence in Spanish and the mob roared. If Hindle had been a more intelligent man he would have laughed with them; instead he stalked over to the Land Rover, brushing down his military denim trousers as he went and drove away in a spectacular cloud of dust.

"You went too far," said Maria whose mouth was still quivering at the corner. "He is a dangerous man; he thinks everyone is against him."

"I'm very dangerous too," Harry said and felt seventeen as Maria started to giggle. "He'll just go back and read his war books and manuals and mope his Sunday away. People like that love their little dramas, Maria. My father was the same. They make mountains out of mole hills."

"Mole hills?" said Maria frowning. Harry felt like kissing her. Taking her by the hand he walked her past the *cantina* and towards the house of Petroni. Besides his own it was the only large house around.

"Señor Hindle is not with you?" said the beaming Petroni as a maid brought in coffee and sandwiches. "That is a shame," which Harry knew meant that it wasn't and he liked the little man as they sat on his patio looking out onto an orange grove. Petroni patted Maria's brown knee indulgently as one would do a favourite child. He was an old man, no one could say how old, who like almost everyone else in the area had made his money out of smuggling. Now he had retired and even his former enemies seemed to accept it, but he still knew everything that happened on the river and on the borders and his pale blue eyes twinkled when Harry asked him about the gossip. He wore a Paisley patterned shirt without buttons that stretched down almost to his knees. One hip had been crushed in a river battle with a rival, and Harry found it hard to imagine that today when he looked into the kind face above the withered body in the wheelchair.

"Do not leave Sergeant Hindle here when you go. I do not think it would be safe for him." Petroni snorted. "They would send someone else surely?" Then he saw the hurt look in Maria's eyes. "Pardon me, I am sorry. Anyway I'm sure you are stuck here till you die like me, eh *compadre*?" Maria remained glum.

"We have had some good times together, me and Major Harry, when we both were young and I rode for Don Lorca with a red bandana on my hat. You remember how we met when we came after that thief Giuseppe? How you played the Beatles to me on your radio?"

Harry nodded: it had been 1966, June, and after listening to the World Service they had ridden out to track down an Italian immigrant from Buenos Aires called Giuseppe. Lorca and his ten mounted retainers had been most courteous and Harry had strict orders to bend with the breeze. The man had stolen a sack of cocaine.

"Your Aché could follow a man under the sea. We found him on a little island at the mouth of one of the rivers that join the Paraná. We ate and drank and it was like a picnic, yes?" Harry nodded again. "And then we fought, charging across the shallows and one of our men was killed. Then Harry's Indians crawled onto the island like snakes and wounded Giuseppe in the stomach. He moaned for hours, but I do not think Don Lorca would have killed him had he not thrown the drugs into the river. Giuseppe had been his right-hand man and after promising to take care of his little ones he put him out of his misery. . . ."

"What happened to Lorca?" asked Maria.

"He was shot by the Argentines smuggling political refugees. They paid him back for Giuseppe. But he taught Harry much about how to deal with people on the river." Petroni smiled, helping himself to a cake.

"Now for our sins which were considerable, eh Harry, we have been sent the good Father Labuschagne. In fact that is what I want to talk to you about." The twisted little man fixed his eyes on a large and very gory crucifix he had looted from a church in his heyday and spoke in a low clear voice, almost like a priest. Harry was all ears. Instinctively Maria slipped away into the garden.

"There is going to be trouble. I have it on good authority that Cortez is going to be poking his nose into everyone's business again. He has some grand scheme to clean up the area but really it is because Father Labuschagne has become too greedy, too powerful. Cortez is jealous of his profits. I think the little shit believes he is Presidente."

Petroni was talking of the head of the secret police, in fact of all police, who had been a smuggler too in his time. Harry munched on an *empanada*. Rumours of Cortez were nothing. But if the vicious policeman was on a collision course with Labuschagne trouble would be an understatement and it could affect them all.

Father Labuschagne had fled to Argentina fifteen years ago from South Africa where he was wanted for killing a white man. The very odd thing was that he actually had been a minister in the Dutch Reform Church. Many people who ran away to Paraguay merely used the priesthood as a disguise. Labuschagne was the genuine article and it made him bitter. He came, so the gossips said, from an old Boer family whose land was purchased by a British mining company when they could not meet the mortgage payments. Bailiffs had come to throw the patriarch Labuschagne off his land and his sons had tried to stop the eviction. Pushing and shoving became all-out fighting and somewhere in the mêlée that followed a man's neck snapped in the iron grip of the young priest. The combatants fell back and the dust settled and under the ancient shotguns of his astonished relatives, for he had always been the good boy of the family (Harry could not begin to imagine what the bad ones were like), Labuschagne struck out for Latin America. In Argentina he developed a religious determination not to be poor, but the only business opportunity was smuggling tobacco and whisky with a fellow countryman. Simple economics had led him to graduate to the drugs trade and the cruel world which surrounded it. He embraced his new church with enthusiasm. Harry heard he sent money back to his family; if so it was his only weakness.

About ten years ago he had moved north to Paraguay and had been firm friends with Cortez. The police chief had taken care of his citizenship and even made him an honorary captain in the Air Force. But Labuschagne's flair for organization had latched onto the Ukranian community in Southern Paraguay. Sullen and leaderless, they were tired of being thrown off their land by the industrious Germans who bought it from under them. It was an echo of his own past and the priest found a ready-made army more than willing to fight with God and a decent income on their side. Before long three of the southern provinces along the banks of the Paraná were under his control. The air strips smuggling loads to Argentina now paid him and not the local head of police who, in turn, could no longer pay his dues to Cortez.

" . . . and Father Labuschagne has a helicopter."

Now that was news.

"A real one or a toy one?" Harry joked.

The ex-smuggler laughed.

"A real one. There are some crazy Baptist missionaries who lend it him. They think he's an ordinary priest delivering supplies to the Indian villages and you have never seen anything like it. It has two loud-speakers which play hymns and preach at you. He has got people to fly it too and it could be very dangerous. But he's got too much to lose to start upsetting anyone."

I hope so, thought Harry. Petroni did not seem all that worried as he watched Maria in the garden. Only the

Argentinians had helicopters and then not very many of them. Perhaps he should take it seriously, except the idea of a priest who smuggled was hard enough to swallow; a priest who smuggled in a helicopter borrowed from other priests was even harder; if the helicopter was then fitted with loud-speakers to bombard the jungle with sermons and hymns in English, Spanish, German and Guaraní, that could only happen in Paraguay.

"Would you like a Scotch?" asked Petroni. "I have some Chivas Regal which my cousin brought me. You must take a bottle. Or would you prefer a straight malt?" The helicopter was not so absurd after all when you could get such fine whisky in the middle of nowhere.

They both heard the diesel engine of Harry's Land Rover clatter up the drive and scrunch to a stop. Hindle had returned. Whatever sulks the sergeant was having when he drove off earlier had vanished. He seemed excited: "Radio message sir. Mr Chambers is in town. He wants to see you. Lucky I drove back sir."

"Yes Sergeant," said Harry, distracted, reading the transcript. "Let's go back home." They collected Maria and said hurried goodbyes to a disappointed Petroni.

"Who will eat all my cakes and sandwiches?" he asked, pressing Maria to take a plate of biscuits into the Land Rover with her and waving to them, a grinning impish figure in a wheelchair. "*Felicitaciones, amigos,*" he shouted.

Harry clutched the radio message written in Hindle's painstaking copperplate. He had not seen the Fat Man for two years. It cheered him up immensely and he didn't mind the bumps. If they were really to let this humble servant depart in peace he almost felt like praying. He had never been a man for sleepless nights but it had worried him of late what would happen if the world found out about his secret.

Some would treat him as a criminal, but what would wound was that others might think of him as a "Missing Link" figure and examine him scientifically, the very last trace of Imperial Man Doing His Duty. The prospect was terrifying. There was no doubt the British government and the Americans and the

Germans and Lord knows who else had prevented his guest from being brought to justice as a result of a sordid deal in a beer *keller*. But if it were ever found out he would be the most visible person to blame, even though he was only obeying orders.

Hindle screeched to a halt as they came upon a bullock cart with high wheels that nearly blocked the road.

It was encouraging that Chambers, the Rio man, a Falstafian figure who usually visited others to drink them out of house and home should summon him to the city. It must be important. Perhaps his posting was finally to be reviewed. At least from what Petroni had told him this morning Major Harry Copeland-Smith MC of the Scots Greys would have a bargaining card. If there was to be a battle between Labuschagne and Cortez in his own backyard wouldn't that affect the security of his prisoner who would be better looked after by a younger man? He chuckled to himself as Hindle put the Land Rover into low ratio on the rutted path up to his house.

Chapter 3

"*¿Qué tal?*" was all the tall young *campesino* had said before curling up in his execrable red poncho, allowing his head, which smelt of fields and dung, to slip onto Harry's shoulder. The poncho had a life of its own and soon Harry felt a tell-tale itch but he was crammed against the window and could not move even to scratch. Trussed chickens clucked mournfully under the seat in front. He had been forced to take a field-workers' bus from Encarnación early that morning as the second four-wheel-drive Land Rover was in pieces for reasons known only to Hindle. Harry had bought two seats but the bus had filled with young men riding up to work on the big farms outside the city before going back at the weekend to tend their own. The man on his shoulder slept the limp unconscious sleep of exhaustion. Everyone seemed to be slumped across each other on the swaying old bus, shifting only when it hit a large pothole, and the hard seats jarred Harry's back. He had to sacrifice his privacy. He could not complain; they would only laugh. Gringos were all meant to drive Cadillacs. The man started to snore and Harry wondered if he had sought out his shoulder on purpose.

Things should not be like this at my age, he thought. It wasn't as if he expected to be chauffeur-driven to the embassy in a Rolls but his job, albeit as a jailor to a very sensitive criminal, was vital. The man had never been proved guilty but Harry had seen the evidence and it was overwhelming. Suddenly an accidental elbow in the face was his reward for acting as a pillow to the slumbering *campesino*, now wide awake, as they pulled into Asunción's "bus station", in reality a few ramshackle ticket offices surrounding the Bar San Rocque near the Plaza Venezuela. He pushed his way off the bus and made for the embassy in search of a good cup of coffee from Mabel the cipher clerk. What she had to tell him woke him up very quickly.

A new "ambassador" had taken up residence. Harry of course had heard one was coming but this individual was a senior diplomat, a roving plenipotentiary without portfolio, higher ranking than a mere ambassador. They still called him ambassador as they did the last one, though some said he was only a consul. The previous incumbent, a fat incompetent named Tupper, died of a heart attack after overstuffing himself with excellent Sauerbraten mit Kartoffelklosse at the German Club and then calling on a lady of his acquaintance. He had expired in her expensive arms and was unceremoniously carried out to his car as other paying customers were waiting to sample the establishment's deadly charm. A British Council official who claimed to be looking for a lost dog found Tupper naked with one rigor mortified leg clamped against his chest so the knee was touching the shoulder. They straightened him out and the cause of death was recorded as a riding accident.

The guard who was meant to be in front of the embassy had left his rifle with a nut seller, a gnarled old man having a vicious argument with a one-legged cigarette vendor, selling his wares one at a time by the dank hallway stinking of urine. Nothing had changed.

The embassy came as a bit of a shock to the trickle of Her Majesty's subjects who had business in Paraguay and compared to Harry's lavish house in Paradiso it was a slum. After weeks of searching for demented relatives who had run off to join one of the country's homosexual or nudist communities, rotund sensible ladies from Peckham or Basildon eventually stood helpless on its evil-smelling steps and consulted the tourist map to make sure this indeed was the right place. When they realized it was all hope left them. A bank manager from Southampton trying to locate his Gauguinite brother on behalf of his sister-in-law, fainted at the sight of it and was carted off to the Hospital de Clinicas babbling about taxpayers' money.

The piece of England was on the second floor of an otherwise disused office block, with the empty levels just a tangle of rubbish and decaying concrete. A few of the vendors in that street full of little sacks, coloured ponchos and calm Indio faces made their homes in the damp ground floor, and a line of ducks splattered its way from the street through the puddles to the interior, presumably where Mrs Nut Vendor fed them. It always made Harry smile. The unhappy structure was continually being mistaken for a vet's, either because it looked like another building close by in the run-down port area, or the poor inhabitants liked the joke of introducing a struggling calf into politically sensitive discussions. Some ambassadors comforted themselves that an idiot in the Foreign Office had bought the wrong building, or imagined this must be some kind of consular annex: the wise searched their background for that signal failure, that awful faux pas that had brought them there. White straw hats above the street sellers' ponchos nodded as Harry went past. The poor of Asunción hated all gringos and to be acknowledged in quiet contempt was red carpet treatment indeed. The new man must be worse than usual.

"He is *loco*," said Mabel, who was not usually given to insults, pouring him a large cup of coffee made on the stove with creamy milk and heaps of sugar exactly how he liked it. Mabel was a long, leggy German-Paraguayan with blue amorous eyes just into her forties who after her last husband had died had virtually been adopted by the embassy. Mabel was not her real name which no one could pronounce and people whispered she was a countess. Her current affair was with the boyish commercial attaché, though it had crossed Harry's mind from time to time to invite her down to Paradiso. Just for a holiday, of course, but Maria would kill him.

"You are looking so well, Major. You have the secret of eternal youth. That is what comes from playing host to. . . ." She stopped and smiled.

"The Ambassador?" asked Harry. "Is he in?"

She patted Harry's neatly combed hair as she pulled up a chair and sat down. "No, not yet. The man is a pig and I should know, I have been married to two. You once told me that only people they want to get rid of are sent here. This new man thinks he has been sent to reorganize things. If you want there is some whisky in the cupboard." She pointed to a green painted box halfway up the wall in the dismal little kitchen off the main filing room. "You know he's called Sir Reginald Tough. He was in London before he came here and before that he was in Vietnam and Hong Kong. You don't think he will send me away do you Harry? He said I was 'irregular' the other day but everyone stuck up for me and said that as most white people here spoke German I was vital. They won't get rid of me will they? I can't stand all those dunces in the Deutsche Institute. I could not bear to work there, not for a minute."

Harry took her hand, regretting Maria for a moment.

"I don't think you have anything to worry about my dear. They send them here to put them out to grass or because they have gone barmy. London is only interested in protocol and the occasional economic report if that. Once he's been ignored for a year or two Tough will calm down and go quietly potty like me. I think I will have that whisky. Not that I usually drink in the mornings, down country you know, but I'm meeting Mr Chambers."

"You won't sneak on me will you?" Mabel shook her shiny brown hair and reached the bottle down, her blue dress lifting.

"Thank you," said Harry. "You have made an old man very happy. What has Reggie done? Anything serious yet?" Mabel looked businesslike for a moment.

"First I must tell you Mr Chambers says go to the Da Vinci. He wants to see you before you see Sir Reggie to talk privately and does not want the Ambassador to hear. They do not like each other." Harry poured a generous measure of Scotch into both their coffees as she examined a carefully painted nail. "Tough is not the usual sort I think. He drinks very little and talks of doing great things and the others do not have the heart to tell him there is nothing to do. Already he has been complaining about the furniture and the fact that as a senior diplomat he should have much better quarters. He has taken the old residence outside town and has the builders in." They both smiled. No one would choose to live out there. "Then he drove up in the old Rolls-Royce that has been in the garage at the German Club for years taken in lieu of debts from Señor Tupper but he managed to get it back and insists on parking outside where it gets in the way of the barrows. Yesterday he went out and someone had put a little black and white pig on the front of the car which was eating the windscreen wipers. It was so funny. He bellowed for the guard to do something and even ordered the man to shoot it. The guard said he wouldn't as it was not his pig and everyone laughed. Then the noise scared the pig and it peed on the car. You should have seen His Excellency's face."

"I can imagine," chuckled Harry, thinking of the rancid breath and the rotten sack-like ponchos. How they would despise such a man. They had obviously surpassed themselves in Whitehall this time.

"And also," said Mabel slowly with a mysterious smile, "he seems to know about you. He wanted the file on you and we told him there wasn't one and to ask Mr Chambers. He wants to know what you do Harry."

"What I bloody do?" Harry heard the words leave his lips with uncharacteristic violence and Mabel looked alarmed. "Sorry Mabel." He was glad of the excuse to hold her hand again. "Bloody cheek." At the other end of the long room of green cabinets which housed confidential files and where the last ambassador had once found a donkey after a long lunch, there was a rumbling commotion like an approaching storm. The new ambassador had come in followed by the commercial attaché. There was a row, an almighty row, in progress to do with security and the fact that anyone off the street seemed to be able to walk into the embassy.

"Best to go *liebling*," said Mabel planting a wet kiss on his cheek. "I'll take him a cup of tea and you sneak out past the filing cabinets, please. Keep your head down. If he knows I have been talking I am for the high jump." She drew a finger across her neck where the wrinkles were just beginning to show. Laughter lines creased the corners of her eyes; she was a happy woman. I could take this one to England, thought Harry.

"But what did Tough want to know about me? What time do I meet Chambers?" he whispered across the cabinets. The reply did nothing to reassure him.

"Everything," said Mabel. "And Chambers says to wait."

Harry seemed to have been sitting for hours with one cup of coffee at the Da Vinci bar while a busy young man scowled at him from the counter, took repeated swigs from a bottle of beer and turned the jukebox up three times. Old folk and gringos were bad for business. Harry couldn't care a damn, and smiled at the man who began manically polishing glasses as his customers started to drift in. The Da Vinci was the place for Paraguay's idle young rich and had a balcony overlooking the Calle Palma just off the main square. The clothes were quaintly behind the times; one of the two girls asking for banana milkshakes at the bar was wearing flared jeans and worse still were the shapeless Paraguayan copies of *Vogue* chic. But the Da Vinci did make a stab at being a place for the young. The American football shirts behind the chromium-plated bar, the posters of Debbie Harry and the Rolling Stones, and even the Snoopy doll were an attempt in a bare concrete shell to transplant the customers to New York or Europe for the length of time it took to drink a milkshake, yet something always disturbed the plan. Harry was the disturbance today. But on others lepers had wandered in from the Chacarita, the sprawling riparian slum, or poor Indians who had escaped from the Association de Parcialidades Indigenes reservations and pathetically tried to sell little bows and arrows to non-existent tourists, or policemen with small jealous eyes and with large guns which they propped against the bar: all these were enemies of the Da Vinci's potential.

Trams clanked past below with little boys hanging onto the sides. It was a noisy city and an unashamedly wicked one at present enjoying a boom, largely on the profits of smuggling.

Harry had been told that half of the economy was "black", whatever that meant. He toyed with his coffee, not a patch on Mabel's. He knew plenty of smugglers, and Scotch was cheaper on the streets of Asunción than from the embassy. Asunción was a town where you could buy anything from a washing machine to a bearded lady at unbelievable prices; a pueblo at heart despite its self-satisfied government buildings and stuffy attempts at modern architecture, reminding Harry of Madrid before the war. Casablanca must have been a lot like this too in its heyday. A 1930s setting for a 1930s sort of chap. As he looked up the jukebox had been eclipsed, blotted out by a sweating, smiling man in acres of grey flannel suiting.

"Sorry about the cloak and stagger, Major," said Chambers with an ingratiating smile. "They've outdone themselves with the new boy. I suppose you popped in to see Mabel?" Harry nodded. "Knew you would." The Fat Man first tried one chair and then another while the café owner looked worried about his property as a small wooden structure groaned under great weight. "Got all your notes about going home."

The smile vanished and he frowned accusingly at Harry. A snarling Rock and Roll single from the 1950s jumped tracks on the jukebox.

"I think you will agree, old man, that given the present lunatic they have sent us, it's not exactly the best time to send you back home for the hols with a label in your lapel. He's forever complaining and he's hardly unpacked. That's why I'm here. Mabel will have told you Sir Reginald is completely barking. It's a wonderful story."

Gloom descended upon Harry. "I think I have a right," he said trying to be calm as the café owner stomped over bringing two bottles of beer. "I at least have the right to some date for retirement, something to look forward to."

"Ah, I thought you would see our difficulty. It's very hard to find another veritable Atlas to take over your position and don't think for a moment that we have not considered other options regarding your man. I think that's why they sent Hindle – now I don't know mind, they don't tell me everything you know. Handling a problem like this with lots of different countries involved is like trying to unite Europe. And we have a few more MI6 bum boys about to wash their dirty linen."

Harry was angry. The beer spilt as his fist hit the table. "I hope my loyalty is not in question. Because if it is . . . " The smile returned to Chambers' face. He knows, thought Harry, knows instinctively that thumping tables is as far as I am prepared to go, the bastard. I'll play the cards Petroni gave me later. A tram nosed down the busy street and a policeman blew a whistle. He was the real prisoner as Chambers droned on about experience and the trust he had built up with the myriad facets of a difficult country. It would take another twenty years to replace him. Somehow behind it all, what he really disliked was the implicit threat that they could leave him high and dry.

"I'm as much in the dark as you," lied Chambers, his several chins quivering and his oyster eyes looking carefully at a pink ashtray. "But I'll keep batting for you; you have my word. Anyway I thought you liked it here with that marvellous house of yours and things. Old Tough is raising a hell of a stink about you, but don't worry we will cover your tracks."

"You're making me sound like Jack the Ripper."

Harry looked at the bursting bubbles on the top of his beer. Surely they must understand. He was like a scientist who had worked with deadly toxins or radioactive isotopes pleading to be retired before a careless clumsy move brought on by old age killed him. It was as much in their interests as his. He was about to beg. Harry was no good at this sort of thing.

"Cheer up," boomed Chambers. "England is an awful place, wouldn't touch it with a bargepole. It might be easier to persuade them to retire you somewhere else . . . But let me tell you about old Tough." A policeman came in and the youngsters mostly departed leaving comparative quiet as Chambers, his jowls wet with beer, gleefully chuckled out the story of a monkey called Sidney's Tamasin and how Tough came to Paraguay.

As usual, the Fat Man had jumped from the very serious with ease. "Once upon a time," he began and with a sigh Harry resigned himself to the story. Sidney's Tamasin, perhaps the smallest monkey known to science, had long been regarded as extinct until the Vietnam War and Captain Eisenhower Goodfellow was walking "point" for his own patrol on the Mekong Delta.

"Imagine the scene," said Chambers. "He motions to his men to halt and they follow his gaze into the gloom waiting for Charlie to fire back, except all they see is the minute simian with a Prussian Blue backside. Sidney's Tamasin. 'Dat sure some monkey man,' says a marine. Can you picture it?" Chambers slurped at his beer.

"Now Goodfellow is a zoology student – don't worry old chap you'll see the point of this in a moment – Goodfellow is a zoology major with impeccable military connections going back to the War of Independence and was so concerned about the monkey he pulled a few strings. What had been a free-fire zone was suddenly silvan bliss. They murdered the trees everywhere else but the monkey had its own private wood a hundred miles square. Of course the Cong moved in when they discovered it wasn't a trap and set up a large prison camp in the area after the war. That's where Tough came in.

"He'd been several years in Hong Kong and was knighted for being the only diplomat not on the take. But before that he was in Malaya and got the nickname Stuffer. He'd stuff anything at the drop of a hat. Taxidermy I mean. One minute an animal was free and happy, the next it was nailed to a bloody board in Tough's study. He even broke off the negotiations with the guerillas over a particular lizard he wanted to send to the British Museum. Now, he went on a deputation or whatever you call it to try to free some black bods from the prison camp in the jungle where the monkey lived."

Chambers handed Harry a paper translated with some licence from the Swedish. This Foreign Office "digest" contained an account of Tough's visit to the prison camp with the Nobel prize-winning veteran who had written the report, a Red Cross worker and a progressive senator from Louisiana. Despite the fact the Swede had more experience, Tough insisted on "taking charge". The prize-winner had taped everything and had transcribed it with painstaking Scandinavian thoroughness afterwards.

"I think we ought to get straight down to business," Sir Reginald had said to Captain Vin, the commander of the camp, as five black American prisoners had been paraded in front of them. The Swede, a Professor Lars Person, had described morale as very low, Harry read, scanning down the page through the usual attack on American imperialism by Captain Vin. The ambassador then countered through his "neurotic looking" Khmer interpreter, "who had a crossbow on his knee and was part of a tribe converted to Catholicism and was fanatically against the communists. The use of such a man was a mistake." It certainly had been. At a delicate point in the negotiations Sir Reginald, renowned for his amateur work with small animals, saw the bright blue bottom of Sidney's Tamasin.

"But staring in the direction of the prisoners," continued the report, "Sir Reginald pointed and shouted: 'I must have that monkey, I must have that monkey!' This of course caused some alarm." Despite himself a smile spread across Harry's face. "'I want that one, that little beggar,'" Person faithfully recorded. "This brought protests from my colleague Senator Brett of Bloomsville, Louisiana who thought, as we all did, that he meant one of the prisoners. 'That's racism. That's no way to talk to the negro fightin' man,' said Senator Brett. Then Sir Reginald answered: 'No, no, no it's a monkey damnit. Can't you see it's a monkey? I want to take it home with me. Stuff it if I cannot take it alive. It may be the only one of its kind.'"

A prisoner had thrown himself at Captain Vin's feet. "'Please Captain Vin. Don' let that white motherfucker stuff me. I withdraw what I said about the food. I wanna be a communist just like you Captain. Don' let them take me.' Then Sir Reginald turned to his Khmer interpreter. 'Surely you can see it? The little monkey, the one over there. It's coming down the tree. It's helping itself to scraps from the soldiers' table. It's quite tame.' Unfortunately," concluded the report, "Sir Reginald was not experienced in dealing with tribesmen and before he could stop him the man had shot the small monkey with his crossbow and then shot a second poisoned bolt into Captain

Vin. The Vietnamese, who liked the monkey and were exceedingly fond of their Captain, opened fire and we were lucky to lose only the misguided Khmer and poor Senator Brett. Needless to say the coloured prisoners refused to have anything to do with our delegation and we were extremely lucky to leave the country ourselves without incarceration. I protest in the strongest possible terms and insist that Sir Reginald. . . . "

"Good God," said Harry.

"What's more," said Chambers grinning with all of his three chins, "Person was an old friend of the Duke of Edinburgh and in the World Wildlife lot. They kicked Tough out and so did the Royal Zoological Society. The FO sent him to Iran but that didn't exactly work so they pulled him back to Blighty. He then hovered around corridors and you know how they abhor hoverers. Old Sir John Sanders was over at a Lodge meeting in Rio and told me he decided Paraguay was the only place for him. 'You know Chambers,' he said. 'That country is somewhere even a trained diplomat could not make things worse.'" Chambers sat back in his chair and looked at him pleadingly.

I'm not going to help him thought Harry, it's up to them if they appoint maniacs.

"In our experience," continued Chambers, "Stuffer will be house trained in no time at all, but just at the moment he's in a bit of a lather. He wants to make a comeback. Asking all sorts of questions about his job here and about you. About what you do here. He's giving his first party tonight and I want you to go, that's an order. We will think of a plausible yarn to tell the madman. Please be sensible Harry, I need someone to hold my hand. It's at the residence." Both men laughed and it broke the tension. No one in his right mind would hold a party there.

Harry took out his pipe and put it away again, as he always did when he was anxious. He bet a penny against a pound it was Chambers himself who had started the ball rolling, planted his name in Tough's fevered brain for his own manipulative reasons.

"Why don't you just tell him what I do is top secret?"

Chambers put a stubby finger against his lips, letting out a long hissing shhh sound like a punctured beachball and theatrically looked out of the corner of his eye at the policeman. "We want to avoid telling him even that, if we can, dear . . . " Chambers affected a Churchillian camp and often called people "dear" as the great man did his generals.

"I'll go, of course, even to the residence, as long as you promise . . . " His words were cut off by a deafening explosion from somewhere near the main square which shook the café, followed by long bursts of automatic fire and then by silence. For a moment one could almost hear the dust fall. A girl screamed and Harry became conscious of the jukebox again, and Elvis crooning on unperturbed.

Chapter 4

The policeman with the droopy moustache leaning on the bar was the first to move. He ran down the narrow staircase as Harry tried to collect his thoughts, a ringing still in his ears. He, Chambers and everyone else in the café had prudently sought shelter under the tables, and the eerie quiet was punctuated by cries and short bursts of fire or single shots, or two shots close together. The authorities were taking no chances and not until fifteen, perhaps twenty, minutes later did they dare emerge still not knowing if a tiff between gangsters or a full scale coup d'état was in progress.

A man came up the stairs. It was Raul the café owner's brother.

"Anastasio Somoza is dead! The tyrant of Nicaragua is dead!"

Harry marvelled as they toasted the imagined revolutionaries who had carried out the act, yet the picture of their own Presidente Stroessner remained intact above the bar, promising peace and tranquillity and a regime that made Anastasio's look amateur.

"Better get to the car," Chambers said brushing the dust from his lapels. "They will soon be stopping everyone."

Outside in the gutter lay two casualties of police enthusiasm. One was a beggar. The other a mule which had been carrying honey. The beggar had obviously been asleep, jumping up suddenly as the moustached policeman had run out, gun at the ready. Stray bullets from the burst had hit the mule and broken a heavy jar of honey on its back. A sticky tide was lapping over the dead man's twisted shoulders. The smell was sweet and nauseating. "Trigger happy nitwits," muttered the Fat Man waddling around the mess.

They skirted a main square empty of people for even the honour guard had left the Pantheon de los Héroes, where the eternal flame burned. Chambers had somehow commandeered the embassy Rolls and had it parked on a small hill by the Hotel Paraná, complete with a very worried driver. Soldiers stood near the Hotel Guaraní but no one challenged them. They got inside the comfortable old car without a word and felt safe in the all too English familiarity of the battered leather seats until a gun barrel hammered against the window.

"Papers," snarled the man with the gun.

Harry slowly got out of the car and immediately recognized the officer in charge of the mobile police squad armed with sub-machine guns.

"*Hola* Luiz. Are you going to take me in? You have caught me at last. I shot the old cunt."

The young man who had been scowling a moment before and had ordered his corporal to break the window if the gringos didn't open it was now all smiles. He eased his pistol back into its holster, telling the others to stand by; they had overflowed from two Jeeps on the corner. Dark green Jeeps to match the colour of their helmets. On the back of one was a machine gun. Harry breathed a sigh of relief. "How is your old reprobate of a father?" he asked his godchild, turning his back on the car as Luiz brought him up to date with family business and the fact his wife had a week ago given birth to a daughter. He apologized for not being able to assign them a vehicle to escort them out of town.

"Just one question Luiz." Harry knew he could take the liberty. "How did Señor Somoza pass away?"

"No one has ever seen anything like it. They used a British Army weapon," said Luiz, his eyes lighting up as if Harry should patriotically approve. "A Karl Gustav 84 mm anti-tank weapon was found on top of the Hotel Guaraní. As he came to do his shopping they fired it at his Mercedes. Pow! Then they machine gunned the hole. My cousin is in charge of what is left of the car, and the hole. An exiled dictator has many enemies." He shook his head and shrugged. Both knew he was parroting the words of those above him. The police never liked single, apolitical assassins, nor did the government. A grand Left Wing conspiracy would make it possible for Luiz's superiors to round up whoever they did not approve of, from Encarnación to the Chaco, rather in the spirit of the incinerated Somoza.

"*Adiós padre*," shouted Luiz as Harry got back into the car and drove off. Harry had taught him the alphabet.

"Golly," said Chambers, "didn't know you had a family here." The driver roared up the street as if in a getaway car. He realized how lucky they had been. Harry felt the soft cushions against his back and relaxed.

"Godchild," corrected Harry as they sped out into the country. "His father was doing the same sort of job around my neck of the woods when I came over. We are still good friends. Bloody lucky it was Luiz; another patrol might not have been so understanding. After an assassination everyone is fair game. Anyway it should liven up Tough's bloody party."

In one way Harry was pleased with himself, showing off with Luiz, firmly demonstrating this was his patch, an area where he was known and where he knew the ropes, where even creatures of the night like Luiz – who at twenty-five had had more experience of violent death than the entire population of most small English towns – respected him. Yet this was exactly what Chambers wanted: to show him no one else could cope. As they neared the residence he caught the Fat Man looking at him with that wicked little half smile Harry remembered well from the time he had holidayed in Rio. Here was an extremely clever, venal individual whom he liked a lot and feared more than he cared to admit, and the dark eyes gave nothing away. Chambers didn't let people become a problem. Perhaps that is what Hindle is for, he worried: if I become too much of a headache.

They came to a small gatehouse and were waved in by a man with bare feet and a dappled pig, both standing by the broken-down shack. From the shack to the red-brick house, built it seemed fairly recently, probably by a German who had seen pictures of North Finchley Bastard Gothic, was an avenue of rippling palms, a kind of oil palm which anywhere else would have had a pleasant effect. But no palm is at its best when a dozen or so black vultures with greasy white necks and evil beaks are gathered in its fronds. The trouble with the house was a large swamp on the other side of the road into which the vultures waited for unlucky animals to fall and drown. They reminded Harry of divorce lawyers. The last ambassador, Tupper, who refused to live there had called the place Dunroamin, which was apt, and it had been left to rot.

Harry had been told there had been British-owned houses on the spot since the last century. All rotted and fell down and were regarded as monuments to gringo stupidity as most inhabitants attempted to drain the swamp and shoot the vultures, snakes and other vileness which only made things worse. Drainage channels were dug leading away from the mire. But as the swamp was the lowest point for miles around this only had the effect of enlarging the morass when the rains came. Likewise, one could blow away vultures and vipers all day with the Holland and Holland and all one did was use up cartridges and attract more vultures, vipers and other carrion from far and wide. The steamy thickets were alive with creatures enthusiastically waiting for others to drop dead. The residence had an extremely depressing effect on even the most robust of human souls.

A few workmen lounged in the afternoon sun and a maid came out to stare sullenly at them as they bumped onto the concrete parking area at the side of the house. Park anywhere else and you were sucked slowly into the mud. But there was an orchard beyond the house full of orange trees and guavas, where coloured lights were being strung. Sir Reginald was holding the party to impress Paraguayan society. Harry was not sure if such a thing existed, and if it did he doubted whether it could be charmed by the most capable nuncio to drive out of Asunción on the day of a very interesting assassination to gossip by a swamp. The maid grudgingly showed him up to a room to wash and shave and despite himself he drifted off to sleep on the bed, only to be woken by a strange and disconcerting hissing in the darkness. At first he thought it was one of the swamp's more terrifying inhabitants coming to look for Dunroamin's new owner. When after breathless seconds he managed to operate a bedside lamp the reptile turned out to be Chambers.

"I say you're going to miss the bash old man. Don't forget Tough's wife's here. She's even more peculiar than he is. Quite a good turnout really considering the venue. The Americans have telephoned to say they will put in an appearance. The dagos must think it's the safest place to be at the moment with everyone waving cattle prods in town."

Harry could hear that the band had started, and a small trio of voices and guitars competed with it in a lilting song about love and death and yet more death. He sighed. One of the pleasures of living out in the middle of the jungle was not having to go to affairs like this, although they were far better value than the average European diplomatic thrash and it was quite common to find someone murdered in the shrubbery afterwards. Mabel told a story of how she talked to a Major General once for an hour at a barbecue given by the Acuerdo National, the official opposition, only to realize as a waiter held champagne in front of his sightless eyes that he had been poisoned. Mabel was a born diplomat. Tough would be mad to get rid of her.

"Must I?" Harry said as Chambers handed him a crumpled jacket and tie.

The fact that a man like Sir Reginald had a wife, poor coot, intrigued Harry who once had one of his own, Cynthia. The girl nursed him back to health in a little cottage hospital in Hertfordshire after the Dunkirk evacuation and four machine gun bullets in the leg which still gave him a slight limp. Cynthia had thought the wound rather dashing and in the end had proved far harder to get rid of than the bullets. They had married during the war and lived in a tiny mock Tudor confection in Radlett with roses growing up the wall, while he worked at a military intelligence establishment nearby; when he was at home. She had developed from a kind, well-endowed nurse to being a fussy and, dare he say it, plump wife who nagged him constantly. The marriage, made in hospital, had become a casualty after only a year, yet she always wrote to him without knowing where in the world he was before she finally gave up and they divorced.

In her purposeful handwriting she had explained that her decision was so that he would grow up. Now she lived on the Isle of Wight, no doubt a pillar of the WVS and the local Conservative Association. A petty niggle began to take root in his mind. Perhaps his masters wouldn't recommend a knighthood because of what he did to dear old Cynthia? It might be better to retire somewhere like India as Chambers had suggested. He took a glass of punch from a silver tray, noticing as he passed that the waiter had his trousers undone. Harry spotted Lady Tough immediately.

"Of course, I met poor Mr Somoza in London and all I can say is that he was a charming man who had his country's interests at heart. It's his poor widow I feel sorry for. And it must have been such a painful and unexpected way to go . . . " Lady Tough was addressing a grim-faced group of army wives who did not understand a word she was saying; just as well, thought Harry.

In the next little group under the blue and red fairy-lights the same subject was being discussed with much hilarity, and it was generally agreed in a mixture of Spanish and Guaraní, that the old lecher, not content with his own mistress and foolish enough to dally with the escorts of some of the most eminent gangsters in Asunción, had stepped over the borders of etiquette and got what he deserved, and for an assassination the matter had been carried off with a panache and originality rarely seen these days though the army were right to round up Leftists, just in case.

Harry had ceased to be amazed by the country's politics where it was not only possible, but desirable and sometimes extremely vital, to hold conflicting views. A small commotion among the vultures and just the faintest whisper of a splash signalled something had been unfortunate enough to fall into the swamp. A rotten silty smell blended with the barbecue smoke and there was a clumsy flapping in the palms. The vultures were ready for their supper. So were Lady Tough's guests who looked expectantly at a smoking fire on which a wire mesh had been spread with unwholesome meat as canapés were handed round and the wife of the Interior Minister, brought up in the deprived Chaco, wrapped them carefully in her serviette and placed them in her handbag while deftly continuing the conversation.

The nearest thing to nobility, although Asunción was full of counts and the occasional Ruritanian king, was a white-haired man with a spotted bow tie and lacquered cigarette holder who was related to Generalísimo José Félix Estigarribia, hero of the Chaco War. Harry had seen him before at parties and always wondered if it was his pedigree or his penchant for elegantly exposing himself which got him invited back time after time. Lady Tough fussed over him and after kissing her hand he begged to be excused and walked off to relieve himself in the bushes, deliberately selecting the higher drier ground. His wife looked bored and worked a tooth pick round her gold front teeth while the Estigarribia seemed to be having trouble with his flies. Here it comes, thought Harry, and as the band struck up a pre-requested patriotic song the old man turned and ceremonially exposed himself to the entire gathering with a delicacy born only of frequent practice and good breeding.

"Bravo!" shouted his wife clapping her hands and looking about her at the thirty or more guests who did not show the slightest flicker of surprise. Harry moved closer to Lady Tough, who seemed to be the sort of woman his wife Cynthia would have grown into, a bustling mass of corset and face powder forever falling on its own dignity. As he was about to introduce himself Lady Tough began to scratch her ample backside and before he knew it an interloper in an orange overall had stepped in. Harry decided it might not be a bad thing; the contents of the overall were well known to him.

"Not quite what you're used to I suppose. Hardly Kensington what? Younger country and all that. . . . "

Lady Tough scowled at the newcomer. "What my guests do

is no concern of yours, young man. Are you here to mend a car or to plaster a wall? Don't you think it's time you went home? Do you usually drink your employer's wine?"

"Now, now, Lady Tough," said the orange suit masterfully. "You don't recognize me do you? You shouldn't get flustered at a new country's customs. They are always exposing themselves, especially at parades. Something to do with their Indian heritage. Do you know seventy per cent of Paraguayans are of Indian descent? Some of this lot's grandfathers actually ate people." Lady Tough was bristling, about to call out the guard. "You don't recognize me in my Number Two fancy dress, do you? If you think about it, I usually wear a kind of frock. A long black number? Full length? Yes, I can see you've got it. We met in church on Sunday. I'm the vicar of St Jude's remember, you invited me. I say is that you lurking by that tree Major? Come and vouch for me. I'm about to get kicked out because of my Number Two dress and evil ways." Harry came forward and Lady Tough made a gurgling sound of welcome.

"We had a bit of a panic at the service, didn't we?" continued the man in the Belisha beacon suit. "Haven't seen you in town for a long time Harry but it was fun last Sunday. Some *campesinos* were turning over an old melon patch and a snake got into church. Certainly took everyone's mind off things spiritual. I think it's still in there, in the organ probably. Of course I don't believe it was dangerous, not like those around here from that swamp."

Lady Tough looked down quickly at her feet.

"Do you often have snakes and gardeners running through your church, and why are you dressed as a mechanic?"

Harry smiled as Lady Tough wrestled with her composure. She had scowled at him almost immediately. A more considered scowl than that she was giving the jolly priest. Sir Reginald had obviously been telling her about him. He tried to put himself in Tough's place, being moved to a new posting with a sewer of a consulate and a residence with its own swamp, knowing there is a mysterious high-ranking Englishman connected with the Foreign Office, with his own private army, palace and nubile mistress, whom no one seems at all willing to explain. Would Cynthia have come to Paraguay? She would most likely have looked it up in the *Reader's Digest Atlas* and decided against it as it didn't have a coast or something equally bizarre. Yet if she had come and they had had children, his masters would have had to move him by now and found someone else to keep his finger in the dyke, so to speak.

The vicar of St Jude's, a handsome man with blond hair and blue eyes, looked more like an out-of-training film star than a priest. "Oh no," he bowled on. "I can't mend cars and that sort of thing. I only wear this if I've been up to La Trinidad, the leper colony just up the road. That's one of the better ones they let out over by the salad bowl. Hope you don't mind me bringing him."

Harry laughed. "Do you still see old Rosas up there? Hasn't he a reputation for murdering priests?"

"That's why I wear the suit. He goes to get his gun as soon as he sees dust in the distance or hears a Jeep, and he rules that leper colony just as he used to rule the streets of São Paulo. It must be the only settlement for the chronically sick with a protection racket. I'm sorry Lady Tough, you're new here. Rosas was a Brazilian gangster who first introduced drug trafficking, or so it's said, on a large organized scale to Asunción, now without rival in the world. But he got into a trial of strength with a man called Napoleon Cortez – no, don't laugh, that's his real name, poor soul – who had just taken the job of police chief. Mr Cortez didn't bother with the normal formalities of arrest and killed all of the Brazilian's top men, bottling up Rosas himself in Asunción where he sought sanctuary with a priest and fellow countryman at that.

"Unfortunately the papist was in the pay of Cortez and spirited him out to the church in the colony at La Trinidad, where he was waited on by lepers. Of course he caught the disease, and in such a terrible form that he cannot leave. He is said to want to make one last journey to shake the hand of Napoleon Cortez before he dies, which really should have been years ago. I should not say this but I think it's the hate which keeps him going. That's why he shoots priests. He doesn't believe I'm a proper priest, being C of E and I play chess with him, but if I went in there in full fig I would be carried back as dead as a doornail. I say Harry, you don't think my leper will contaminate the salad?"

"Every chance I would have thought," he said. He turned to Lady Tough. "You must let this young man be your guide. He's a mine of information."

"You've been here a long time Major," said the ambassador's wife slowly. "I would have thought you would have been the best person to consult. Just what is it you do all the way down there in the south?"

People had started to dance on the boards in front of the improvised band stand as a waltz struck up. I'm blowed if I'm going to answer her, thought Harry and the Reverend unexpectedly came to his rescue.

"Oh, what Harry does is terribly hush-hush," he said putting a carefully manicured finger to his lips.

"Terribly hush-hush," repeated Harry, spying the considerable form of Chambers at the buffet. "I'm sorry I must go and meet Rio's answer to Harry Lime. Not every day there's an assassination you know. Goodnight Rev. Tell her about the War of the Triple Alliance."

Almost before he had finished speaking the personable young vicar, his fingers toying with the chiffon sleeve of the large lady's gown, began to tell the story of the dreadful war in which Brazil, Argentina and Uruguay with a little help from Britain slaughtered most Paraguayans, leaving only twenty-eight thousand men. Women outnumbered men by nearly four to one. It was the starting place for most conversation about Paraguay and used on new visitors to try to explain and justify the strange and dangerous state they found. The war had taken place in the middle of the last century and standards regarding the sanctity of life had probably declined since. The sly Reverend used the epic for a different reason, a sermon almost, on how he was faced with temptation at every turn and how it was only human to fail and to give in to sin. Harry had heard it all before. As he walked over towards the broad back of the Fat Man at the refreshment tables the vicar had his arm round

Lady Tough's shoulders and was pointing out the fetching silhouette of the swamp set off against the sunset.

"I wouldn't touch too much of the fodder, Chambers. The randy vicar of St Jude's brought along a leper from La Trinidad. Are you sure that's a sausage?"

Chambers looked savage as he threw the morsel away and foraged for something in a jar. "I'll have to raid the kitchens later," he said sulkily.

It was probably not the best time to have a quiet word on the security of his prisoner, on the feud between Cortez and Labuschagne, on what Petroni had told him, but he might not get another chance. Harry was about to open his mouth when Chambers spoke first, anticipating what he was going to say. "While you were snoring your head off . . . Just what do you do down in Paradiso that makes you so tired? Can't be anything official." He grinned at Harry. "While you were in the land of nod I have been hard at it old boy. People believe there is going to be a lot of blood. I hear prophesies of drug wars and worse. Warlords vying for territory now there is chaos among the gangs after the assassination. The Lebanese gangsters blame the Syrians who blame the Turks who blame the Italians who blame the Koreans. Things are such a mess I can imagine only one man can be responsible: Cortez. The first time this happened we nearly had to pull you out and sent you new bang-bangs so you could hold the fort. In the circumstances we couldn't possibly let another man take over, even discounting Tough. Your role has always been one of delicate negotiation with these madmen. What I'm saying Harry is we cannot have a balls-up, not after so many years. Let it go quiet again. Please."

Harry felt sick. The arguments he would have used to provoke his retirement had been used to justify his staying. Yet he was partly flattered. He was not sure when he had last heard Chambers say "please" in such a sincere way. The Fat Man was right: it was a subtle art to hide and stay hidden if one ran away to Paraguay. Somoza had learnt that lesson on the streets of Asunción all too well when a rocket had not only snuffed out his life but made his memory ridiculous as well.

"Have you spoken to Cortez?" he said suspiciously as a man nearby took the corned beef out of several sandwiches and stuffed it into his mouth. There was a Rotary Club badge in his lapel.

Chambers dabbed his lips. "Mr Cortez, thank heavens, is your province. You know he's barking and I think that German Rudel and you are the only Europeans he sees. I'm told he's a galloping hypochondriac. Cortez is another reason why you can't go for the time being. But he won't live for ever."

Harry winced. "I wouldn't let him hear you say that, or anyone here for that matter. No one is untouchable where Uncle Napi is concerned. I would not be at all surprised if it was our esteemed Head of Investigaciones who put Somoza out to celestial pasture."

The Fat Man looked uncomfortable. It was no joke: Napoleon had the power of life and death, even over Chambers once he stepped across the border, though he seldom exercised it nowadays and lived for considerable periods of time on reputation. "Yes, they do say he really detested Somoza. Probably thought the man a health risk." The great chins wobbled with attempted mirth.

A family of raccoons sitting on a low stone wall had taken over from the man who had been eating the middles out of the sandwiches and the large male was washing the bread off in a silver punchbowl. A horrible cocktail of smells blew in from the swamp.

"Don't worry, Chambers. Napoleon will have far too many things on his mind to spare a thought for our little problem, who, I might add, is in rude health. *Cave*, here comes His Excellency.

Sir Reginald Tough had none of the charm which was many ambassadors' only qualification and his long nose, staring eyes and hunched shoulders made him appear a bit like a drawing Harry had once seen of a Jabberwocky. The face was etched with failure despite the knighthood awarded for sneaking on his chums in Hong Kong. The Foreign Office had sent him to the right place if they wanted to get rid of him; they didn't suffer fools like Sir Reggie wisely here. The fools themselves suffered, often terminally.

"Hello Chambers. Pleased to see you have emerged from the woodwork at long last, Major Smith. Glad you could come." He produced a paper from his inside pocket with a flourish. On it he had scribbled some notes. "We have such a lot to sort out I hope you don't mind if I come straight to the point. We don't have a file for Major Smith and the reason we don't have one is classified. Even the classification is classified. Surely I can be told the reason for his presence in this country?" he demanded. "If not I wish to know exactly the protocol on the question of seniority with Mr Smith."

"Major *Copeland*-Smith," Harry corrected. The diplomat glared at him.

"Well, by any name . . . Just what is it you are doing here, Major? All I could find to enlighten me is a series of irregular diary entries by the late Mr Tupper who died in very mysterious circumstances. He seemed to be of the opinion you received extensive military supplies and have what amounts to a private army of Apache Indians."

"Aché Indians," Harry chipped in again. "The Apache have always preferred North America, bless them."

Sir Reginald's medals quivered. "Chambers, really, I will not be treated like this. I require an explanation. . . . "

The man was not going to be easily appeased but Chambers launched into a practised response on how Harry had a few native "trusties" up his sleeve from the "old days" when it was thought necessary to protect missionaries and expeditions and that sort of thing. Not even an infant would have believed such a pack of lies and the ambassador shifted irritably from foot to foot as Chambers eulogized on Harry. Suddenly there was a gunshot.

"*Mi Patria o Muerte*! My Country or Death!" cried Admiral Alonso of Paraguay's riparian Navy shooting his antique revolver in the air. Many copied him, and in the drained swimming pool a vulture made the first tentative moves towards a guest who had been very, very still for far too long. Two of the Minister of the Interior's young aides were handing round a silver wine coaster full to the brim with cocaine while other officials had already passed out. The fairy-lights in the trees revealed that only the vultures had maintained a modicum of dignity, and girlish screams came from behind the house. Lady Tough and the vicar were nowhere to be seen.

" . . . I say you know they have just opened a new Korean restaurant in Asunción. Great cooks the Koreans, lashings of garlic and do splendid things with tripe. But of course you must know that from all your extensive experience out East," Chambers was saying to Sir Reginald who was somewhat green about the gills. He had a look of hatred and envy in his eyes and they were fixed on Harry, not a nice expression. It was clear Tough had decided he was to be the scapegoat for the ills that surrounded him, thinking that by uncovering a scandal he could get sent elsewhere. Little did he know what can of worms he was trying to pry open. Harry smiled blandly in his direction. Tough's eyes were glazed and he began to sway.

"Excuse me sir, are you all right?" asked his aide taking his arm. People had left the dance floor and the crush pressed around them. Sir Reginald nearly fell over one of the collapsed revellers. "Fuck off lackey and look after that young CIA whipper-snapper over there," commanded Chambers pointing to an effeminate man by the punchbowl who seemed to be deep in conversation with a tree. The aide obeyed.

" . . . moreover it was a British Army weapon!" Tough was now shouting. "I rang the police myself when you were having a siesta. What do you think of that? A British Army weapon. What do you think of that? I understand you have weapons at your disposal Major . . . " His voice trailed off. "I'm worried about my wife. Where is the old thing? Often has a drop too much at these occasions."

The aide, horrified, glanced over at Tough and tried to direct the American's attention away from His most unsteady Excellency. He'd been well and truly nobbled. They had put something in his drink or spiked the canapés. "Now see here Major Smith or whatever your name is . . . Just why do you need this private army?" Even if Harry had been inclined to tell him the unlucky man picked that moment to crash to the floor.

"Reminds me of one of those brick factory chimneys being blown up. He fell absolutely rigid. Remarkable. I hope he's not damaged that unique nose," said Chambers.

Harry thought it time Tough kept his nose to himself. Ambassadors should know their place and this one obviously did not. He looked down at the mud-splattered failure of diplomacy.

"Wouldn't it be a lot easier to tell him about me and Paradiso? Issue some kind of 'Order of Battle'. You are always good at that sort of legal thing Chambers. Make him sign the Official Secrets Act again, upside down, nude or something instead of him asking all these questions. Other people might start becoming interested, especially at the moment."

"You certainly are an innocent old thing at times Harry," said Chambers. "I wouldn't trust that fellow to do my washing. Don't worry we will deal with him. I shouldn't think he will want to be reminded of tonight." A photographer with a badge saying "ABC Colour" came over with an ancient plate camera and an even larger flash gun. The young man asked permission and pointed the vast piece of equipment at Tough. The flash blinded them for a moment and then Harry heard the crackle of a radio. The CIA man was now seen to be speaking into his left lapel. Oh God, thought Harry, the madmen cometh.

He was right. Through the chilly night under a canopy of stars came the sound of a siren and people started to vanish, even driving in the direction of La Trinidad rather than towards the dreadful sound. They feared Cortez's police. But the raccoon stood unperturbed by the punchbowl as did the more important guests. It was only the CIA chief's security convoy. He had decided to come out for a talk with Harry as he knew what the Major did, and his secret, and it caused him many sleepless nights.

It always amazed Harry that Americans could never do things quietly. Three cars drew up, all of them Cadillacs, and determined agents jumped out and surrounded the house, the remaining guests and even the vultures before their boss poked his nose out. In his white jogging suit and crewcut the seemingly easy-going middle-aged man looked just how American diplomats are meant to look; dignified and concerned. Except Harry knew that the man had responsibility for "dirty tricks" for the whole of Latin America. He took a dim view of anyone who disturbed his grim plans.

He shook Harry's hand and then Chambers' purposefully, as if starting a judo throw. He oozed Christian concern in the direction of Sir Reginald.

"He's been asking a few questions hasn't he? Not that I mean to admonish you in any way," began the sinister American. "But my boys cannot help overhearing what goes on, though we never interfere directly unless it's absolutely necessary. Is he some kind of lush? His files don't show it. It's really good to meet you again Major; keeping in trim I see. He's not getting too much of a problem is he?" Harry did not like the way the man was looking at Tough, like an expectant undertaker only a few corpses ahead of the Official Receiver. It gave him the creeps.

"He's breathing, sir. I thought for a moment we had a termination." The booming voice came from an intelligence man with immense shoulders. "Eye movement sir, but weak life functions."

"You didn't stamp on him did you Karl?" snapped his boss. "Get him inside and lay him down. Be careful now."

Tough was picked up like a sack of potatoes and carried towards the house. One of the band came up and asked if he should continue and was waved away. Under the Monroe Doctrine, the party had been completely invaded by Americans. Bloody cheek. Harry kept his mouth shut. No wonder all gringos were hated. A small huddle of high-ranking government officials were protesting to a secret serviceman, who merely smiled patronizingly and told them to go. Have a nice country, thought Harry. He could forgive them if they weren't so bad mannered.

"Sorry to drop in on you like this," apologized their leader.

"Very sorry. But having lost one of our *enfants terribles* today on his way to lunch, a man to whom we had promised protection, I got to wondering about the security of the other, more sensitive charge. Then my boys told me your new ambassador was being inquisitive. Do you need some help? Do you want us to take the prisoner off your hands for a while? None of us is getting any younger."

Chambers was looking blankly at Harry as the radios crackled around them. Could it be possible what he had just heard? Yet the Fat Man seemed none too pleased. Why? he wondered. His was not the sort of problem one could give away every day and surely this was no time for transatlantic rivalry. Why not get rid of it? Let the Yanks have him.

"Perhaps we should talk in the car," said the CIA chief. "Things will warm up after this Somoza tragedy." He cast a suspicious glance towards the raccoon who glared back at him alone and defiant from the wine-stained table.

Other revellers who, like Sir Reginald, had eaten narcotic pastries were stacked in neat piles by the secret agents, while one liberal assembly member was quietly knocked unconscious by Karl for refusing to stop screaming at what he had seen in the swimming pool. As they were driven towards Asunción a plish, gurgle, grunt announced that something even nastier had taken over the swamp night-shift from the vultures.

The party was over.

Chapter 5

Harry woke at seven sharp, as he always did, in a rather spartan but adequate bedroom of the Hotel Paraná, where he had returned after declining an offer of a bed for the night at the US embassy. In his delicate position he could not be seen to be taking too many favours from the Yanks. Last night the CIA had poured them pre-emptive whiskies in glasses the size of fruit bowls, but Chambers had been in no mood for a cosy chat. In the most diplomatic of language he had accused the Americans of wanting to take over the job in Paradiso to save face after their cock-up with Somoza; he had been under their protection and now they couldn't find all the bits. No, Harry's methods had worked up until now and that was the way the British Government wanted things to stay.

Harry did not want to contradict Chambers in front of the CIA, but it seemed the Yanks were using his name and that of his charge to cover up their own bungling and if he played his cards right it might be his ticket home. If things did get tricky the CIA would have to step in anyway, but for the moment Harry argued that the assassination was not part of any general unrest or threat to his man. Somoza had brought it on himself by buying into the rackets of Asunción with the hundreds of millions of dollars he had stolen from Nicaragua – a move never likely to prolong his life. His terminal mistake was to steal the mistress of the brother of Napoleon Cortez, head of the Departamento de Investigaciones. A real danger was that Napoleon had become a gringo-hater of late and was capable of anything . . . In the end the Americans were in a fine lather. Harry's prisoner, they said, was of international stature and could not be at the whim of a corrupt police chief. Then to Harry's horror it was decided that he, as he had known Cortez on and off for most of his years in Paraguay, should go and see the monster. It was not a prospect he relished.

Harry yawned, got out of bed and put on his grey suit and Surrey Cricket Club tie, admiring himself in the mirror before rushing down for a quick breakfast of coffee and cherry cake. He wanted to get the meeting over early if possible. He felt a pang of fear as he returned to the room, sat on the bed and asked the switchboard operator for Cortez's direct line. He could tell from the operator's slightly breathless voice that she knew who the number belonged to. Harry was now through to a secretary. Then he heard a stern interruption from the other side of the office. The brisk ratlike man behind the huge military desk had heard Harry's name and demanded to see him. His appointment was for 8:30 and he arrived damp from the rainy wind blowing in off the river.

The long, low one-storey building of the Departamento on La Nuestra Señora de Asunción was probably the most understated piece of architecture in the city. Other ministers sat enthroned in hideous temples of gaucho baroque while Cortez, who was a good deal more powerful, had this strange whitewashed building near the river, a rambling building whose sides were about a quarter of a mile long with soldiers smartly patrolling each corner and doorway. Some said it had been a monastery and the death cells were once the cells of monks. No one walked on the pavements by it; no one went near it. Every family in the country had some dreadful story to tell about what happened inside, and about the man who ran it.

A well-rounded duty sergeant, who but for his paramilitary uniform could have been straight out of an English country police station, politely showed him to a waiting room with white tiled walls, two simple wooden chairs and a table. Harry was in the everyday business end of the Departamento and he could smell the cells under that part of the building: the sickly sweetness of urine, the stench of the monkey house. It clung to your clothes when you left, if you left. Once inside Harry always felt his stomach tighten and a dryness come into his mouth, even though he had been there a dozen times before.

Two guards entered and asked him to come with them and marched quickly down a long corridor off which stretched the administration departments. These men in their khaki drill were from Napoleon's personal bodyguard. They were clean shaven, unlike most of the country's police, and very smart. Napoleon was a stickler for discipline and detail, and Harry admired that. A meticulous man who had no time for fools. He wondered what Cortez thought of the new so-called ambassador.

They approached a security check and he was made to turn out all his pockets and leave his suit jacket with a woman in blue gabardine who, like a cloakroom attendant, handed him a ticket. Down the corridor he came to a pair of swing doors and a man gave him an expert body search. A little further he had to walk through a metal detector, a grey plastic arch. Cortez loved his security: a series of tests on the way to meet the devil incarnate.

They turned a corner and came to a courtyard, and the smell of orange blossom replaced that of frightened men. Beside cloisters fashioned by priests was a little garden. A humming-bird darted over what Harry knew to be a fish pond but he could not quite make it out as they hurried past. In the garden were more guards – with ugly Uzi sub-machine pistols held unstrapped and at the ready – as there were every ten yards down the corridor. These too were Napoleon's superior brand of secret policemen. They had no chairs and did not loll against the wall, were young and, Harry supposed, keen. It always surprised him given their reputation, not that it should have: the Waffen SS must have been composed of the same kind of fine keen young men; or the Inquisition, which had operated from within these walls.

The guard on his right pressed a button next to the massive wooden door at the end of the corridor and smiled as Harry turned to look at him. He wondered what the young man's father thought of his profession, himself probably a banker or small merchant boasting in his cups about his powerful son as his friends listened reverently, but hating him just a little. It was a paradox that Paraguay was such an efficient police state but had a population who loathed the police.

A bell rang inside. His guards left him as he stepped through the first door and was searched again by an older man. A second door opened, and behind the large military desk which never had a scrap of paper on its leather top beamed Napoleon Cortez who stood up to greet him with the sweetest of expressions. He came to the centre of the room but did not shake hands. He never shook hands for fear of other people's germs. Harry knew that.

Napoleon returned to his side of the desk, took out a packet of Kleenex tissues and wiped his long fingers. He was a smart precise little man, nothing like the rum-soaked, stubble-faced stereotype of the South American secret policeman. Such creatures did exist, but in small towns in the north until one excess too many led to their removal, usually in a wooden box. Most were sufficiently frightened of Cortez to keep their noses very clean indeed. He held up a manicured chalk-white hand at the other side of the vast desk for Harry to remain silent as he pored over a file taken from his desk drawer. A guard had come into the room, standing motionless by the door. Napoleon touched the file as little as possible, as though it had been exposed to smallpox. It was Harry's file.

Harry knew the stories behind the absurd name. The real name was unpronounceable. He was the child of a family of Balkan origin and had been sent to Asunción's Military Academy. There his polo-playing peers had teased him with the nickname Napoleon because of his size and pride. At first he had sulked, but finally began to sign himself Napoleon and expand his talents to measure up to it. The generals who ran the establishment grudgingly passed him out third in his year. Napoleon regarded not winning the Sword of Honour as a personal slight.

But the generals sought to make short work of the arrogant young officer. It was the mid-thirties and Paraguay was engaged in the Chaco War with Boliva. Napoleon was put in charge of dispirited bands of Indian *macheteros*, armed only with cane-cutting machetes. The function of these troops was to draw and deplete enemy machine-gun fire. It had been a suicide posting, but, luckily for Napoleon the Bolivians were on the offensive at the time, sending raiding parties into the Paraguayan lines. Everyone was a target and he and his *macheteros* did not have to charge the dreadful machine-gun nests. In this breathing space he hit on a plan to discourage raids which earned him his second name. His Indians were told to lay ambushes for Bolivian stragglers who were then subject to specially devised *cortes*, combinations of machete strokes which caused a slow, lingering death as the soldier tried to crawl or drag himself back to his own lines at night, followed by silent Indios in soot-black ponchos ready to do the same to anyone who tried to help him. Men screamed for hours, sometimes days. The least severe of the *cortes* was the *corte de rodillas*, a slash behind both knees which severed the tendons: the most horrific, the *corte de chalaco*, or waistcoat cut in which both the arms were severed and the belly slashed to expose the intestines. Bolivian troops soon showed a marked reluctance to attack Napoleon's *fantasmas*, his company of ghosts. Prisoners of other units were threatened with a visit to "Señor Cortes" which soon became Señor Cortez. Señor Napoleon Cortez.

It was in the Chaco that Napoleon also learned his techniques for extracting information. A logical commander, he was not interested in cruelty for the sake of it, only its effect. Traditional methods such as castration tended not to make a captive garrulous. "Bring me information, not balls," he said. It became clear to him that asphyxiation was the greatest fear, and it could be controlled. Two of the standard tortures still used in the building where Harry was now had been born in the Chaco. The *pileta*, in which a person was rocked back into a tub of excrement with his arms bound to his knees, and the kiss, or *beso de Judas*. This entailed the captive's mouth being forced open with a stick and a thin strip of leather poked down his throat. Water dribbled down the rawhide would make him start to choke. In this way Cortez was able to pinpoint Bolivian machine-gun positions and ambush them. The exploits of his men were Paraguayan folklore. From his earliest days Cortez seemed destined for the office he now held.

"I see it's raining outside." Cortez took out a pair of old-fashioned round glasses and placed them carefully on his nose. His pencil-thin moustache formed a sharp black line above a sardonic mouth. "I could have sent a car for you, only the Departamento cars tend to upset people. You're not going to smoke are you? Good. What did you think of our little excitement the other day? Very spectacular wouldn't you say? Like your Fifth of November."

"A most terrible thing, Mr Somoza's death," Harry said carefully, looking for a sign, "but I cannot see he will be missed, except, I am told, by Asunción's ice-cream salesmen. But in one respect Somoza is what I have come to see you about. My bosses are worried that this incident might mark the beginning of a policy to remove foreign exiles. I hope you don't mind me speaking frankly. Some groups, it is said, want to clear such fugitives out of the country and we were worried it could affect my prisoner."

"I have heard that too," said Napoleon affably, as if they were two elderly men in a street café discussing their families. "But you may be sure it isn't true. Not a word of it. Somoza brought me headaches with all his money. We did not want them. He stirred up trouble. He was a threat to order. Your prisoner is different. That is a matter of honour agreed long ago. A matter of personal concern to me and the *Presidente*."

"Thank you for the reassurance Señor Cortez," said Harry. The large brown eyes continued to examine him and it was hard to look away.

"Every year, Major Copeland-Smith, I think you will return to England; every year you do not." Cortez toyed with his moustache. "You stay here with us and become a little more Paraguayan. I don't think you want to leave. Does Mr Chambers want you to leave? I think not. I cannot see him or your precious Americans giving Paradiso to that thick-headed sergeant. Do you want to go home, Harry?" Napoleon sounded sincere.

"I haven't really thought about it much," Harry lied. "I expect it's all in hand. I have talked it over from time to time. I'm not getting any younger and haven't your stamina, Señor Cortez. I do know that we don't want to hand the job over to the Yanks."

"Have you ever thought of us taking him off your hands?" said Napoleon suddenly. "He would be just as safe because no one goes against the wishes, the very secret wishes, of our beloved *Presidente*. Not while I'm alive." The eyes seemed to grow larger. "It's a possibility we could discuss, yes? You could go home to England and grow roses." He smiled. "You could take Maria?"

Harry didn't like the mention of Maria. But the eyes became even more benign. "Sometimes, Harry, I think you do not like me. We are friends are we not? Have I ever gone back on my word? I do not think you like me." Harry heard a slight movement from the guard behind.

"Oh but I do," he replied quickly to the man they called the Animal of Asunción and whom every beggar said was a psychopath in a barely audible whisper and with a certain amount of national pride. "Oh but I do."

"You can call me Napi, my close friends do." Harry was amazed and cautious. An insult could send one straight to the cells.

"Thank you very much," he said.

"Napi. . . . "

"Thank you very much . . . Napi."

"You do like us really, don't you? When you are sitting in your house with your Maria? You do like this country of ours?"

"Yes Napi, I do like Paraguay."

"I *love* Paraguay."

Harry was beginning to feel uneasy. "I share your sentiments entirely, er, Napi. And now I can take it that my prisoner is secure I had better get back to the shop, so to speak. You must be very busy." He was about to get up but Napoleon raised his hand.

"Don't be in such a hurry, Harry. I want to tell you about

my dream. About my vision of a better Paraguay after I am gone." Napoleon paused, looking for an answer. Harry was aware he was walking on eggshells. "I know many gringos joke that we are a dirty little country and cannot exist without foreign aid and smuggling drugs. I want to put an end to that. Now we have the largest hydro-electric scheme in the world at Itapúa. We will make millions selling that electricity. The dam will give me the power to cleanse this country. Do you know what I mean, Harry?"

He almost said yes, but bit his tongue and raised his eyebrows instead. Thankfully Cortez continued.

"Yes, I have a dream. Let me explain it slowly, it takes a while for gringos to grasp things. Today I have the government monopoly for water and electricity supply, Hydrosana. If anyone wants to take a bath or switch on a light he will have to have permission from me. Do you realize what a small percentage of this country has proper sanitation and electricity? Not nearly enough! Without these things we take for granted it is easy to catch diseases or fall over and break your neck. So I have set up the Committee of Public Safety and Sanitation and am going to take the fruits of Itapúa to the nation, *pueblo* by *pueblo*. Everyone will have lights in their houses and a lavatory to flush with Paraguayan water. Of course the people will pay me for the service and we will no longer need the criminals, the drug dealers. . . . "

Harry could hardly believe his ears.

"Of course certain people cannot be permitted to remain," continued Cortez. "I dislike very much your neighbour Father Labuschagne. I dislike him a lot. He has been lining his pockets with the money of Somoza. He has established his own little kingdom in the south, and that is not my vision of the New Paraguay. An essential part of the country should not be controlled by a foreign opportunist. You must help me, Harry. Be part of my dream. I will be frank with you. I need an excuse to convince the *Presidente* that Father Labuschagne must be removed. At the moment the *Presidente* wants no more violence. He is hoping for a Papal visit. But if Labuschagne was to threaten you in some way. Even attack your fine house . . . It would be a matter of honour to protect your prisoner. Help me Harry. I want to leave behind me a country with peace and tranquillity where everyone has proper sanitation. Do you know more people were killed in the Chaco by disease than by bullets? But for my dream to come true I must remove these gangsters who would oppose me."

Harry could picture a column of Napoleon's mounted troops, harnesses jangling and machete sheaths slapping against their horses' flanks, forcing lavatories, even bidets, on frightened *pueblos* and razing those to the ground that did not want, or could not afford, to be connected to Cortez's private sewage system. Pissing in the bushes would be a seditious act. Surely the man could not be serious

"We hold the future," beamed Cortez. "We hold the future in our hands every time we go to the lavatory!" Cortez laughed. Harry thought the safest thing to do was to laugh with him. He abruptly became aware that he was laughing by himself in the large echoing room.

"So you think my plans are a joke?"

"No, er Napi, I think they are very sensible. You would be better rid of the drug trade . . . Lavatories would be good for Paraguay."

"So Paraguay is a dirty little country then? You insult the honour of my country bathed in the blood of many heroes. Because you are a gringo you think you can come in here and tell *me* I am dirty. Guard!"

He had walked into a trap baited by the madman. He could not win. Harry was about to protest he had diplomatic immunity when a blow to the side of his head put out the lights. The last thing he remembered was that the friendliness in those large brown eyes had vanished. Instead it was like looking into the wilderness of the Chaco.

He was brought round by the throbbing pain in his head. He must have been out for some time. Twenty feet above him on bars open to the sky a guard stood. He smiled and spat when he saw his prisoner stirring. Harry looked around him. There was no bed, table, chair, wash basin or crucifix. No doors, only a small exit and entrance hole for a channel of intermittent water to take away his filth. Bread and water were lowered to him in a bucket. Yet thankfully no one came to beat him, to torture him with electrodes or partially drown him. They knew he would co-operate. The four vile days he spent in the pit were to remind him that this was Paraguay and if Cortez so ordained he could spend the rest of his life there – which, in that cell, would not be long.

When they ordered him to climb out up a rickety, ancient ladder and dragged him to the Departamento's infirmary, he expected torture. Instead he was bathed, thoroughly disinfected and returned to Cortez's office.

"You don't need to say anything this time," said the little man. "Don't worry, I informed everyone you spent a few days on my *estancia*. No one is looking for you. But to business."

From behind the great desk he stepped towards Harry and dropped a satchel round his neck. It was of good leather and the kind Departamento motor cycle dispatch riders used. He had seen them before. Napoleon placed a sealed envelope inside.

"Deliver that to Father Labuschagne for me. It will annoy him. If you do as I say, now and in the future, you will get home in one piece. It may put your prisoner under threat but if you don't obey me . . . " He paused. "We now have nothing to lose by telling the world your secret. We do not need your aid."

He had been bundled out of a Jeep by the bus station. He felt alone; not even Chambers could help him. He felt numb, then angry, but later strangely pleased. At least you have got out in one piece, Harry old boy, he told himself. More than that, his prisoner was under real threat. Surely they would have to move him. . . .

Chapter 6

Labuschagne was a man of immense proportions. He towered above Harry. His shoulders could fill a door and his walking stick was the size of a stave. The knees of the black, well-worn suit were wet and muddy. Had he been praying? At his devotions somewhere on his small island in the middle of the lake which shimmered in the sunlight? It was whispered Labuschagne prayed aloud in his native Afrikaans as no one could understand the strange rasping language. It was said he had once shot a man in the leg for talking in church and nailed another to a tree for taking a sacred Madonna from a peasant shrine. Harry had heard all the gossip and had always tried to keep the priest at a distance. Now that was impossible. The terrible man had a smile on his ruddy, deeply lined face.

"So, you have become Cortez's messenger-boy. I had a better opinion of you than that, Englishman. You have become unclean."

They were standing on a jetty and a cold breeze stirred the reeds, making Harry shiver. His heart beat faster as Labuschagne stared at him. The bulbous, broken nose and heavy jaw made him look like a retired boxer. But then you met the eyes, fierce blue eyes with an Arctic coldness about them. Even when the thin mouth smiled those eyes were angry, and the voice was as deep and doom laden as only a preacher's can be: "Why do you risk your life coming here, Englishman? You have lived hereabouts long enough to know I shoot trespassers. And you have disturbed me at my morning prayers."

Harry fingered the satchel, which he noticed for the first time had the Departamento's stamp on the leather. It was a week since his release from the cells. Where he had not admitted to being, not to Maria or anyone.

"That's for me? From the little worm Cortez? Give it to me." A large hand reached forward and Harry noticed it had been dreadfully scarred around the knuckles as the satchel was pulled over his head. He instinctively stepped back and the priest took the lapel of his jacket in his other hand. "Stay where you are little man. I wish to take my time reading this. Guard him."

And with that he let go, turned on his heel and walked up into the rambling red-brick construction which was his home. Initially built as a hotel with German money in the 1950s, it had been inspired by the Hanging Gardens of Babylon, but the effect was more of an irregular Aztec pyramid whose reddish tinge looked out of place against the green of the jungle. It ascended from the lakeside in a series of garden terraces to a wooden hall at the top of two vast staircases. Harry had rowed across in a little boat that morning with two burly Ukranians, one nursing an M-16, and it was difficult to be scared when the building ahead in the breaking dawn had all the reality of an artist's impression. That mood had passed the moment he had caught sight of the preacher.

Harry sat drinking sweet black tea from a small glass which the guard took back to the hut and replenished from time to time, and stared in the direction of where Labuschagne had disappeared into his strange home. Then on the wind he heard singing. He looked at the hut; they must have a radio, yet it sounded like a hymn tune. The two guards clattered out onto the jetty, where they had placed a chair for him, and looked towards the far shore. Harry had the odd sensation that the singing was coming from the trees at the other side of the lake. It was unmistakable now.

Jesus wants me for a sunbeam
To shine for him each day . . .

The hymn was getting louder and Labuschagne re-emerged from his lair.

In every way try to please him
At home, at school and play . . .

Quite suddenly the words were mixed with a low thudding roar as a squat black helicopter skimmed the trees they had been peering at and then thundered overhead, scattering small bromeliads and orchids from the trees on the island. So Labuschagne did have a helicopter; Petroni, bless his socks, had been right. The jetty was just in front of a flat area of soft grass with a cross in the middle, obviously the craft's landing spot. After what was meant to be an impressive tight turn around the lake, the aircraft made a rather troubled landing dangerously near the first of the jutting terraces. Harry saw Labuschagne shake his head and nearby he caught laughter above the noise of the rotors from two young men in American military uniform. The pilot was doubtless one of the Baptists who lent the helicopter to Labuschagne.

The engine was switched off and now there was only the whisper of the rotor blades. "That motherfucker is going to put our bird smack down in the River Jordan one day and we'll be out of a job," he heard one of the Americans say. It was the slow drawl of the South and the man and his companion walked over to the guard post where they were deferentially handed little glasses of tea. Both were dressed in army fatigues. The man who was speaking had a purple silk scarf tied theatrically around his head. His companion was heavily built, dark and soulful. To Harry's surprise the man in the headscarf put his arm around the other's shoulders and planted a tender kiss on the side of his swarthy face. The sort of kiss Harry would have given Maria. The Ukranian guard's jaw dropped and he quickly looked away. So these were the men that flew the helicopter for Labuschagne, by the look of them refugees from the Vietnam war, no doubt first class judging from the Air Cavalry badges on their fatigues. But he wondered if the good Father knew what they got up to when he wasn't looking. The blond man was nibbling his friend's ear when his eyes caught Harry's.

"Hi," he said. "'Scuse us. Do you work for mad Captain Rasputin and the Magic Castle or are you a tourist who he is going to murder and dump in the lake?" He would have come over to Harry except another Ukranian had emerged from the guard post, grunted and gesticulated with his rifle barrel that the man move away. "All right, all right," said the American and stepped back, still smiling.

"Don't mind us, man. We're just the hired help. We're on a working honeymoon round the world before returning triumphally to the US of A. John here is going to be the first gay President of the States and I'm going to be First Lady. Rasputin picked us up at the Brazilian border. Someone had told us there were emerald mines up there. What a rip-off. We ended up working for the National Parks Department which does a heavy number in cocaine." His partner dug him in the ribs. "Don't worry, man, this guy looks all right. Labuschagne wouldn't let him over here if he wasn't." There was something in the last remark that made the hairs on the back of Harry's neck prickle. The American kept on talking, fast and incessant. At a guess he had been chewing coca leaves. " . . . Rasputin saw our true righteousness and brought us down here. Set us up high and wide. I hope you are not in any trouble with him mister as he really is a mean sonofabitch. What's your name?"

Harry answered, if just to stop the monologue. "Copeland-Smith. Major Harry Copeland-Smith."

The man began to sing: "I'm Just Wild About Harry," drumming in time on his dark-haired friend's shoulders. "Where's your army, Major?" he giggled. "Have they gone and left you all on your ownsome?" Harry noticed the man was wearing a small earring from which hung a tiny gold swastika, the Hindu good luck charm, not the Nazi symbol, he hoped. "Wait a minute," he continued. "You live in that big white house don't you? The one we are meant to leave alone. We know you, Harry. . . . "

Harry was sitting bolt upright in his chair dreading what was going to come next when there was a shout from the terrace.

"Sorry granddad, got to go. You know the score. Work to do, buckets to fill, gooks to kill."

The smile had gone and the two ran over to where Labuschagne was talking to another man, clearly a priest, who had climbed shakily out of the helicopter and was now being hurried to a small motorboat on another jetty. The flying preacher looked pleased with himself after a productive morning bombarding tiny Indian villages with hymns. Obviously he believed he was onto a good thing. Father Labuschagne gave him protection; he loaned Labuschagne the helicopter. According to Petroni, all the Baptist insisted on was that the loudspeakers and multi-lingual tapes, made at the Church of the Living God Inc. at Amarillo in Texas, be turned on at every opportunity over populated areas. Evidently Father Labuschagne was only too glad to comply.

The minister was hardly across the lake when a procession under the direction of the two Americans, who seemed to have the function of two altarboys in some bellicose mass, started from the sheds near the main building out towards the helicopter. First came a trolley bearing a drum of what Harry deduced was gasoline. Next an evil-looking machine gun came out, followed by two men carrying another, then by others with boxes and pans of bullets and clamps for mounting the weapons. Even at this range he could see the blond man's tooth-filled grin. A long metal boom was brought out with what, as far as he could make out, were rockets. By the modest standards of this part of the world Father Labuschagne had his own air force. The preacher had gone inside again.

Rocking backwards on his stool on the jetty of rotten wood, Harry had the feeling of being a man who had half walked the plank. As if the pirate captain and the crew had left him wobbling above the sharks while they went about their deadly business. Suddenly there was a roar from Labuschagne and a Ukranian taller than the rest ran up the stone steps of the terrace and disappeared inside the building. Only minutes later he and four more men jumped into another motorboat and were speeding towards the other bank, armed to the teeth.

Someone somewhere was going to suffer; there was an anticipation in the faces of the men that said so. The guards of the jetty sensed it and exchanged a few guttural words. One of them brought him a larger glass of tea and a piece of black bread when it was lunchtime; there was a silver spoon with what looked like cherry jam in the tea. Why hadn't Labuschagne called for him? He must have opened Cortez's note by now. Harry noted the black jackboots of the guards and remembered seing a file on how most of the SS Ukrania "Galizien" division survivors had made their homes around that area, especially in Capitan Boda, the village near the lake named after a Ukranian veteran of the Chaco War. Other villages had names like Bela Tzerkow and Lemberg. In the early afternoon, as mechanics continued to tinker with the helicopter, the motorboat and the men returned. The leader walked straight inside, but wearily this time, not briskly.

At last the priest sent for him.

The walls of Labuschagne's office were mostly glass and looked out onto the lake. On the untidy desk was a Bible and a Luger pistol. A smile had returned to the priest's face.

"As you are a creature of Cortez, with whom I now seem to be in dispute, give me a good reason why I shouldn't kill you and throw your body in that lake. Or do you think your British Government will protect you down here? Why do you take sides against me?"

Harry took a deep breath. The tone was playful but he had no doubt the man meant what he said.

"Cortez made me do it; bring that to you. I didn't want to. I do not take sides. I've never interfered with your affairs, you know that. For the life of me I do not know what he put in the bag. I did not break the seal. If you kill me you will give him the excuse he needs to attack this place." His voice faltered and the eyes of the priest were on him.

"Shall I show you what he sent?" Labuschagne said, and turning the envelope upside down shook out a captain's epaulettes and a certificate of citizenship onto the crowded desk. "I think he is telling me I am an outlaw. I do not know what deal you have made with that filthy little man but whatever it is you will come off the worse. I should know. He double-crossed me once too often, so naturally I worked with other people. Somoza had enough money for all of us and now everyone knows it was Cortez who shot the goose that could have laid golden eggs. And," the voice was angry, "he has seized all my warehouses with their contents."

Labuschagne got up and glowered across the desk at Harry.

"I have known some terrible men in my life Major, but Señor Cortez is the lowest. For he is not content with telling me he has my property. He tells me who told him which of the warehouses I was using and where the drugs were. Exactly where to go." Harry went cold. "Don't worry Major, I know it could not be you. Perhaps you *would* tell him, but you did not know these things."

He handed Harry an inventory in the precise copperplate handwriting of a Departamento scribe. At the top of the list by the word "informants" was the single name: Petroni. Harry felt sick. The blue eyes bored into his face.

"He was your friend wasn't he? My men tell me you used to go to his house on Sundays. Now look what you have done to him. The question is, what should we do to you?"

"People know I am here," Harry began unconvincingly.

"Humbug, Major," said the huge man and laughed. "I think that's the English word. But you see I have long arms and if I decide to I can kill you at a distance and all your little Indios. If I were you I would have nothing more to do with Napoleon Cortez. And I should not bother to call on your friend Petroni in the future. He has had an accident. We should thank God he saves us from such things. You may go, Major. Just remember that I am a lot closer to you than Cortez."

Labuschagne then led him down to the jetty.

"Don't forget Major, I will be here for ever. Cortez can only last a few more years. He's too old. If I were you I should think about going home to England while you still can. Remember I still have not decided what should become of you. Do not get mixed up in things you cannot control. I have always liked your fine house, Major."

They bundled him into the boat and the giant stood on the shore smiling and waving as Harry rowed as fast as he could for the opposite bank. It seemed to take an age, and at first he did not appear to be moving at all. Splosh, splosh, splosh the oars took him slowly to the far side. For a moment he thought they had put him in a boat on his own to use it for target practice. He looked around for leaks and wondered if there were piranha in the lake. The black-clad figure was still waving from the shore and Harry's breath was coming quicker now, his jaws clamped tightly shut, rowing for all he was worth. Father Labuschagne knew all about scaring someone; it had been part of his business for years.

Only the scrunch of the prow in the reeds of the opposite shore brought him back to reality. He felt a fool and had to push off again to get the boat to the little jetty. The grinning Ukranians who had been watching his Land Rover shouted after him as he ran for the vehicle. Once inside he had the glove compartment open and the old Webley in his hand, almost kissing it. He switched on the engine and drove off in the direction of Paradiso. He knew what he would find.

When he reached Petroni's house the screen door was slamming in the breeze and a man was carrying a table out to a Toyota pick-up truck. He saw Harry and hesitated about going back into the house, then he got into the pick-up and set off in a flourish of red dust. It wasn't until the engine was out of earshot that Harry heard a low moaning sound and went inside. In a chair before the French windows leading out onto the garden he found the old lady who cleaned for Petroni, her head in her hands, making an eerie sing-song noise. There were no tears on her face. She looked at him as if he were another murderer or looter.

"Petroni?" he remembered saying and dull-eyed she had pointed to the door which he knew led to a damp basement where the smuggler had tried rather pompously to establish a wine cellar. It had been too wet and all manner of creatures had moved in; he had laughed about it at the time. Harry had enjoyed the crooked little chap's friendship. Better get it over with, he thought, and strode to the door and turned the handle. In the gloom at the bottom of the stairs was Petroni's wheelchair, one of the wheels battered in. He turned on the light. First he noticed the bundle of clothes, then a shoe and a leg. A rat rustled and he saw the head, mercifully with the eyes closed but no longer connected to the man's shoulders. The body resembled a puppet which had fallen apart at the extremities. All that was left of the trunk was a blurred collection of offal. Petroni had been cut to pieces with machetes, the usual and accepted punishment for informing on another smuggler. Poor sod, was all Harry could think as he strode out and got into his Land Rover, desperately trying to keep his mind on his own problems but feeling sick. He counted himself lucky that the smuggler's eyes had not been open. He would never have forgotten a plaintive last stare which asked him why.

The people of Paradiso would now no longer respect him. As the town's *Mbareté*, its protector almost, Harry would be held responsible for the death in the sense he should have prevented it. More people would leave and the town would rot away all the quicker. If Labuschagne could do that to Petroni he could do it to anyone.

It would not be long before he sent the black helicopter against Harry; he had to. By killing Petroni he had deprived Cortez only of a crippled pawn. The police chief had already taken Labuschagne's most important piece, his banker, by blowing Somoza to the four winds. Now Cortez's agents would spread the rumour of the South African's latest humiliation: the return of his commission and withdrawal of citizenship. Labuschagne would then sit down with a Dutch gin and his Bible and wonder how to stay ahead of the other smugglers on the river. To maintain his position he had to be respected, he had to be feared. In attacking Harry he knew he would step on toes he had never intended to but it was a risk he would have to take; to save precious face and hurt Cortez. The eyes of the river would be on the priest, watching for weakness. Harry sighed. An atttack would be exactly what Napoleon Cortez had planned.

Poor Petroni. As he drove quickly home a phrase of his father's kept ringing through his head and he breathed in sharply to stop the tears forming in his eyes: "Never get too fond of your pets Harry, they'll all have to go when you go home to England." How many more of his "pets" would suffer before he went home from Paraguay? He cut the thought from his mind. Let Labuschagne come with his damned contraption piloted by a bunch of nancy boys. He'd be ready for the bugger.

He was trying to concentrate on his plans with all his might, but he still felt like a Judas.

Chapter 7

The bottle of water was in the usual place where Maria left it when he looked intent on a long night with the whisky. Harry tipped it up on end against his mouth and watched the bubbles through the thick green glass. He had drunk half of it and his mouth still felt as if it were full of ashes, and behind a bone-dry tongue was the guilt which always haunted him if he had more than his ration of three large ones. Harry had downed more than three large ones last night as he sat and pored over maps of the area, going through long-made plans of what he would do if Labuschagne attacked. The whole problem was such a worry it had made him drink. What if Labuschagne had walked in as he lay there sozzled? The guards might have stopped them, Hindle afterwards looking at him as if he were unfit to command. To Hindle one apple scrumped meant you were a thief for life. But the question was if they could stop a raid at all.

The room looked lovely. Springtime sunlight danced in through the windows and onto the bed where his scrawny legs, thin as a beggar's, stuck from under the covers he had pulled off Maria, whose ample brown body slept the sleep of the innocent. Watching the gentle rhythm of Maria breathing, her plump limbs twitching with satisfaction at her dreams, was pure pleasure. He noticed she had woven a tiny blue-green iridescent hummingbird feather to a strand of pubic hair, an Indio charm. He had not been paying enough attention to her, but Maria would regard that as her own fault; faultless Maria.

She was only part Aché, but the huntress of the tribe's lore, their Diana, had finally captured her man with such decorations of feathers, albeit more elaborate, after many attempts to make him notice her, planting flowers in his path as he went every day to the stream to drink and presenting him with magic emeralds as gifts from the stars. She had sacrificed to the Tigre, the jaguar god, to the Alligator and to the Fish Man, who was now usually replaced by pictures of Christ or of the Pope, until one day she saved a hummingbird who was defending his nest against a snake. The huntress killed the snake and out of gratitude the hummingbird, regarded as the bravest and manliest of all birds, told her the charm of the feathers and let her pluck one out of its tail as it flew. As soon as she was seen by her intended it worked and they married and lived forever on the river bank. Harry knew one Aché shaman from the village did a roaring trade, often painting small hen feathers when he couldn't find a hummingbird. But Maria believed and he found it a delightful legend. He kissed her nose but she sleepily rearranged herself and refused to wake. Harry could not get his mind off the more pressing problem of Father Labuschagne and what would happen if things got rough. Maria would have to go, but where?

He swung his legs over the side of the bed and picked up a well-thumbed hardback copy of *Summer Lightning* by P. G. Wodehouse he had recently lent to his prisoner. One could see it had been in the valley: red and black splatters and traces of exoskeleton showed how beetles and tiny scorpions had met their deaths in between pages celebrating pulchritude and pigs. Poor old things, he thought, and went off to shave in the dressing room next to the bedroom. As he stood up his head ached as if he had bumped it on a low beam. He really must lay off the hard stuff. But at least he was cheering up. Perhaps after a shave he could manage a tango with Maria. He looked down at the quiescent creature between his legs and decided against it. At his age if you don't succeed you might never try again. Better wait for a good following wind when his liver wasn't so full of whisky and his brain full of funk.

He heard a low moan from Maria and gently closed the

bedroom door. They were very much like a married couple despite the difference in their ages, which never seemed to bother her at all. He was glad Hindle wasn't a dashing young cavalry captain with nice manners. In that respect it was fine he was a small, ugly, hairy bore.

Maria loved to shave him if she was up first and got it totally wrong. Shaving was a male ritual for him, as sacred as her hummingbird feather. He was convinced that if he didn't go through the lathering with the badger-hair brush from Harrods and the gentle but precise scraping with the cut-throat razor something would go wrong that day. The blade had to be stropped correctly and the water and the soap in the shaving mug had to be just right. The pearl-handled razor had belonged to the first cook and general underling the Ministry of Defence had sent him. He was called Bert and was given to bouts of severely manic behaviour, which had not been in any of the files, due to being hit in the head by shrapnel during a wartime night canoe raid on Bordeaux. Eager to please at first, he had made a very trying cook as he would suddenly throw himself to the floor screaming.

Every morning Bert had shaved elaborately with the pearl-handled razor in front of an ornate mirror. Harry had caught him whispering to the glass, pressed against the wall so as not to be reflected in it. The mirror had been very important to Bert. Somehow it had come through the war with him and, although it looked as if he had won it in a shooting gallery on Blackpool sea front from among the pot dogs and the other tinsel treasures of the Golden Mile, it had the significance of an idol. Harry wished he could have made out exactly what Bert was muttering to it.

Then one morning the rusty nail which held the mirror fell out of the damp plaster wall and the glass shattered against the floor as Bert was shaving. One minute he was grinning at himself. The next his foam-covered face was gone.

"I've cut off me head!" he screamed, dropping the razor and running round the house and off into the thick thornbush. They looked for him, of course, but not a trace was found. Now Harry used the madman's razor. He fancied it kept him sane to reflect on the tragedy of Bert each new day.

When he had been put into Military Intelligence during the war it had seemed a very good job, full of chaps from the bright Cambridge colleges, looking longingly at each other, trying to be quietly dignified. He had risen with remarkable ease as everyone else had desperately wanted to be safe and developed lock jaw when the CO mentioned "special duties" or SOE or "volunteer". To Harry it had been fun, most of the time spent planning in a beautiful country house near Hatfield, with the occasional burst of training punctuated by drops into France and Germany when the leg had got better. Such a life made you feel like a spectator not having the hard slog of the infantry, as the son of a Lord might feel roughing it in the coal mines for the summer vac but still having the security of his other foot on the silk Persian carpets of the family drawing room. Years later they had picked Harry for his present mission, they said because the war had equipped him emotionally and intellectually to deal with any complication. He had liked the sound of that. He pulled on his trousers, then his vest and shirt, and sighed. At the back of his mind was the unflattering thought they had forgotten about him.

He went downstairs to breakfast. Maria was wearing her green dress with a pleated skirt and had a yellow scarf around her neck. God, how he would like to buy her some proper clothes in Europe! He could just imagine her wide eyes: she would be so grateful.

"Do you want your bacon and eggs this morning?" she asked.

"Toast will be enough."

Harry took a nut of butter out of the water-filled dish and spread it on the toast before covering the result with marmalade. The toast-rack was silver, as were the little dishes, and he sat at breakfast alone, usually reading something English like Waugh. This morning it was Kipling, the first book he had put his hand on, an Indian edition from the 1930s with a swastika etched in gold leaf on the cover, the same sort of symbol as the American pilot's gold earring. The reading was to assure himself that everything was right in the world and a British God was in a heaven where no undesirables were permitted to loiter; to reinforce his prejudices and calm his fears.

"Carmen tells me Mr Hindle has taken the boys out on a training run," said Maria. "Are you going down to the village?"

"I thought I would look in on the schoolhouse before going up to the prisoner. I have to see him this morning. If you are not a good girl I will give you to him. He will eat you up in one mouthful."

There was fear on Maria's face although she knew he was playing with her. The chief said the devil sat on the prisoner's head and shoulders, commanding whoever looked at him to run in fear and horror. Harry thought this remarkable as they had no idea what the man had done and they probably wouldn't believe it if he told them, just as he did not believe in their demonology.

Maria reappeared with a large straw basket covered with a blue and white cloth and he shook his head. "They will all grow up to expect everyone they meet to feed them," and then he smiled as he saw her look down. She would normally have had a large family by now, but in the decade or so they had been together she had never once become pregnant, which was strange as Indian women were usually so productive. Unless, and he did not like the idea one bit, he was incapable of fathering children. He was almost tempted to dally with one of the other Indio girls to prove his own potency but a bond had grown up between him and Maria. He had felt like a child molester in the beginning with a teenage mistress and that was why he allowed her indulgences, like the children's school. The twisted bamboo building that let in the rain and all sorts of vile jungle creatures attracted waifs and strays and was more like a small orphanage. A foundlings home funded by the Foreign Office, to say nothing of the Americans, the French or whoever else contributed to keeping the prisoner under wraps.

She put her arm through his as they hurried down the curving path towards the river. Maria was laughing and

Labuschagne was a nasty memory, a bad dream. She had brought his Kipling so he could read to the children. He translated it into the simple Spanish Maria taught them.

They stopped and hailed the two guard towers above the entrance to the dank, secret valley and Maria drew her shawl embroidered with red and yellow roses around her as they both looked into the shadows and felt a cold wet breath on their faces. Unconsciously they quickened their pace until they reached the point where the Aché had hidden the locking pin of a rifle from Hindle during weapon training. Harry told her the story again and they laughed. It was good to be out on such a morning.

The only thing that Harry had against the Aché was that they were the untidiest lot he had ever come across. Years ago the tribe had abandoned the idea of living in neat straw huts for shanty style constructions of oil drums, boards, earth and lianas held together with spit and faith. The general disarray drove Hindle up the wall, and Harry had come down on the sergeant hard when he started calling the Aché gipsies. "Like calling someone corporal in the sergeants' mess," he had explained, rubbing in the difference in rank. Still, if he did not hate Hindle he might start hating the country.

"Good morning to you," he said as a grinning Indian poked her nose through a gap in a wattle and daub wall, plugged at one point with two copies of *Fortune* magazine from the house. She was offering him a plate of wild pineapple and he took a piece. Proudly pinned to a tree above her chicken run was a picture of John Travolta, her love of the moment even though she already had ten children, none of whom went hungry. What she could grow or raise was supplemented by Harry's monthly ration of flour and salt and sugar and other staples. When he was sent military spares, the Aché could feast on the exotic delights of tinned foods such as sausage and beans or apricot pudding, all the way from some Aldershot store and cooked before they were born and parcelled in with the machine-gun barrels and big ends. She disappeared into the hut without a word, as Indians tend not to say goodbye.

The schoolhouse was on top of a cleared mound and inside

he could hear the children singing a Spanish hymn being led by one of the more educated mothers, a former maid who could read, write and sew. Frightened eyes looked from under fringes as his boots crashed and splintered across the reed matting meant for tinier feet. As he cleared his throat and said "Good morning, children" one of the little girls let out an awful wail and had to be nursed by Maria.

He opened his Kipling at the Rikki-Tikki-Tavi story and forgot to change the name of Nag the cobra, much to the delight of the older children as it was the nickname of their easy-going chief. When he altered Nag's name to Ja Ra Ra, a snake they all knew and hated with a head as big as a man's fist, he heard the steady nasal breathing of infant concentration. No matter how many times he read them the story he sensed waves of relief when Rikki-Tikki finally did his work and they felt able to talk again. The Aché took story telling seriously.

You should have been a bloody missionary, he said to himself, frowning at the delighted faces as he always did, part of the gringo ritual, part of the Major's magic. "I have to go and see my man now," he said taking Maria's hand. "I'll see you back at the house."

"Be careful as you go up the valley. The guards may be drunk and shoot you, thinking you are a bad man," she teased. The children laughed although they did not understand.

On a warm spring day, approaching noon, the walk was not an unpleasant one. The path by the stream was totally cleared now. No roots to climb round, no boulders to scramble across, but the jungle did attempt to subvert the beaten earth path in places and it zig-zagged from side to side, the next bend forever hidden behind a dripping wall of foliage. Above the trees, as he went deeper into the box canyon, rose dappled grey cliffs made of a different rock from the friendlier local red sandstone. Harry brushed away a spider's web and a large green and yellow creature, quite harmless, fell to the floor and scurried away to lay another trap. The sides of the canyon seemed to press in as he got to the halfway stage, not more than twenty feet across, and there in front, built on stilts over the stream, was a small green guardpost. The creosoted wood was covered in moss and several sorts of orchid grew in the gables. He called out in Guaraní.

"Pass Major." The high-pitched voice belonged to Jeronimo, a young man who was Harry's favourite Aché. He suspected that, as with Maria, he was a half-breed with sharper European features. He recalled distant arguments between his own mother and father: "God, Maude, can't you accept for once that the wogs are clever, not as clever as us mind but bright, quite bright." It made him chuckle. Jeronimo was clever all right.

"Skiving again Jerry," he said nosing into the gloomy hut and seeing a brown wiry man devouring a tin of emergency ration Spam. A sliver of the luncheon meat had fallen into the British Army issue General Purpose Machine-Gun sight, the only clean object in the hovel. Behind Jeronimo in the darkness, another Aché was curled up like a dog fast asleep, and the Spam-eating Indian, dressed only in the traditional loin cloth as he too had been recently off watch, continued his messy meal. The hut had an unmistakable herbal smell of marijuana.

"I heard you coming, Major sir. I was not asleep. I am a vigilant guard," he said with a charming wink.

Harry wondered what London would say if they knew that their secret was guarded by a stoned Indian. But that was not exactly true. Hindle always put the best men at the bridge at the start of the valley and on a platform above the huts where the prisoner lived. Still, he would like to send them a photograph of Jeronimo. Normally he would have let them get on with it. But today things were far from normal.

"Look alive both of you," he said with an angry edge to his voice. "Any more smoking on guard and you will be cleaning rifles until your hair is grey. Understood?" He spoke in English to counter Jeronimo's familiar Guaraní.

The drug-enhanced image of eternal jankers was too much for the Indian and he cowered back. Harry extracted the Spam from the rear sight of the machine gun. "Now wake up your friend and get on with it."

The trouble was the more he educated them the more rebellious they became. Jeronimo could be a pest. He left them in a flurry of mock activity pretending to check the ammunition.

Up the track the canyon opened out dramatically into a clearing a hundred yards wide surrounded by steep cliff walls which were overgrown with trees on the top and sides. A few tall trees grew in the middle of the valley. Labuschagne could not land his helicopter here.

Two huts were built into the west wall of the canyon, both covered with rotting camouflage netting. One was longer than the other and had a veranda. It was used as a laboratory. A mould-spotted white could be seen where the netting had fallen away. The other smaller hut where the two men lived had originally been painted a more cheerful pink before the camouflage cocoon had been ordered by Whitehall. An Aché in a highly visible red shirt and white trousers squatted by the door, his rifle propped beside him. He had seen Harry and lifted one hand pointing to the tree tops. A piece of red material was quickly waved up in the branches and Harry knew everything was fine; one man, even in a bright red shirt, could hold the place against an army. At least he hoped so.

The Indian nodded at the laboratory indicating that the two men were in there and about their business. He picked up his rifle and affected a military pose. Harry stopped at the door and, as always, wished there was a bell to ring. He pulled aside the fly-screen and went through the inner door.

He could have been in a home counties cottage hospital apart from the view through the windows, and one expected a fierce sister to appear and scold one into a waiting room. Except a notice board by the first door was not honoured with any notices: no rotas, no congratulations of nurse so-and-so on a birthday or a baby. In fact there were no nurses. There had been one at the start, Harry recalled, when his man had first arrived from Argentina, but she could not stand the claustrophobic nature of the valley. She had also been mistaken about the man she had come to work for and had gone back to live with her father in Chile.

Harry clumped down the corridor in his heavy walking shoes, peering through one round glass window and then another until, over a tangle of tubes, bunsen burners and pipettes, he made out two figures examining something in a tank. One was a large chap with big clumsy hands, the type of person you could tell was easy-going just by looking at him, dressed neatly in a simple brown shirt and corduroy trousers he seemed about to grow out of. He had the remains of what had been blond hair which, when Harry had first seen him, had been popular with the local girls and some of the orphans in the kindergarten had been his. But that was past. As Willy had grown older he had become fussy, almost effeminate, and now was only devoted to his master's every whim.

Harry had never understood the relationship but he knew it went back to a shared childhood. The other, smaller man stood very erect by the tank as Willy carefully probed among the leaves with a long stick. There was a sudden commotion and Willy jumped back, bringing shouts of rage from the dapper little man dressed in a scientist's white coat, which accentuated his dark features under a spiky crew cut of black hair, even though he was seventy. Harry could see the piercing blue eyes that made him appear younger. Blue was the wrong colour really; they were almost violet and had the strangest effect on people. The Indians hated to look at him.

Harry knocked out of habit as he walked into the room.

"Good morning, Doctor."

The eyes snapped angrily at him. "It's now afternoon, Major, and could you tell me why we cannot go down to the river to collect specimens? These are useless." The man's command of English was perfect.

"Sorry about that. Had a spot of bother with one of the warlords in the area," Harry replied. "Father Labuschagne is on the rampage. I'm sure I've told you about him. Got a bee in his bonnet that I'm some kind of threat. You'll just have to stay put until it blows over I'm afraid. Better safe than sorry, eh?"

"Typical," growled the old German. "Not a year has gone by without some fanatic trying to kill us. Now the locals have turned against you. That is what you must expect if you employ Indios, whom they hate. Indians who would run away if anyone said boo."

"They did not run away last time," Harry said, adding under his breath, I wish I had let them take you then, you pompous little swine. He wondered exactly what was in the vivarium tank.

The Doctor had always been good to the local German community, poor dirt farmers whom he helped when Harry would let him, lancing the odd carbuncle, delivering a baby or two and even a calf. On more than one occasion, when Harry had deemed it safe, he had attended the old Paraguayan lady from the vegetable shop in Paradiso who had terrible sores on her legs. But he had left his bedside manner behind this morning.

Once he had been very handsome. In youth Josef had an effeminate beauty that led to the nickname of Valentino. Now, though he looked hardly more than fifty, exile had deepened the lines, the type of lines a man gets from worrying too much about himself, a turning down at the sides of the mouth and a pinched look at the corner of the eyes. A bitterness had crept over the face, which one would expect but usually had to catch the man off guard to see. For Josef was a very proud man, always standing ramrod straight. When he was talking or listening his face was constantly in motion, his darting eyes giving the impression of dynamism. As he spoke he made you feel, when he was in a good mood, as if no one else on the earth mattered to him, and you believed it, unless you shut your eyes and held the frozen image of the face in your mind, a twisted face of a twisted man. But there was no denying his charm and the old goat was still fond of women. Harry had let some from the German families visit him in the early years at a remote hotel. But these had had to stop.

"Major are you listening to me?" the Doctor rasped. "As you know I have started to make a study of comparative religion and require some more books. The ones in your library are useless. Shouldn't a man have the things he wants in his old age?"

Oh he should, thought Harry, as he came under the cool stare of the most wanted man in the world. After all these years he found it hard to square the individual who stood before him with the infamous war criminal, the man they called the Angel of Death. To Harry it sounded melodramatic, rather like something from a medieval mystery play. The only trouble was he knew every charge against the German, and more, was true. Here he was only ever referred to as Doctor Josef, or Josef, or the Doctor, without ever uttering the jangling surname which still haunted many dreams. But that was not out of guilt, fear, or respect for the dead; merely a question of security.

Chapter 8

Harry Copeland-Smith always felt a sense of rampant unreality immediately after he saw the Doctor. Today Josef had been in a bad mood yet on other days he could be perfectly charming, and about once a week he came to the house for dinner, if everything was quiet and there were going to be no interruptions. He was surprisingly witty and told many stories at his own expense from his childhood in Günzburg with poor old Willy, who came from a long line of family retainers and was not the brightest of men. Josef teased him unmercifully, referring to the big affectionate man as "The Pole".

It had been drummed into Harry, when he took the assignment after the war, that it was not his place to act as judge to the man he protected, merely to be a benevolent jailor. Josef was not eager for unsupervised freedom, and would have a short life expectancy if he ventured back to Europe. An innocent would not have put up with the conditions in that little valley.

Even before the Allied invasion of Normandy, they had known just what the man was doing, if not the numerical extent of his crime. However, Cambridge double firsts had swopped red files with Harvard men late at night across leather-topped desks in shelters safe from any doodlebug, and it had been decided to recruit the delicate-featured man to their cause, concerned not so much with locating Nazis after the war as having access to SS files on other undesirable elements who could be a threat to a new Europe. To be fair, it was not the Allies who had made the first approach. The Doctor had done that through a Catholic priest.

Harry left the two men peering at the unfortunate creature in the tank and started back down the track. If I'd actually seen the gas-chambers I would probably feel differently, he thought as he passed Jeronimo's smoke-filled guard post and shouted a greeting. But I didn't and I don't and that's that. I've never really felt sad when anyone has died; friends in the war, parents. There must be something wrong with me. Perhaps Josef and I deserve each other.

He got back to the bridge and hailed the guard-towers again. What would he have done in the Doctor's place? Got the hell out of there and no mistake with that maniac Hitler ranting around, but he knew a lot of people who would have stayed. Many of his colleagues had been intellectually sympathetic to the Third Reich.

The callousness of the decisions made by Sir Peter Broom's team still sent a tremor of excitement through him. "New Broom for a New Europe" had been a cynical sort of motto but there was a commitment underneath not to bear grudges against the Germans. At first Harry had been ignored because he had left Oxford without a degree to join up, and having won a medal seemed to indicate a dangerous level of emotional involvement. But he had worked hard and meticulously, and when contacts were being made with Nazi Party members he was in at the start, demonstrating a clinical understanding of the problem. At the time he had never thought it was odd that no one cared what Josef had done. Only after he came to Paraguay did the enormity of the crime strike him, under that immense sky where there were villages full of Germans who saw nothing wrong with Adolph Hitler.

Maria greeted him in front of the house with a Scotch and soda. "You have a letter. The messenger brought it for you all the way from the embassy, Harry. I hope you don't have to go. You look so glum. You are not mad with me?" He wished she hadn't poured the drink for him; that meant one less for tonight.

The envelope was bulging and the messenger's hired white Volkswagen beetle was in the drive, its motor turning over slowly. He did not recognize the messenger, a seedy looking character, and the car was not right. They used an old Ford, not a hire car. He was glad to see Hindle standing by his outhouse like a country farmer, a trap-shooting gun hugged in his arms. He was making the driver nervous. Harry nodded to Hindle, who cocked his head to one side like a gun dog, and went inside the house.

He could have whooped with relief when he found the letter was from Mabel at the embassy, a clandestine communication that she dare not pass on by phone or send through usual embassy channels.

"Call that boy in and give him some grub, Maria. Tell Hindle he's OK but get one of the lads to watch him in the kitchen just in case." He busied himself with the letter.

Liebling,

I put in a note for you from one of your disreputable contacts from the Chacarita barrio which is so filthy I cannot read it and refuse to handle it without a bath. Why I am writing to you is to warn you about His Excellency who has been on the warpath ever since that party you all went to and didn't take me.

I think I was the only one stuck in Asunción that night. You were very naughty and I heard you all got properly drunk at the US afterwards. Swine. Ever since that crazy man has been asking for a file on you and raves because you have not got one. Then he finds even why you have not got one is hush-hush and raves all the more about a conspiracy. He has threatened to sack my poor commercial attaché and has written countless letters to Mr Chambers. Now His Excellency has been introduced to Nabout the Lebanese gambler at the German Club who says you are a drug smuggler and white slaver. The gambler's boss is that strange man Albert Rattucci who is said to have connections with Labuschagne. Tough believes everything he is told. Be careful.

Love and more than kisses
Mabel

Usually her letters went on for pages and pages, but not this one and there was something in its brevity that made him take it seriously. She was warning him there was more going on than Sir Reginald's tantrums, and while Harry welcomed any attention that might lead to his retirement Mabel saw danger. Two elderly men were very vulnerable in southern Paraguay and Chambers' shadowy masters might decide Josef and himself should no longer be a burden to the taxpayer. It was unlikely, though, because the German had taken meticulous precautions and Harry had duplicated some of them for his own protection. There were documents in bank vaults in Vaduz, Liechtenstein, telling the whole story. How the Doctor spent the five years after the war as the guest of the Americans in Bavaria, and how on his betrayal by a former SS chauffeur he had been spirited through Italy by poisonous little priests to the Columbus Hotel in Genoa. He had been taken to Argentina, and Harry pulled up his own roots in England and joined the Doctor in Paraguay in 1957.

In the years after the war, the Doctor had been debriefed by a secret Allied committee, and a very grateful one at that, because Josef, it was said, had a vast memory and kept detailed diaries of his own interrogations in the camps. They recorded the secrets of communists, artists, scientists, bankers, soldiers and spies, usually under torture, before they were sent to the gas-chambers or the scaffold. The strain of these interviews was such that the Doctor lost two stone in weight. Harry had once accidently burst in on one late at night in Germany, the pale face of Josef illuminated by the desk lights as a stenographer clicked away at a little machine and heads nodded below a curtain of cigarette smoke. Then the stenographer had stopped and scowled at him and the others had turned round. He had excused himself and quickly shut the door. It had been like interrupting a church service or a seance. In return for these nightly communions Josef obtained signed agreements promising him security and protection for the rest of his life, which had also gone into the bank vault. Harry did not know the signatories, but it would be a very brave young Turk indeed who tried to upset that particular apple cart in the Curzon Street offices of MI5. In his way the Doctor had been as valuable as the German rocket scientists, they said. The "confessions" he acquired formed the basis of much Allied intelligence work in the years that followed.

Mabel was sweet to be so concerned. He loved the idea of Sir Reggie rushing from pillar to post and getting himself deeper into the Asunción mire with second-eleven gangsters like Rattucci and Nabout. Once they had run Asunción, but now the Italian and Lebanese "families" had to kowtow to the likes of Labuschagne and Cortez.

At least Albert Rattucci had a sense of humour. He had come to Paraguay after falling out with the Mafia in Miami, and that organization had let him live because he quickly convinced them of Paraguay's potential. An elegant silver-haired man in 500-dollar suits, his one passion in life – apart from putting other people down – was breeding Fancy Rats, rodents with fluffy ears or spots or suchlike. Much to the other gangsters' chagrin, he called the Asunción syndicate, of which the humourless Nabout was first lieutenant, the Fancy Mouse Club. Albert was an acquaintance of Labuschagne and probably the man who lost most when Somoza was assassinated. Somoza was going to invest a substantial part of the 200-million-dollar earthquake aid fund he had stolen from his country in a more efficient way of smuggling heroin through Asunción to New York, claiming he was only doing it because the Americans had let him down. Poor Anastasio, so serious. Rattucci was not above insisting that government officials bring Nero, his favourite rat, offerings of cheese. Harry had a soft spot for Rattucci.

He also had a soft spot for the sender of the other greasier epistle in the packet, or rather the man who had dictated most of it onto the thick brown rotten paper which smelt like it had been wrapped around green hides, and probably had.

The letter was from a contact in the *barrio*. It told in a simple, direct way that Cortez and his aptly named Committee of Public Safety and Sanitation had begun its work. Napoleon's men had gone into the stinking *barrio* slum of the Chacarita, partially flooded as it was by the River Paraguay, and all but destroyed it. They had pulled apart the tin shacks and little houses made of old vehicles and floated them away on the muddy waters of the river. Most wore the uniforms of health officials but this did not stop them shooting dead five people who got in their way. The whole of Asunción's underworld was looking for a sign that Napoleon would extend his campaign against the gangsters and drug warlords like Labuschagne. The destruction of Chacarita was Cortez flexing his muscles. It showed he had persuaded the *Presidente* that cleanliness was next to Godliness and the chances of a papal visit would be improved if first he flushed out the country's filth. To Cortez Labuschagne was part of that filth. It meant that open bloody warfare would break out in southern Paraguay between Labuschagne and Cortez all the sooner. To the violent priest the only form of defence was attack; the nearest target Harry, who he thought was a stooge of Napoleon.

Labuschagne also had further supplies of drugs hidden in the Chacarita now under Cortez's lock and key. The little man was making a fool of him. In Paraguay if you were powerful you were occasionally required to prove it. This was far more interesting than Sir Reginald and his gangsters. If Labuschagne did attack it would mean the CIA would have all the excuse they needed to take over the protection of the Doctor completely. In Washington's corridors of power they would be heroes and the bungle with Somoza would be forgotten. Harry sat back against the cushions of his settee and lit a pipe: things were moving faster than he thought possible. All he had to do was keep his head, literally.

Harry could imagine Labuschagne pacing his study and peering through the window at the evil black helicopter, wondering who first to send it against. A saner man would try at least to make a deal with Cortez, offer to become part of his plans, for as the priest himself had said the man could not last for ever. But that would not be Father Labuschagne's style, especially as he had already been baited by Cortez, teased by having his citizenship revoked and his commission sent back in an army satchel around the neck of an Englishman. The police chief would know how he hated Englishmen, and while there were many obvious targets, such as property and smuggling launches belonging to Cortez along the river, it would make biblical sense to Labuschagne to send his helicopter against the man who delivered the message. Harry walked slowly over to the drinks trolley and poured himself a large one.

Perhaps it was wicked even to think about it, but doing a bunk was in his mind. But there was Maria, to say nothing of the bloody Indians. He could not deny he had become very attached to the girl and after all was said and done the Aché were his responsibility. He looked at the whisky in the glass.

Josef had changed in the last few years, he mused, glancing out of the window at Hindle and two Aché who seemed to be digging a hole near the flagpole. Overall he had mellowed since Harry had known him. When they had first met in Germany he had become used to the periods of cool aloofness interspersed with outbursts of rage which left the Doctor and anyone around him at a loss for words, as if a thunderstorm had suddenly broken overhead. The rages blew up so quickly and were of such violence that Harry at first thought the man was insane, quite mad, and if he didn't crack under the hours of painful interrogation he would be finished off by the loneliness of exile. His own sense of duty was such that he had never considered how the loneliness would eventually begin to affect him. Harry had presumed, quite wrongly he now realized, that it was these spikes of anger that had led to the legions of deaths in the extermination camps, the horrible experiments, the unspeakable cruelty. But after observing Josef year in year out, Harry had come to a different conclusion. The rages were human; it was the other side of the man, the quiet, obedient side, which was frightening. The discipline that enabled him to confine himself to the hellish valley with his books, Willy and his experiments had a chilling facet to it. Had there been the same stoic acceptance of the dreadful purpose of the camps which turned duty into atrocity? The idea that Josef had only done his duty had a deadly fascination and Harry began to toy with it, searching for something that proved the Doctor had added, personally, one dram of cruelty to the vicious camps. Would the same things have happened if he had not been there? Even his experiments on twins were not original, nor was injecting blue dye into brown eyes. He had been told to experiment to produce a master race and had dutifully done so. What was horrible was that he was not unique, not a monster, and that any ordinary man could have replaced him.

Harry often found himself comparing his fate to that of the Doctor. Was he not where he was today because he too had obeyed orders to the letter? He had obeyed orders for so long he now felt downright guilty about attempting to engineer his own retirement.

Harry put the glass down and opened the stiff catch on the French windows and went outside. He picked up a stout stick propped against the house and walked across the garden and down towards the river. He wanted to see if Hindle had done anything about the defences to the Doctor's valley. Not that he had become fond of the old devil but, retirement or not, it would never do to let him get his backside shot off.

Yes, Josef had mellowed but in the last months he had seemed to acquire a calmness that made Harry almost envy him. Perhaps his latest project, a study of comparative religions, was a sign he was finally changing his views, since arriving at three score and ten years is a difficult age for anyone.

Harry stopped and looked down at the river. A heron was picking its way along the rocky side of the torrent. He hoped it would not get too close as it was easy to get swept away at that point just below the house. Smoke rose from the direction of Paradiso. What would Josef have made of looking after him, guarding Major Harry, all these years if he had done something dreadful? It was an intriguing thought. Probably there would not have been all that much difference, though he doubted whether the Doctor would have had much patience with Hindle. In many ways they were very much alike, from the same sort of family background and class, having had the same sort of schooling and military training. They had similar tastes in music and art and painting, and both wanted to be respected. He had expected to be faced with the man's snivelling remorse after a few years in the valley. Instead, ever resourceful, the German had his doctorate and medical qualifications smuggled from Germany and put them up on his wall. He had invited Harry for a game of chess to admire them and had not been pleased when the Major laughed.

But he sometimes did show his deeper more tender feelings, and not just when listening to music. Harry had seen him cry once at the funeral of an old German, who had lived in Hohenau and with whom Josef had played chess. He had read the lesson in the church and no one from that tight little community thought there was anything incongruous or wrong in him doing so. Many were born in Paraguay between the wars, and for them what had happened to Germany may as well have been on another planet as they stood there in torn breeches listening to the precise reading of the Twenty-Third Psalm.

When the Inspection Committee of Germans came to call in the early months to make sure the Doctor was alive and well (if he had not been they had strict orders to release all the incriminating documents which had been stored away), Harry had inquired if there were any old comrades in the locality who might help against raids by Jewish extremists. The result had been two elderly Waffen SS men, one crippled, and a mangy dog that had bitten Willy. Josef had roared with laughter. The myth of the vast supportive SS comrades organization, the *Kameradenwerk*, was mostly Harry's own creation. He was rather proud of it. It was something to chuckle over on rainy winter evenings. He would read sensational newspaper articles about secret jungle armies and remember the two men and the mangy dog. Someone from an English newspaper had once got very close to finding SS Captain Eduard Roschmann, Butcher of Riga, up in Lomo Plata near the Bolivian border in the Chaco, where he lived among the Mennonite Christians, an industrious member of an industrious community. The reporter was on the trail of Hitler's deputy *Führer*, Martin Bormann, who had been killed in the last stages of the war. Roschmann had put on a virtuoso performance, taking on the identity of Bormann and giving the poor reporter a long and garbled interview. When the story appeared it was easily and quickly discredited and had the effect of making Nazi-hunting unfashionable for a while. In the early days, Harry himself had even pretended to be the Doctor, as he did not look so very different from him, in order to throw a group of Argentinian Jews off the trail. When they confronted him in a hotel lobby, where he had checked in under Josef's often assumed name of Gregory, he had answered their charges with such English politeness that they invited him to take tea with them, apologizing for the "mistake".

Indians were stacking sandbags near the entrance to the valley, and a machine-gun post had already been constructed. Harry couldn't really recall what he had said to Hindle last night, but it must have sunk in. He often wondered if the place could run without him; well, he supposed it would have to if he retired. Satisfied with the preparations he quickly strode back up the hill looking over at the Aché village. In the last resort there was a six-man steel bunker under the laboratory.

Chapter 9

"We are as ready as we'll ever be for Labuschagne sir," said Hindle as they took a rare cup of coffee together two days later. As he spoke the first drone of an aircraft could be heard on the mid-morning air through the open French windows of the drawing room. Was it the helicopter? Yesterday all the gun crews had gone on alert as an Argentinian Air Force light plane, a Pucara Hindle had said, passed harmlessly to the south, oblivious that if it turned north it would have run into a determined if not very effective cloud of anti-aircraft fire. Harry had been equipped to take on a threat from the ground, a group of Jewish Defence League commandos or suchlike. He had no real anti-aircraft weapons, no rocket launchers fired from the shoulder, and he damn well wished he had. There was a troublesome .50-calibre machine gun by the house, but of a much older vintage than the guns on the helicopter Labuschagne would send against them; then there was a handful of light GPMGs, some rusty old Brens, and the riflemen whom Hindle had grouped into firing parties the like of which Harry had not seen since the 1940s. He commended the Scotsman, who admitted sheepishly he had dug up the knowledge from an "old pamphlet" – meaning, of course, one of his War Picture Library comics.

The sound of the aircraft grew louder, becoming the unmistakable thudding of a helicopter. Harry went into the garden and blew his police whistle, a remedy to the problem of communication with the Aché, who hated radios. He then tried the walkie-talkie while Hindle went to supervise the heavy machine-gun crew.

In a sudden explosion of sound, the black helicopter roared overhead, a swarthy, grinning figure leaning out against the port-door gun. The house shook as the chopper made a low pass and swooped down the hill into the valley towards the river, the Doctor, and the Aché village. The machine guns and rifles down by the river began to engage the helicopter. Harry held a pair of binoculars to his eyes to see if the machine carried any rockets. If it did he might as well start waving the white flag now. In a moment of inspiration he got Hindle on the walkie-talkie.

"Get Duarte or one of the responsible ones to run up the Union Jack on the flag-pole. You've got one I hope. Might discourage them. Quick man. Over."

"Yes sir, over." He probably thought Harry wanted to go down round the flag or some such patriotic rubbish.

Duarte sprinted to the end of the garden on the second pass, when again the helicopter held its fire, and had the familiar flag up before the third. Surely they would not shoot at the Union Jack? But it had exactly the opposite effect from the one he had hoped for. The set of French doors just to his right exploded into shards of glass as heavy-calibre bullets ripped up the wooden floor and tracer rounds set the carpets and curtains smouldering. "Fire! Get the bloody buckets in here!" he shouted and two shaking girls followed by Maria threw water on the furniture and fled. "Down into the cellar with you. Quickly, go," he said when the little fire was out and ran to join Hindle watching the pink tracer from the river guns pursue the helicopter and overtake it. They must have got it Harry thought, but it flew on and turned again. Tracer was so damned deceptive.

Their cantankerous American machine gun was belt-fed, unlike those in the helicopter, and the rounds frequently jammed. Hindle attempted in vain to hold the sights onto the black shape as it jumped like a clay pigeon from the treeline, allowing only one burst at the most before it was above them. Again the tracer made them think they had a hit until the very last minute, and then the world was engulfed in dust and flying metal. Harry coughed. As the dust cleared he saw that the last burst from the dark man, obviously a master gunner, had missed them by inches, digging a deep furrow in the red earth. As the boom of the engine died away he heard the helicopter's speakers crackle into life with "The Battle Hymn of the Republic". Then chattering fire came from the valley again, and this time the helicopter turned its starboard weapon against the Aché village, banking sharply and pouring burst after burst into the undefended huts.

"Hindle, tell the men to hold their positions."

The last thing he wanted was a stampede back to the village.

"Don't worry sir, they are good men."

Harry didn't doubt that, but he didn't believe they would stand by him if their village was being machine-gunned. He had not put any protection down there, thinking first of Josef and then the house.

"Mine eyes have seen the glory of the coming of the Lord;
He is trampling out the vintage. . . ."

The helicopter came on again, and this time Harry thought he could make out the blond maniac who hugged the machine close to the ground. They fired another burst at the house and the heavy bullets smashed into the orange tiles of the roof. The run had been over so quickly that Hindle had not been able to fire. His knuckles were white with rage as he gripped his weapon. It was not his kind of war. There was an explosion in the valley as one of the ammunition stores was hit. Whatever their sexual preferences, these men were professionals.

Harry grabbed the radio and tried to get through to the chief who had a detachment of men near the road. Was this just an airborne attack or had Labuschagne sent in men to take the place lock stock and barrel?

"See if we can hit him this time, Sergeant," he snapped, handing his place by the gun over to Duarte and concentrating on the walkie-talkie.

"Yes, I am here Major," said the solemn voice of the chieftain who distrusted and hated the radio, for reasons, probably metaphysical, that Harry had never been able to fathom.

"Any sign of movement on the road Chief? Over."

"The road is clear and peaceful. We see the smoke from our village. Do you see the smoke from our village Major? There is so much smoke and my brothers are anxious."

"I see the smoke Chief, over."

"We must stay here and watch our houses burn? Why must we do that?"

"Because men might come on the road to kill us all after the houses have burnt. To kill your wife and children."

"Your house is not burning," observed the chief calmly.

Harry wanted to tear his hair. He wished the chief would learn proper radio procedure, proper military procedure come to that. It was like dealing with a child and anyone's guess if he would obey orders. Harry dropped the radio as dust enveloped him again, a stone thrown up by a bullet caught him painfully in the front of the chest. Hindle's bungalow exploded and caught fire. "Ma hoos!" he heard and through the smoke he saw Hindle turn towards the smouldering ruins. The prolonged burst had more or less torn away one side of the prefabricated building.

Duarte, the man who had raised the ill-considered flag, now lay dead in the dust, his chest ripped open. The wound moaned as air escaped from the body, giving the impression the man was still alive. Hindle looked down horrified. Harry had seen it before. The gun was unscathed but had jammed on the moment of firing. Hindle gazed at the bungalow where his papers rustled in the breeze. It had always been such a tidy dwelling and, but for a picture of a large-breasted lady in the lavatory, something of a tasteful one for an army sergeant. Everything was exposed: the man: the red corduroy bedroom slippers under the bunk, the carefully tended plant, the picture of Hindle's mother and father, the hand-painted Airfix model of a German Tiger Tank. All these private things were under public scrutiny, like poor Duarte's lungs.

The next time the helicopter jumped the horizon they were running down to join Jeronimo and the men in the riverside battery. Hindle clutched his trap-shooting gun, his prize possession, bought on a trip to Posadas in Argentina and completely useless against helicopters. "Bastards," he could be heard to mutter. "Fucking bloody bastards!" It was strange. The raid had transformed the martinet Scot into almost an acceptable human being

The machine overflew the valley, unscathed yet again, not even deigning to shoot back, and was circling the village, dropping parachute flares to add to the fires. Harry wondered if the chief was still on the road. The radio was broken and even the whistle was bent. He must get them all into the mouth of Josef's valley; they could not risk another death, though God knows how many casualties there were in the village with nothing but banana matting roof to protect them.

"Get into the valley, the canyon, all of you come *on*!" he shouted at the sandbags. As Jeronimo's head peered over the top he saw he had a sub-machine gun. "Don't shoot," he said needlessly. Jeronimo smiled. "I wouldn't shoot you, Major. I cannot even shoot a big helicopter. What has become of me?"

"Too many women, too much weed, Jeronimo. Quick – into the canyon. Bring the weapons. *Move!* Set up a firing position here behind the bridge. They will not be able to see us with luck. Come on, jump to it."

The sandbags surrounding one machine-gun position were stacked at the narrow mouth of the small valley and an extra gun was dragged up to the tree platform. As the helicopter thudded over it stitched a neat line of fire where the sandbags had been. Beside Harry in the gloom beneath the trees a young Aché shivered with fear. It was the first helicopter he had ever seen and it was now over the village where his sister was in the little school. Harry wondered about Maria up at the house. If the attack continued he would soon have to start making plans to abandon ship and get Josef away.

The helicopter banked away from the village which, by the smell of woodsmoke, was well alight, and had come back to look for them. They want me, thought Harry. Labuschagne has told them to get me. He would like to send my head back on a platter to Cortez. What a bloody country!

Above him the lovers had switched on the Baptist's sermon: "I care not what you have done in the past," pleaded the Bell helicopter with a Texan accent. "I care not what you have done in the days of sin with your face turned away from the Lord."

If I was home in England now, thought Harry wistfully, the most excitment I would ever have in an afternoon would probably be firing someone, not being fired at by a hostile sermonizing helicopter, piloted by two homosexual psychopaths with orders to kill me because of a tiff between a local smuggler, who just happened to be a priest, and the toilet-obsessed chief of police. If he ever got home he promised he would never ever be bored again and instead view the blessed condition as a sacrament dispensed by God only to a lucky few. Water and pebbles spurted over the sandbags which they were trying to reinforce with earth as the door gunner fired at random into where he thought they were hiding.

"Hold your fire!" shouted Harry.

"It does not matter what you have done, turn to the Lord and you will have life everlasting. This is the solemn promise from the Lord on high. This is the voice of God. I am talking to you, yes you. Stop slouching and look up and listen when I'm talking to you. That's right. This is not just any God but the one and only true God. If you put your trust in Him today He will bring you food and great wealth. . . . "

That was stretching it a bit far. Harry put his hands over his ears. The Aché next to him had his fingers almost boring into his brain as the sound of the aircraft beat into the valley. It was hovering now, blotting out the sky, stationary above the river and pouring out bursts of fire first right then left into the bushes, hoping that the bushes would fire back and give away a position. Harry had to admire the Americans' bravery. Suddenly the sermon spluttered off and became the friendly voice of the blond pilot.

"Hello sinners. This is God again. Are you down there Harry? I'll bet you're down there somewhere, you sonofabitch. Sorry about all the damage and that but old Rasputin says it will be a good deal worse if you don't stay out of politics. Personally I'd not stop running until I got to Rio, but you know me. I like you Harry, so no hard feelings. Only next time he might make us bring rockets and we would have to off you for good. By the way it's a fair old mess down in the *pueblo*. Dig my Spanish? Bye *viejo*."

Hindle fired as the helicopter roared away over the trees and into the smoke towards Paradiso. If the shot struck home it did not hit anything of consequence and if it was noticed the odd couple didn't view it as unfriendly.

"Idiot," said Harry, his contempt for the sergeant returning.

"Sorry sir," said the little man. "I thought I might hole his fuel tank."

"Well, thank God you didn't. It would have blown us all to kingdom come. And what if you had winged him and the door gunner judged the direction of the shot? These men know what they are doing Sergeant."

"Yes sir," said Hindle squirming. He had obviously not been in this sort of war before. Stalking around Crossmaglen looking for the IRA was one thing; being attacked from the air was something that assaulted the senses, filled your nose with dust and turned your knees to jelly. He recalled his own reaction on the beaches at the Dunkirk evacuation with the Stukas whirling in. They could drop a bomb into a bucket of water. Dreadful screaming things.

Josef! He had completely forgotten about him.

"Hindle, go and send a message to Mr Chambers in Rio on the special frequency. The gadget is pre-set." There were some things even the sergeant could not cock up in the age of automation.

Harry pulled Jeronimo, who was grimacing at a minute flesh wound on his upper arm, to his feet and pushed him up the valley. As he reached the first guard-post he saw Willy, one fat arm holding the other as if it hurt. He feared the worst.

"He's not shot is he? The sods haven't got Josef have they?" Harry blurted it out as if he were asking about a friend, a comrade close to him, a jolly fine chap instead of a mass murderer. "Is he hit?"

Willy screwed up his face and raised his good arm, grasping

at air as if he were trying to find words there. He stood still for a moment and then said: "No, he is not wounded, not scratched. There is nothing wrong with his body but he is in shock. He smashed up the laboratory and let the reptiles out of the vivarium. Then he hit me with an iron bar as I tried to stop him burning his notes. I have not seen him like it since the war."

"But he's okay?" said Harry. "He's not hurt himself or tried to hurt himself, that kind of nonsense? Can I send anyone up there with you?"

"I don't think you quite understand me, Major. It was the helicopter. . . ."

"Yes, yes," said Harry. "Got you in one. We are all pretty scared stiff of the things. Look, take Jeronimo and calm Josef down. Tie the fool into a chair if you have to but don't let him out of your sight. I've got to go over to the village and see the damage there. I'll be back as soon as I can. Was he all right when you left him? Was he still smashing things?"

"He was tearing a paper into quarter-inch pieces and laughing, actually laughing. I said he needed to see a doctor and he laughed all the more . . . Please hurry back from the village. I am sure they can cope on their own. Josef is usually so calm and precise and balanced."

Willy turned and hurried back towards his master. Harry ran off towards the Aché village. He met the chief at the water-pump in the centre of the hovels.

"Did you know such a thing could happen?"

Harry was conscious that his authority was slipping. Feared ones, *Mbareté* like himself, are not meant to cower in the bushes when a fire god comes. What had he done to provoke such wrath? That's what he was really being asked.

"I think Father Labuschagne from Capitan Boda who sent the helicopter does not like Indians," he said. The chief looked about him. The huts behind him were burning with a whoosh of flame.

"He wanted to kill you, not us." The chief was not a man to be put off.

Several injured had already been laid out on the open patch

of ground by the pump. A boy with a limp, who wanted to go to medical school one day, was treating the wounds, mostly burns caused by the flares and tracer. Miraculously only two people had been killed – two old ladies who had been too frightened to run from their home into the jungle. The hut had been a traditional one of bent-over saplings and straw woven by the old women themselves. It had burnt in seconds, leaving the two bodies huddled together. Men stood around and nodded their heads. Women began to wail.

The warriors looked at the two small, pathetic corpses with no more outward emotion than if watching manioca roots cook in the embers of a fire. But Harry could sense an ugly change of mood as more and more of the men stood with their toes against the circumference of the ash circle, and an old man, older than the others, began to bang a drum. The young ones glared at Harry accusingly. Their eyes said that he had let them down; it was his fault, his carelessness with their lives had brought a disaster which so easily could have been much worse. The chief stepped forward and put his hand on Harry's shoulder. It was not a kindly gesture; more of a warning.

Really it was incredible none of his Indio guards had been killed in action over the years. Today Duarte and the two old girls were the only casualties. Was it such a high price for them to pay for his protection? Was it too much of a sacrifice for him to expect in his schemes to get home?

Tatugi's home had been scattered into the trees by stampeding pigs. A large black pig looked at Harry from the centre of the wreckage by a gaudy calendar decorated with roses, naked girls and sticks of dynamite, advertising Emilio Santos' blasting equipment: he had allowed one of the boys to go and work in the Bolivian mines when he pleaded to leave. He had come back with a cough and a calendar and a hatred of cold. The pig was lame. One of its trotters had been burnt and it looked at him with bemused contempt. What a bloody nightmare. Was the Doctor worth all this? *Was* he? Yet in many ways the attack was what Harry had wanted. London would have to do something now, and he could not afford to get sentimental about a bunch of natives.

He must get Hindle to bring down the body of Duarte; it must not all be on his shoulders. He went back to the river and saw a party of Aché was still at work strengthening the sandbags at the mouth of Josef's valley and he had to stop twice on the steep hill up to the house, the blood thumping in his temples as he looked down at the pall of smoke. Out of the north wheeled the black and white wings of a vulture.

As he reached the start of his garden proper he found himself looking into the barrels of a shotgun.

"You kill my husband."

The kitchen maid pulled the trigger. Nothing happened. Then she discovered the weapon's hammers and Harry threw himself to the ground, yelling for Maria. There was a loud explosion and pigeon shot peppered the bushes he had crawled behind. Then another bang, and he felt a sharp pain in his backside. His hand reached for the Webley, then let it go.

"You have killed my husband. You will die!" shouted the woman who he thought was called Catrina. "Maria!" he howled and a third explosion blew a hole in the little hedge, splintering the pungent cinnamon bark and leaves, morbidly reminding him of embalming fluid.

On his front porch Maria screamed, and had his right knee not given way as he stood up sending him ploughing into the bushes again, another shot at kidney height might have caused him a long, painful death. Maria came running and swore at Catrina in Guaraní.

"Stop, you pig woman! Stop!"

"I will shoot the murderer and his whore. Whore! Whore!" shouted the hysterical woman. She was rummaging in his cartridge bag as Maria dashed over and knocked her down, thumping her across the nose with the shotgun.

"Now don't hurt her, there's a good girl," said Harry, and passed out.

Chapter 10

The next morning Harry woke up with his head aching. So did his leg and something noxious and smelly had been smeared on his buttock wound. He tried to recall the outcome of the fight between Maria and Catrina. Maria must have won or he wouldn't have all this gunge on his behind. He twisted his head round and regarded his rear, which seemed to be covered in a greyish slime that stung. Perhaps this was a punishment for wrecking their village. God, what a disaster of a day. He was glad he had passed out before anything else could happen; there was a lot to be said for the ostrich outlook.

His bottom didn't seem to be badly hurt. There was only a long deep cut which bled as he touched it. He gingerly got out of bed, putting his weight first on his good knee and then on the one that had given way. The knee ached rather more than his backside and he would not be able to do the Highland Fling, but nothing seemed to have come adrift or fallen off. He shuffled across the carpet to his dressing room. If the boys in Whitehall could see me now, he thought: a scrawny old man, naked as the day he was born except for his bottom plastered with grey river mud, herbs and things he cared not to think about, they would probably retire me on aesthetic grounds. Not a very pretty sight. He set to work scraping with the blunt side of the razor and then rubbed the old blue face flannel with hyacinth soap and dabbed away very gently. It took ages to get every last painful speck of mud off and a collection of unmatched Elastoplasts over the wound. He had only smelled anything like that ointment once before, and that was when he had found a long-dead alligator in a trap down by the river.

Harry dressed, shaved and put on his trousers, and was beginning to feel human again when a thought sent a twinge of pain through his new wound. Josef! He never went up there. Willy said he was very disturbed. He had not checked. He looked at his watch and was horrified to see it was ten. By his bed was a stone Indian mug which smelled spicy, probably a sleeping draught. He went downstairs.

He remembered the chatter of bullets ripping up the floor. Yet he felt no desire to revenge himself on Labuschagne, only to cut and run. He recalled the reaction of the Indians; they all wanted revenge deep down, like Catrina. They had learnt too much from the white man.

He opened the front door and then the screen doors which kept out the flies and made his way down the garden. He didn't like waking up and not knowing exactly when the lights had gone off. It reminded him of being a freshman again, inching across quads in the first blast of a hangover to apologize to some tutor or other for making a noise or breaking a window. He could never remember any of it. He must have looked innocent for he never got sent down. He focused on a patch of grass and tried to imagine he was in Oxford. But it was no good; here the grass was greener.

A neat row of sandbags had been built along the entrance to the little valley, and two Aché stripped to the waist looked grim in a machine-gun nest they had constructed under Hindle's supervision. On its rim sat Jeronimo deep into the rhythms of a small tape-recorder rescued from the ruins of Hindle's hut. Harry wondered if the sergeant knew. Surely Jeronimo wouldn't take Hindle's tape without asking, although he could not imagine the Scot lending an Indian anything. Combat certainly had a funny effect on people. He remembered that Jeronimo had been "wounded". The loan of the tape, which sounded like Elvis Presley, might be Hindle's reward for courage. Or Jeronimo was even more courageous than he thought.

"*Tepeho*," he grunted. Jeronimo didn't look up and the

guards nodded as he worked his way gingerly through a gap in the sandbags. Elvis was singing about his dog as Harry made his way into the valley and the first checkpoint. Here an Aché had red paint on his body and was obstructive, pointing the GPMG at him and cocking the weapon when he did not announce himself properly.

Harry was almost glad to see the sergeant arguing with a group of guards outside the white laboratory building. Hindle was annoyed.

"Look, don't piss me about. Get in there and shoot that snake. It is not a god, it's a snake and I want it to be a dead snake. If it bites me . . . Just get on with it."

The order was delivered with such venom that the snake-hunting party, which included the argumentative Tatugi, sloped off into the lab though with no intention of killing the lethal Ja Ra Ra. Harry knew all about the Doctor's snakes. Indeed it was the only thing he would allow him to experiment on as snakes did not have the ability to scream.

His buttock hurt like hell and his bad leg was giving him gyp. The sergeant started to mumble about the message he had sent and how the decoded reply meant Chambers was proceeding with all speed. He limped past them.

"Must have a word, sir!"

"Not now Hindle."

Inside the hut the smell of damp was stronger and mixed with the incense of mosquito coils. There was also the sickly sweet smell of eau-de-Cologne which Josef employed to conquer the deathly stench of the place.

He stepped along the narrow corridor. The blinds were still drawn and he had to blink to adjust to the dim light. A mumbling was coming from Josef's room. Harry pushed the door open and made out the stubbly head and kneeling outline of his charge. What sounded like a chant in German suddenly stopped.

"Do you want to join me in prayer?" said a clear voice in English, without a trace of mischief. "I suppose the others have told you. I hope this is not an embarrassment."

Something was very wrong.

Two steps round the furniture-crammed hut and Harry had his hand on the cord of the blind. It snapped in his impatience and flew up with a clatter. Before him, with a smile on his lips and a rosary in his hands, was Josef.

"Bloody hell." In the circumstances it was all he could think to say. He felt weak. For a moment his mind was empty. His knee threatened to give way. His hand touched the arm of the chair by the window and he dropped into it with a bump.

"Christ!"

The searing pain catapulted him across the room.

Josef crossed himself.

Harry had sat down hard on a hastily nailed together cross and two mosquito coils the resourceful German had erected as a makeshift altar on the armchair cushion. He clutched at his re-opened buttock wound and crashed into the table. His bottom was on fire.

He steadied himself against the wall, breathing heavily, warm blood trickling down his leg. His knee was about to give way again. It was a bad dream.

"Please believe me, Major, I did not intend this," said Josef with a sympathetic smile and a gesture of the hand towards the overturned furniture and the altar recently desecrated by Harry's backside. "I do not have the words. . . . "

"Neither do I," said Harry.

"I mean I do not have the words to express my joy. Not at your little accident of course. No Major, forgive me. I cannot explain to you my joy in suddenly knowing Jesus. He wants to receive me into the Temple of the Lord. That is why I built the little altar."

It was a trick. It had to be a trick. What on earth was the old devil up to?

"We'd better put you on the first plane to Jerusalem then. Nothing like starting a new lease of faith with a pilgrimage. You must know that. I've no doubt the Israelis would gratefully restage the crucifixion for you." Harry looked the man hard in the face and the blue eyes shone back. "Come on Josef, stop this nonsense. We were all shaken up a bit by that raid. Let's just get back to normal; we have enough trouble with the natives and we may have to move you."

The Doctor was minutely examining his hand.

"You are making fun of me and I am not going anywhere. I have heard the voice of God and I need time to decide what He is telling me to do. Then if you like I will go to Jerusalem and face, as you say, the music. I agree I deserve to be punished and can probably never attain a state of heavenly grace."

"Heaven wouldn't be a popular place if they allowed people like you up there," said Harry crossly. "I'm sorry Josef, forgetting myself. But you have to stop this playing around. That 'voice of God' you heard was one of the maniac Baptists who lend their helicopter to Father Labuschagne. The helicopter has loud-speakers and was flown by a psychopathic young homosexual who thought it a good joke to turn on that hymn singing and the sermon while he was trying to kill us all. So you see it was all a bit of a lark. They were trying to kill me, not save you."

Josef actually smiled. The expression lit up the whole face and he put one hand on Harry's arm.

"Harry, believe me, it matters not how one is called. What matters is that I have been. God has been on my mind for some weeks now and I would be the first to admit, as a philosopher, that not everything in this world is ruled by logic when it comes to getting at the truth. I have denied the Almighty too long and God has often to resort to strange and absurd techniques to get one to believe." He clutched at Harry's sleeve. "I *will* go to Jerusalem and face all the relatives of the people I murdered. Yes, I confess it. I murdered them all. I have done many awful things and must make amends."

Josef's eyes, full of messianic zeal, pleaded with him. Harry looked away at the German's crumpled cavalry twill trousers. How absurd to be converted in cavalry twill trousers, he thought. Thankfully Josef had exhausted his sermon for the moment.

He heard voices outside, among them Maria's. Harry noticed that Josef was kneeling again, praying. Better let him be for a minute. It was some time before they went out.

*

Maria, nervous of Josef, had brought sandwiches for lunch, beef sandwiches with mild sweet mustard not butter. She had passed round plates and even brought a salt pot with a lid under which nestled a little silver spoon. They sat in a ring outside the huts and munched silently. A strange communion.

"You should have said Grace," said Harry sarcastically.

"You will become tired of making fun of me," the convert said patiently, wiping a film of mustard from his upper lip.

He was clean-shaven these days but when he had first come to the valley he had both a moustache and a beard for purposes of disguise. However, they had proved impractical in the climate. Hindle said that he even shaved his armpits as a precaution against lice, which Harry personally regarded as going a bit far since there was nothing wrong with British Army louse powder. Maria pulled a face at him, distributing the spare food onto the plates of Willy and Hindle, who each stole a sly glance at the other's sandwich like school-kids.

Josef became increasingly agitated. "I have done many awful things," he repeated. "It is wrong that you should continue to risk your lives to protect someone like me. I release you from your bargain."

"Nothing's changed as far as I can see," said Harry. "If you want to practise your new-found faith that's fine by me. We can build you a little chapel up here and arrange for you to see a priest. But you know as well as I do you are not going anywhere other than the places we take you for your own safety. We would be made to look very wicked indeed if the world found out we had been protecting you all these years. Very wicked. Perhaps that's what you want – or is it that you don't trust our security any more? That I can understand and Hindle has already notified Mr Chambers to come down here post-haste. We might even go back to Argentina for a bit. I hear it's a much safer country under this new junta. . . . "

Josef was on the verge of losing his temper, making darting little movements like a clockwork toy. He never put on an ounce of weight such was the nervous energy he burnt up every moment of the waking day: it must be like hell on wheels inside that brain.

I've done a lot for you, you insufferable little prick, thought Harry. He didn't loathe him for what he had done, that was too big; it was the colossal lack of dignity in scurrying from country to country, covering his tracks, making up stories and identities to elude pursuit by the relatives of those he had butchered and burnt. He had never appeared to be frightened, not shaking with fear, but they both knew it was there, and Harry would like to bet the present silliness had something to do with that concealed terror. He had seen men go blind from fear during the war. One minute they could see perfectly and the next they were tapping about with a white stick, not shamming but completely in darkness because they could never face up to going into occupied territory ever again, their minds wanted to go but their bodies mutinied. But Christianity with Josef was a considered type of funk, just another ploy to get more attention or a better and safer billet. Did he think the helicopter was theirs, part of an elaborate plan to kill him and be rid of the bargain they had struck? Yes, the little rat could think like that and pretend to be mad. In some respects he wasn't far wrong.

Harry reached for his pipe. At least five times it had been debated whether to try and kill the Doctor, probably using a subtle skin contact poison, or – the most plausible – infecting him with a contagious disease, a strain of malaria, and actually summoning the old Germans who had been appointed his guardians to come and watch him die. After his death from "natural causes", the plan went, these guardians would destroy all documents incriminating the Allies. But the Americans had thought the plan far too risky.

Harry prised the two halves of his pipe apart. Josef had started to say something to Willy; he was talking about faith. He had never asked the Doctor in detail about the camps. They had been mentioned from time to time but only as one would talk about a workplace. The Doctor had not volunteered anything, so today was historic as it was the first time he admitted he had something to answer for – which made Harry's job harder. He had never really doubted that Josef was guilty. He had read all the available files and compiled some of them himself. But prior to the Doctor's outburst he felt like a barrister defending a known villain. Now the villain had confessed, all in the privacy of his cell, and this was the moment the honest lawyer packed up his brief and said: "I am so sorry Mr Jones but as you admit you committed all these dreadful murders there is no way I can continue to act for your defence. Good day sir."

But Harry was not an honest lawyer, he was an Army officer.

Now Josef started to weep. "I killed so many people. So many and for what? For the name of science, for the cause of progress. I had more power than anyone on earth ever should and it robbed me of my dignity, robbed me of my soul . . . I realize that now." Harry saw Hindle nodding, transfixed by those deep blue eyes, by the charisma of the man. "I must make amends, but how? I cannot continue to skulk here if I am ever to retain my dignity, my self-respect, my soul. You must understand Major, it is a question of honour. It would be impossible for you to imagine all I have done, hundreds of thousands . . . women and children and babies. To do that you have to make yourself nothing. I refuse to be nothing, that is why I want to go back and stand trial. I don't care if they tear me to pieces. It's no good hiding from the Lord. He found me here in this valley and He will not let me go. He has wrestled with me and won. He has. . . . "

The voice was rising to an hysterical crescendo and Harry's bottom began to throb. He sighed. Religion was something you did not talk about at mess dinners. The manuals and training lectures had never dealt with the possibility of miraculous intervention in an operation.

He put his head in his hands, praying Chambers could perform a secular miracle and extract him from this madhouse. God appeared to be otherwise engaged.

Chapter 11

The roar of two trucks shattered the peace of the afternoon. In the back of each were half a dozen American marines who peered out with a day tripper's curiosity from under their crew-cuts. For no initially apparent reason the driver of the first truck pulled off the gravel drive and rolled down Harry's immaculate lawn to the flag-pole. He stepped from the cab with the Stars and Stripes in his hand. Harry was striding down the garden as the tubby figure of Chambers emerged from the passenger seat, waving his hands at two Aché pointing their rifles at the patriotic driver's head. A sergeant leapt from the back of the truck with his own rifle at the ready while an officer rushed from the second truck to join the fray.

Chambers half turned: "Cooee Harry. Help! I think I'm in the middle of an aboriginal international incident. Put that flag away you stupid oaf. Put up that gun," he said to the driver and the sergeant.

Harry, somewhat breathless, called the Aché off. With a shrug they went back to sit in the small dug-out under the Union Jack, the flag a friend of theirs put up before he died; poor Duarte. More Aché were coming up the path from the river.

"Colonel Paris Stebling at your service Major," said a mild man in his late thirties. "Sergeant, get this truck back on the drive." The marines obeyed, though without respect. "We will find somewhere to put the flag later," the Colonel added weakly to the disappearing backs. "I'm sorry about this misunderstanding, Major. My sergeant and I are in Psy Ops; we had to put the team together in a rush. Your guards on the road were so polite to Mr Chambers, I had no idea the Indians here could be so, well, aggressive."

"Probably the very last words of General Custer, what?" said Chambers.

Stebling did not laugh. He was considering the problem as a psychologist.

"Do you think it would be appropriate to give them some sort of present?" he said after a few moments.

"No, Colonel," smiled Harry. "The boys do exactly what I tell them to." One of the older Aché took out his machete and began to sharpen it for effect. "And I think they are well past the coloured bead and chocolate bar stage, although they like American cigarettes. Please leave that flag alone, by the way. It is my order that it stays there. Sergeant Hindle will show you where you can set up camp. Now I have to talk to Mr Chambers and I'm sure you have a lot to do. And for God's sake tell your men to be careful."

With that he tapped Chambers on the shoulder and set off towards the house. Throughout the afternoon they were kept informed of the American latrine-digging, tent-pitching, bar-b-que-building and loud untidiness by a string of Aché runners. The invaders even erected a sign saying "Los Angeles City Limits". Harry listened to the bulletins with satisfaction: it would not be long now. He was trying to imagine the lay-out of his projected Cotswold rose garden, his local pub, the thwack of leather on willow as they played cricket on the village green, when Chambers brought him back to reality.

"I'm afraid the Yanks are chasing their tails and foaming at the mouth as usual," said the Fat Man. "Complete hysteria. It was all I could do to get away with this small party of marines. They seemed to want to send a division, and still might. The Doctor has to be kept down here at arm's length while his state of mind is assessed. They seem very sensitive about his Christianity."

Chambers shifted on the settee among the sea of secret papers he had brought with him. He had the job of writing the report on Josef, if the man's present claims were real or faked, and somehow had to keep the lid on the situation. To Harry's horror his help was viewed as indispensable. Obviously he should have never mentioned the Doctor's conversion to Christianity in his own coded radio communication with Chambers. He should have just said Labuschagne was preparing to attack again and it was imperative Josef be moved. The last confrontation with Josef must have affected his reason. He shouldn't have tried to gild the lily. Chambers had been so amazed he had made Harry repeat the message three times and informed the Americans immediately.

Harry nursed his glass of whisky and wondered, on that sultry afternoon, how long it would take to drink himself to death, and exactly how painful it would be spinning off into oblivion on a tide of amber nectar. They would bury him here, of course, possibly somewhere marshy down by the river and the land crabs would dig him up in no time. A stinking rotting gringo corpse with a life of its own. If I'm being morbid, he pondered looking at his whisky and gulping some more, I have a damn right to be. He had expected to be in Asunción at least by now while they found a safer place for Josef. Then they would let him go back to England.

"If I didn't know you better I would have thought you had planned this," Chambers complained. "All of it. Just what did take place last time you went to see Cortez? Is he behind this? If he threatened you with something you should have come straight to me. Nothing like this has ever happened before."

Harry reflected for a moment if the Americans could have bugged the Departamento de Investigaciones and drew himself up to his full height and looked angry when he decided it would be beyond even their technical accomplishments: "I think you owe me an apology, Chambers. You asked me to see the madman and it was a routine visit, indeed friendlier than usual. No one else would see him. You're looking for someone to blame and it's not going to be me."

Chambers looked shocked. "I'm sorry Harry. I apologize. But it's the damn Christianity that makes things so awkward. The Yanks are bonkers about religion and that sort of thing. I keep trying to find a key."

"There is no bloody key," said Harry. "He has turned into a God botherer and that is that. People do believe in God you know, and if I remember correctly there is far more joy in heaven about one sinner who repents than any amount of normal folk. Given what the Doctor was up to in the past they should be having a non-stop party inside the Pearly Gates for the next millennium. Frankly I don't believe it because I have always found the man a calculating bastard. But what can we do? If he insists he's a Christian then he's a Christian."

"Quite so," said Chambers shuffling some papers. "Has he ever tried to kill himself or anything like that? In Germany or when you got here? Any accidents with those snakes . . . You get my drift. If he has been prone to barmy spells in the past it's much easier to understand how he could suddenly hear voices. If not the Americans might think you were trying to get rid of him, to get him off your hands, put him in a lunatic asylum."

Harry took another swallow of malt. "If you turn back in the file you'll find he murdered an estimated four hundred thousand people in one way or another, to say nothing of the interesting little experiments such as trying to turn young gipsies' brown eyes blue by injecting them with a cheap dye."

"Now, now, Harry let's not get bloody peevish. What a chap does in wartime is not really a concern of ours. You're not becoming a bleeding heart in your old age I hope?"

Harry drained his glass and his voice was steady and resigned as he said, "First you accuse me of trying to murder the old bugger and now you seem to be suggesting I've gone a bit soft. The two don't sit very well together. I think we should go and see him."

"I hardly feel up to it today," Chambers said moving uncomfortably among the papers. "I've never really met him you know. You showed me him once through the window. Possibly this Paris chap would be more suitable. If Josef is off his trolley we might be able to make some arrangements on how to get those documents back from the Swiss banks."

Harry refilled his glass from the Waterford decanter. "Of course I would do whatever you ordered, but that would be immoral and rather shabby. Are you suggesting treatment in a progressive Californian clinic for former concentration camp doctors? You know as well as I do he wouldn't live beyond a minute if we had those documents, and from my point of view it would seem silly murdering the chap after all these years."

Chambers was on the edge of getting rattled. An angry crimson flush flooded up from the Fat Man's neck-band, and beads of sweat ran down his nose and onto the papers. Arguments about Josef always ended somewhat rabidly. Harry looked into his glass. Yes, he was really drinking too much and put the thing down on the table. All this had happened because he had asked for help. He must not overplay his hand.

Chambers tapped the papers. "You say here that the Doctor went to see his pals at the Hotel Tirol in 1967 and there was a raid by Jewish extremists from Posadas in which a man was shot and killed. What was Josef's reaction then? Did he go to pieces or anything? Anything significant?"

"He was as cool as a cucumber," said Harry. "Partly because he wasn't there. He was playing chess with one of his SS cronies in a farmhouse outside the village while we waited in room twenty-six for the assassins. One was shot and the other made a run for it, and I believe the Germans got him later. But it was not an official Israeli raid so we did not think it important. The Doctor wasn't in any danger as we'd known a week before that they were going to try something. But the Americans then insisted he stay closer to home."

"And Bariloche," continued Chambers. "What about that? Did he really murder the woman? We seem to have been involved."

"Yes, Bariloche was very messy, very messy indeed, but I don't think you can attribute it to him personally. If anything it was as much the fault of the people about him panicking and I got up there too late, poor woman. From what I heard later she wasn't even positive she recognized him but they weren't taking chances. We did make some mistakes in Argentina, but as you appreciate it's a damn difficult country to work in, everyone thinks that they know best." Harry paused for a few moments; it was the closest they had come to being caught, except for possibly the current pantomine. "It was the only time we were ever worried about his nibs' health. We had been in Asunción with Eckstein and Jung, getting all the papers through as the Americans had told us that a warrant would be issued in Freiburg for Josef's arrest. He seemed a little off his food so a friend of Baron Eckstein's offered us his villa in Bariloche, which is a kind of Lake District in the Andes, Wordsworth country on a bigger scale, a truly lovely place. When Josef realized we thought he was ill it made him quite nasty. He refused to stay in the villa and we had to move to the largest hotel. There didn't seem much chance of his being recognized so I turned in for the night. The town is run by Germans and was half empty. But as luck would have it he started arguing with one of his guards at the bar. A little woman called Eldoc, Nora Eldoc, appeared from nowhere at the sound of his voice and as far as I can gather started to have an asthmatic fit. Josef told everyone he was a doctor and went over to treat her whereupon she promptly announced he sterilized her in the camp. The hired help bundled her upstairs and by the time our man came to wake me up she was dead. 'Heart attack' poor thing."

Harry took out his pipe. "What could we do? I'm sure the police would have been bribable but it might have looked damned odd on the records if Josef had been forced to sign the death certificate. And he was in a petulant mood and quite capable of signing his own name in those days, saying it was not part of his bargain that he should always travel under aliases. I think it was only when Eichmann came to trial that he realized people were still very upset at what he had done. So we took Mrs Eldoc's body to the top of an extremely picturesque cliff that night and bunged it off. We threw it off twice in fact." He smiled. "The first time it got stuck on a tree a little way down and Klaus, the man who killed her in the first place, decided her body would not be bruised sufficiently so we bunged her off again. After running errands like that I would be the last person to want to kill him. The man's almost a bloody hobby."

Chambers stared at him.

"Not that I like him," said Harry. "I don't. But I do know if I'd questioned every order idiots had given me in the war we'd have never put our noses outside the Nissen hut. I've devoted the best part of my professional life to this man, laying false trails and keeping the bastard safe; that's been my job. As to what makes him tick, I don't know. He joined the SS because his mother told him to. That's in the files if you look. His brother was killed on the Russian front and Josef had already served with the Waffen SS in France and Russia. His mother secured him a cushy little number in the camps, and in 1943 he became chief doctor. The family had some sway with General Glueks. Josef had been a Nazi since his university days and was very interested in 'proving' Rosenberg's racial theories. He still is, or rather was, but only with snakes."

The Fat Man was looking at him in a puzzled sort of way.

"Funny lot the Doctor's family," Harry went on. "He never even mentioned a dicky bird when he came back from the wars and they didn't ask. The Yanks were in charge of him in Bavaria for five years though we always had a liaison officer there. We thought that was that, except of course for popping down to question him about some Lefty or other. But then his former chauffeur recognized him living openly with his folks and thought he could make a few bob. I don't blame him really. The next thing I knew we were spiriting him through the Reschenpass-Merano route to Italy. He went to Argentina, then a former SS man suggested Paraguay and I came to do a recce. I found this place in a history book about the War of the Triple Alliance, and the romantic attachment of an Irish whore to the dictator of the time. She managed to go home and retire in one large piece after a life of nursemaiding fascists – and I intend to do the same."

Chambers got to his feet and waddled across to the drinks trolley, pouring himself a soda water and spicing it with bitters. "Did you get much help from the Germans, this ODESSA lot. Are they still powerful?"

Harry sighed. "If you read those bloody things," he pointed at the papers, "you'd find nine-tenths of the ODESSA – or better still die Spinne, the spider – is my creation. A paper tiger, or rather spider. I think I put a lot of people off looking for him with lurid rumours of storm-troopers goose-stepping around the jungle with Martin Bormann taking the salute. His resurrection was entirely my idea. We knew he was dead before the Doctor set foot in the country, long before. Roschmann was persuaded to boast he was Bormann and . . ."

Chambers yawned. "I know, you've already told me that story."

Harry picked up his whisky glass and took a large swig. "Oh, I see. It's becoming a bore is it, a long time ago and too far away, bogey men stalking the green fields of Europe in fancy dress. Well it's all right for you, you've been on the outside living the life of Riley. Down here we just seem to be an anachronism, an irritant that won't go away. Well it *won't* bloody go away." Harry wondered if he was slurring his speech. He walked to the mantelpiece. "I suppose all those stuffed shirts in Whitehall playing with their paperclips think gas chambers are a bit passé in the modern world? If they think it's so bloody boring why don't we just hand Josef over to whoever will take him and sit back and wait for all the yawns? I don't think many people *would* yawn except as a nervous reaction, and Lord knows what the Ruskies might do. They would have a field day; it would confirm all their mindless propaganda. People all over Europe might become exceedingly bored with their governments and entire administrations. Definitely a bore."

Chambers peered down, trying to see the toes of his shiny black shoes. The vast body seemed to be arranged at odds with gravity. The Fat Man swayed forward but did not topple.

"Sorry Harry," he mumbled. "I've not had much sleep since you sent for me. I always yawn when things start to get exciting." Chambers smiled at him winningly. "There is one thing that has always bothered me about this unholy business," he added.

"What's that?" Harry looked through the French windows. American marines were sprawled on the lawn, occupying the deck-chairs.

"Just what was it we obtained from him that was so valuable? I know he is said to have given us lots and lots of lovely info on communists, but for the life of me I cannot find a single specific reference to any one particular piece of information or document or traitor. Did they ever tell you what he told us? Were you present at those interrogations?" Chambers' voice was completely matter of fact.

"No, I just arranged with the Combined Intelligence Services people and MI5 for the specialists from the various departments concerned to question him. When he was brought to England he was always very busy. I was not really on the case at the time, though I had to steer him around London once." Harry felt his irritation at Chambers rising again. "Just what are you getting at?"

The Fat Man pursed his lips. "It just struck me as strange. Small point I know, but did it ever concern you? Knowing the man was valuable to us but not really knowing why? Not being in on the nuts and bolts as it were? Just doing a job blind?"

Harry was not sure how to answer. He wished he hadn't had so much booze.

"It never occurred to me," he muttered. "You just get on with the job, don't you?"

Chambers drifted back to the settee. "I shouldn't worry about it Harry," he said sipping his soda water. "I shouldn't worry about it at all. Couldn't have that sort of information, whatever it was, available to just anyone. I'll have to chase it up."

Harry was trying tipsily to come to grips with the serious question that Chambers had raised: why had he not been told more about the information reaped from the operation he had initially set up and was still stuck with? It was absurd to think it was because they did not trust him. He had done his duty as he thought fit and proper, but he was becoming aware of a monster in the mists. Suppose he had failed, suppose something went wrong and Josef had died or been killed by Jewish extremists and the secret had leaked? The government and their ministering angels might deny they had anything to do with the Doctor or a Major Harry Copeland-Smith and try to say the documents and tape-recordings he had were faked. In such a situation he could imagine a smart-alec reporter asking that fatal question: just what had he been able to obtain from the mass murderer that was so important to prevent him being brought to trial? Everyone would be looking at him, and waffle as he might about the "need-to-know basis of security work" the question would be left unanswered and his credibility damaged. God, he wished he could think clearly. He gazed out of the French windows. The marines were now playing softball on the lawn, and came lazily to attention when they saw Colonel Stebling approaching. Harry turned back to Chambers.

"I'm not going to be made into some kind of whipping boy am I?" said Harry. "Sir Reggie Tough has not been sending angry memos about me being a brigand has he, damn him?" Chambers seemed to ignore him. "Can you still hear me?" Harry shouted at the top of his voice.

The door opened and Colonel Paris Stebling of the US marine corps stepped into the room.

"Sorry to interrupt your – er – meeting but this situation is new to me and there are one or two points I would like clarified." One thumbnail scratched at the belt of Stebling's immaculately pressed uniform while the other hand held his green beret.

"If it's information about the house and grounds you want for purposes of defence then I think we can leave that in Sergeant Hindle's capable hands," snapped Chambers, directing some of the hostility he felt for Harry onto this dark, curly-haired target. "He's an internal security expert and served for many years in the North of Ireland."

"It's not to do with that sir, it's more a matter of conscience and loyalties." Stebling fiddled with his beret. "You see I'm Jewish, or rather my mother is. A lot of her family died in Nazi Germany . . . It really *is* him, isn't it? I was only told to evaluate 'a prisoner' at the briefing. We did not know what we were getting into, and then I read my orders. I don't think I can carry them out."

"Oh my God," said Harry and sat down, scarcely registering in his amazement a sharp stab of pain from the wound on his buttock. "Surely they asked about your background before they sent you here?"

"Negative Major, they did not. As I pointed out, I was not told the nature of the prisoner. I was horrified when I found out. So is my sergeant. The men don't know yet. I respectfully request that I be allowed to talk to my superiors."

"Were you aware of this splended joke?" Harry said to Chambers. "I've been trying to stop Jews getting at the old sod for twenty years and now I am sent one in command of an armed band of soldiers. Have you all gone mad?" He turned to the Colonel. "Do you know what effect this matter would have if it became known in your country? I'm afraid you and your sergeant must consider yourselves under arrest."

The large, determined and altogether honest-looking hand of Colonel Stebling reached for his regulation automatic pistol, and for what seemed like an age Chambers and Harry gave the movement their full and undivided attention as he took the weapon out of the webbing holster and stared down at it. He tried to speak once and failed. We've been sent a maniac, thought Harry.

"Look here old chap, perhaps I was a bit. . . . "

"That's all right Major." Stebling seemed to have difficulty with the words. "You are correct to place me under arrest since I am unable to obey the orders of my country and my President," and with a flourish he handed the automatic to Harry who took it unsteadily, noticing that the safety catch was off.

Chambers was the first to speak, shivering a little in the warm room. "We appreciate that this is a tricky one, Colonel, and I'm sure we can work something out with your ambassador and the CIA over this." Stebling's face clouded at the mention of the security service. "I am sorry that your government has put you in this odious position but I can let you into a little secret. We are actually making preparations for . . . No, I'm afraid I should not really tell you, but suffice it to say that the Doctor will soon wish he stood trial all those years ago. But I appreciate your feelings. I think though it would be apposite in the circumstances if you and your sergeant stayed in the house itself, and I would be obliged if you would go now and fetch him. We will have to screen the rest of your men, of course. You are a man of honour, Colonel Stebling, and I don't for a moment think you would do anything to harm us but formalities have to be observed, if only for it to be recorded that you refused to do anything you believed might help a Nazi war criminal. Forgive the Major for being a little hasty; could you give us a few minutes alone to discuss this? You have rather sprung it on us. I should be glad if you would not say anything about this to your men and order your sergeant to do the same."

Cowed by Chambers' polite English ways, Stebling agreed. He closed the door behind him.

"Now that is awkward," the Fat Man said. "I think you've been under-occupied today, Harry, and it's made you tetchy. I leave the solution of the Stebling problem to you. You're the expert. I'll go to Asunción tomorrow to find out who was responsible for this cock-up." He struggled to his feet. "And now I suppose I must prepare myself for an appointment with the Angel of Death."

Chapter 12

It was quite hot, only a shadow of the oppressive heat of summer proper but uncomfortable just the same. Harry went into his dressing room, filled a basin to the brim with cold water and stuck his head deep into it. In about ten minutes he was sober, as much from considering what to do about Stebling as from the water. Chambers had not suggested killing the man in so many words but that remedy had always been part of Harry's standing orders if someone threatened to blow the whistle on the operation. And though the Colonel might promise on his mother's grave to be sworn to secrecy it might not stop him revealing something in a year, maybe two years' time, casually one day in a dimly-lit bar about a conspiracy led by an Englishman. Soldiers always blabbed about operations they disagreed with. Harry sighed. At the beginning of the week he was contemplating retirement; now he was anticipating murder.

He put a sports jacket on, sent by Dunn and Co as a Christmas present to himself after he had forwarded his measurements through the embassy, and surveyed himself in the mirror. All he really needed was a riding crop, though he never had been one for horses; he preferred the Land Rover these days. Horses never lived up to one's expectations, being smelly, bad tempered, disobedient or slothful, like a lot of women really. He stooped down and retied the knots on his dark brown brogues and admired himself again.

He bounced down the main staircase feeling none the worse

for the whiskies. Chambers was already there, clutching a Dictaphone in one hand and mopping his brow with another, not having changed out of the grey suit which he seemed to have been born in; Harry had never seen him wear anything else and would have been extremely surprised if he had. His own tweed was a bit heavy but what the hell? He took out a comb and smoothed his hair across his forehead.

"I didn't know we had to dress up to see him," Chambers complained. "You look as if you're going to a shooting party."

Harry merely raised his eyebrows in reply.

"Hindle telephoned down," the Fat Man went on. "He's been up with Josef. I think he prefers him to the Yanks by what he said. Doesn't like Americans, your Mr Hindle."

Harry whistled and stepped out, making Chambers bustle along behind him down to the river. He hoped he would fall in.

A US marine corporal stood at ease by the entrance to the valley and kept peering up into the trees where he had seen two Aché climb into the branches; he scowled at the two Englishmen as they went by. Against regulations he had taped his rifle's magazines together. It must be hard, thought Harry as he passed him; it must be hard to come to a place not already previewed in *Time* magazine.

"I don't think these ordinary marines are a threat. We will keep an eye on them though," he said.

Chambers wheezed as he opened his mouth to speak. "I'll need two men to guard my files when I go back to Asunción and try to sort out the present fiasco. Bloody hell, what was that?" Something long, thin and reptilian sped past the Fat Man and down the valley towards the nervous corporal. "Only a rat snake, I think," said Harry.

Chambers stopped. "Look here, old man," he said. "Look here, I'll pull everything out at my end to speed you back to Blighty, you know that. You'll come out of this all right whatever we have to do to keep the lid on. All I ask is you do nothing foolish."

"I think we are all getting a bit too jumpy," Harry said. "Come on, his nibs will be a bloody bishop before we see him."

Under Chambers' orders, no marines had penetrated as far as the clearing with the two huts which was still effectively sealed by Aché guards, many in tribal dress. Hindle opened the doors to the Doctor's quarters and put a finger to his lips. They ignored him and went in to find the room lit by two candles and the Germans on the floor praying. They were saying the rosary. Where on earth had Josef got it in the first place?

"I lent him it, sir," said Hindle a little guiltily as if he had given the prisoner his gun. "My ma was a Catholic. Celtic supporter . . . " Harry nodded.

They crossed the dim room. "Sorry to interrupt, but Mr Chambers here wants a word in your shell-like ear, Josef. Could we stop for a minute?" He raised one of the blinds and the instant anger on the face of his captive vanished as soon as it had appeared.

"Of course, Major," he said, standing up before taking the reluctant Chambers' hand. "Is it the attack or my conversion that worries you? I still wish personally to apologize for all my transgressions and I need your help. Mr Chambers is in a way an answer to my prayers."

The Fat Man looked non-plussed and gingerly sat down on a chair at the Formica-topped table which was covered in a pile of papers nearly as large as the one he had left in Harry's drawing room.

"You see," said Josef with a tone of meekness Harry had never heard before. "You see I am already trying to make amends. God spoke to me last night and told me to write to each of the people I have wronged, or in the case of the deceased, and regrettably there are many of those . . . " He looked down and wrung his hands, a little too theatrically for Harry's liking. "In those cases I will write to all of the relatives and make my peace with them. Then I will ask God what He wants to do with me and If He wants me to go on trial. It is a good plan, yes?"

Chambers leapt at the idea: "I think that is an excellent suggestion Doctor Josef. We would not object to your writing anything as long as it found its way to the outside world through the proper channels and did not identify where you were or implicate us in any way. I must say I'm relieved you have abandoned the foolish idea of giving yourself up and standing trial."

The Doctor nodded gravely. "For the moment. For the moment I have given up that idea because I am not strong enough. All my life I have run away and refused to face the consequences of my actions, of following orders. I was so careful to destroy all traces of documents with my name on and that is why I must sign my name to each apology I write. Otherwise I could not face myself. It is the only way I can regain my self-respect and honour. Then it is up to God to show me the next step."

Chambers looked delighted; it was undoubtedly just the sort of ploy he had been trying to think of to "keep the lid on things". But his smile vanished as Josef produced a braided whip with nails tied to the thongs.

"I must remind myself of others' sufferings. Have I not often beaten you and been cruel, Willy? Now I have turned that cruelty on myself as an act of contrition. Perhaps if you doubt me, now you will believe I am sincere." The Doctor removed his shirt and turned. Chambers gasped. The flesh on the back was gouged and torn by the small scourge.

"Wouldn't it be better and, in the circumstances, less painful to spend the watches of the night in prayer?" said the Fat Man astounded.

There was a silence in the room and Harry felt he had to say something. The softer option of writing letters to the victims instead of the Doctor attempting to give himself up was far too valuable to let slip through their fingers. They had never envisaged this, always relying on fear to keep the Doctor snug in his bolt-hole; that was common sense. But one look at Josef's grisly back was enough to realize common sense had departed. If they refused the letter-writing demand he might become desperate. Harry didn't relish guarding the man as a reluctant prisoner; he was too clever and had many friends in the villages round about. Old Germans who would never give him away.

"Yes, writing letters is a capital idea," began Harry and the

Doctor brightened. "As I'm sure you must realize it will be a very big job and we will help you all we can. But we must admit you've worried us with all this talk of giving yourself up. I know you are being guided by the heart, but it would have the effect of destroying many of us who have helped you over the years. It would bring down governments. The memory of those camps is still a very real issue. What I am saying is that if we help you we must have complete confidence that you will not try anything stupid. We could not allow it."

He did not mean it to sound threatening but he saw Willy look up quickly and Josef smiled. It was a wry little smile, a calculating one, not the grin of a religious maniac. "I see," he said. "I agree, you have your security considerations. I have always been selfish. I give my word as part of the continuing bargain that I will not try to escape or betray you as long as you let me write those letters."

Josef slowly put on his shirt. "Of course I will need the camp lists. The Jews will have them." Harry glanced at Chambers who nodded that he had heard enough. Great beads of sweat were running down the Fat Man's forehead. The Doctor began to read one of the letters of apology he had already written. Harry felt the airless room closing in on him and opened the door. "Do you need a priest?" he asked as they were leaving. It was Willy who replied: "Josef is a priest." The two Englishmen looked at each other. There was nothing one could say to that.

When they were a safe distance away Chambers broke into a mirthless titter. "Mad as a bloody hatter don't you think? Never seen it like that before."

"I'm almost inclined to believe he is genuine," said Harry. "Lots of people went Godwards during the war. It didn't last. Guilt I suppose. We've just got to keep him happy."

Chambers frowned. "Yes, I'm going to recommend that the letter-writing nonsense goes ahead. It will be a Herculean job and should occupy the old bugger until he dies." He slapped Harry on the back. "There's only the little matter of Stebling to sort out, then you'll be let off the hook to grow roses and retire."

Did Harry believe him? For the first time since Chambers

had arrived he could see a ray of sunshine at the end of the dark tunnel.

At dinner that night, Stebling had regained his composure. It was almost a relaxed affair. Chambers gesticulated expansively with one hand while hanging on tightly with his other to what looked like a gin and tonic. He seemed worse for wear.

"Trouble with this kind of thing, your people did not have time to brief you properly. But they sent you because they thought there was a real threat to this operation, which as you will appreciate is complicated, and all I can say is the person involved has been incredibly valuable to us in ways I will never be at liberty to reveal. Naturally as you're military men we can keep it 'in the family' and there is no danger of any security leak. Do you hold the same views as Colonel Stebling, Sergeant?"

"I just do what I'm told, sir."

Stebling was about to ask a question. Harry could feel the Fat Man willing him not to. "Just what's he like?" The words fell on the silent, suddenly pensive gathering. No one said "who?" Colonel Stebling smiled at those around him as if he were asking the intimate details of an army camp typist. "What's he like?" He waggled his curly head slightly in anticipation and his eyes shone. "What is the Angel of Death really like?" The liberal psychologist had not been able to suppress his curiosity.

Harry drew in his breath and smiled. "Oh he's an ordinary sort of chap. Mad about Charlie Chaplin films and wears women's clothes. That sort of thing. Just any old Joe really." They all burst out laughing.

"Well Colonel Stebling," said Harry after a pause, "I know you can't help us with our guest but there is another little problem I have been discussing with Mr Chambers which could help both of us and wouldn't in any way harm your reputation."

Chambers stared determinedly into his drink as Harry continued: "The thing is Father Labuschagne may still attack again, and although we have the weaponry it occurred to us that you, with your training in communicating with all sorts of guerillas in South-East Asia, could help us with old Labuschagne, who at least is semi-European and has at this present time two Vietnam veterans to fly his gunship. What I propose is that you go and see him, turn up on his island; he would welcome someone in American uniform." Chambers coughed. "Hindle here can go with you. I want to invite Labuschagne over for a pow-wow. You could take him an old Jesuit Bible I found as a peace offering. A quite magnificent work. I'm sure it will charm him. He thinks I am siding with a rival of his but I'm certain you could persuade him I'm neutral. It would look so much better coming from an American. In return, no doubt, Mr Chambers will find some way of glossing over the business this afternoon."

Stebling shot out a hand. "Shake on it, Major. It's a deal."

Chapter 13

It was a dreary sort of day when Harry woke. He turned over and tried to go back to sleep but his thoughts would not let him rest. It was harder to kill a man than most people imagined. It was not a thing you could take lightly. He was not worried the man was Jewish any more than he had been worried Mrs Eldoc was Jewish. Stebling was a threat to his mission and he had orders to remove such threats, however painful it might be.

Chambers had gone. He had heard the American truck start up in the drive at exactly 6:30. The Fat Man had taken a couple of marines along to guard the precious coded report, leaving him to plot against Stebling and his sergeant in peace. It had been agreed that Chambers would tell the Americans about Stebling's reluctance regarding Josef and say he had gone on "a general reconnaissance mission of the area to assess the loyalties of the different ethnic groups". No mention was to be made of the suggested meeting with Labuschagne. Harry hoped one of his maids had relayed the information about the new guards and their anti-aircraft missiles to Father Labuschagne – by way of a sweetheart in Capitan Boda, perhaps – just in case the priest decided to send another airborne sermon. His parish had only one gunship and he was not going to waste it: he would need everything he could muster if Cortez came rampaging south.

Harry dressed and gently lifted the Bible out of his dressing room book-case and undid the heavy locking metal clip, admiring the hand-illuminated plates inside. He sighed. He would be sorry to see it go.

The letters at the start of a chapter took up a considerable amount of the page in the traditional illuminators' way, depicting scenes from Indian life. But what a life! Dressed in brightly coloured clothes they rode proudly on horseback, a literate, Christian, idealistic army living in small farming communities which were safe havens for runaway slaves and where no Marmaluke trod but drew back and bided his time. The drawings showed carefree women with faces like Maria, bathing naked in the streams, washing their simple white dresses, tending their children; and in each representational brush-stroke of the Jesuit revolutionary who had painted it, doomed by an idealism totally out of step with the worldly ways of the Church in Rome, there shone a real love of the Indians. The young Jesuits and their Indian converts had been too successful. The Church stripped them of their authority and even excommunicated some of these jungle saints, and the civil authorities had taken their guns. The Indios fled back into the forest and the dark ages to escape the shackles or the gallows.

Harry always read the book with mixed feelings. The Jesuits brought an end to their communities because, unlike him, they would not scheme and compromise. If they had lowered themselves would there have ever been an ideal community? Would it have been worth a sou? Wasn't it better to have a few brief years of splendour and real freedom? Not in Harry's book it wasn't, but he kept his favourite picture, one of the faithful listening to a young priest under a huge silk cotton tree while in the woods slave hunters lurked. He cut it out carefully with a razor; he would have it framed. Satisfied, Harry went in search of Hindle, now installed in a room in the west wing. He knocked on the door and there was a movement within; the sergeant was up and dressed in anticipation of his trip to Father Labuschagne's.

"Don't stand on ceremony Hindle," said Harry as he walked into the small bedroom. The sergeant sat on the bed looking anything but relaxed. "I have a little problem with the Americans that I want you to take care of for me. Should be a piece of cake."

"I know sir," said Hindle proudly. Had Chambers said something to the man already?

"The thing is," Harry said, ignoring a need for explanation. "The thing is that Labuschagne in his present mood would probably kill them anyway, but we must make absolutely certain. What I propose is to get them unknowingly to take a bomb to Labuschagne. Of course you won't be anywhere near the ferry crossing, let alone on the island, since you'll be looking after the Land Rover, but you can detonate it by remote control as he comes down to meet them. You can see across the lake . . . What the hell's the matter? You aren't becoming a bloody conchie too are you Sergeant?" Hindle's face had gone white. He finally managed to stutter out the words: "No sir, thank you very much sir."

"You are feeling up to the job, not got a dose of Johnny Gypo's tummy? Not feeling apprehensive? That Yank sergeant seems a very capable fellow . . . " Hindle nervously scratched the backs of his hairy hands which in the half light of the room seemed like two small animals fighting in his lap.

"Sorry sir. I got carried away. Just excited at the prospect of some more action."

Harry smiled to himself. A very naïve man would have suggested to Hindle that there were some politicians and citizens who thought blowing up innocent soldiers at a meeting with a priest was the kind of thing the Northern Ireland veteran and his pals were trained to prevent. A cursory glance at Hindle's file would prove him very wrong. The descriptions of what the man had done to a Dublin cinema stuck in Harry's mind. Yes, the sergeant knew all about planting bombs.

"One thing sir," the little man said. "I don't know if I'm speaking out of turn sir, we have not always seen eye to eye, you can count on me all the way . . . But are the Americans on our side?" Harry patted him on the shoulder. "Don't worry. The ones that count are, old man. I'm sorry if I've been a bit of a curmudgeon in the past."

He reached beside him for the book while Hindle puzzled

about what sort of an animal a curmudgeon was.

"Could you make a bomb using the new plastic the Americans brought us and put it in this Bible with a radio-controlled fuse? I know we've got some things like that for if we ever decided to leave in a hurry. Strange, isn't it, how things come in useful," said Harry slowly opening the book at Judges, which showed a pastel tinted group of Indians praying. "Have you got a knife you can use to cut a hole? If not I've brought my razor."

Hindle looked reluctant. "It seems a shame to ruin such a lovely book sir, and the Bible as well. Won't you miss it? It's a nice old book."

Harry looked at him. "That's just the point, Sergeant. The Americans will not suspect anything and neither will Labuschagne's men until it's too late, and this has the added advantage that it locks. We can wrap the key in a separate package."

Hindle stared solemnly at the book. Slowly he warmed to the task. "What I could do, sir, is wire the bomb to go off when the key is inserted. That would be much more reliable in one sense sir. Father Labuschagne will have all sorts of radios and things which might set it off; or I could wire it both ways. The only thing is if I use a gravity fuse connected to the key it will make it more dangerous getting it there."

"It's up to you," said Harry. "Remember, Labuschagne would be a bonus. It's the Americans we must be sure of. Just make certain it happens on the island. Could there be any other problems?"

Hindle's face became more monkey-like than ever as he pursed his lips and whistled irritatingly through his teeth. "Well, I suppose I could make sure that the signal was of a very different type from the radios the island is likely to have. But don't you think if we fail to get Labuschagne as well, and believe me sir these things can go wrong, won't he attack again?" Hindle walked over to a mahogany dresser to take out a kitchen knife sharpened to almost nothing.

Harry shrugged. "Well if he does we have those American blow-pipe rocket things to shoot him down; I thought they were meant to be foolproof."

Whatever he had said about the book, it made him wince as Hindle sketched out where he was going to cut with a stubby pencil and then started, first the sides and then the diagonals, cutting the shape of the Union Jack, gouging out the precious painted innards of the remarkable book, cutting in the pattern of the flag – as used to be done for a snake bite until they discovered it spread the poison faster.

"I'll leave you to it then," Harry said. "Better start out at about ten hundred hours. Then the helicopter will be safely on the deck. I'll pop back to go over the details with you at about nine-thirty. Here's the key to the armoury and the other weapons store in the cellar, and the key to the Bible."

Hindle did not look up; he was absorbed in his work, meticulously vandalizing the book to create room for the explosive, the precious and holy nature of the tome completely forgotten, if it had ever really mattered to him. Harry left the room, hurrying to the staircase which led down to the marble-floored hall.

Breakfast was being served in the dining room so he was careful not to make a noise going through the front door. His shoes scrunched on the well-weeded gravel. He wondered how long it would take for it to be covered in a carpet of greenery without his efforts, or the ridiculous pillars in front of the house to be overgrown with lichen again; he did like the place but would be glad to get home. He heard the crisp sound of leather on wood, or it seemed that way, as if someone were getting his eye in early at the cricket nets, but as he turned the clump of cinnamon bushes it was only Tatugi and some of the other boys putting in fence posts, knocking the post in with a heavy log made of a different type of wood. They stopped but did not wave. He was still out of favour after the raid. Yes, it was time to go back to England though he would miss Paradiso, if not Paraguay. He looked down on the river and the jungle rising behind; every tangled venomous inch had a hold on him.

Two Indians outside the laboratory told him Willy and the Doctor were inside. He found them both writing feverishly at a long Formica-topped table the Doctor had once used for dissection.

"Anything you need?" he said by way of a greeting and was met by a pair of enraged blue eyes. Only then did he notice the crumples of paper in the room, screwed tight and covering most of the work benches and much of the floor. The old boy certainly was not afraid of hard work.

"What I need is a staff of at least a hundred and after these few sheets we will completely run out of paper." Ink from the old Waterman lacquered fountain pen had stained the long and delicate fingers, and he kept wiping them on a white handkerchief. Willy puzzled over lists of names, scratching first his head then his backside and finally licking his pencil and adding or subtracting one. They were all names of important people who had passed through the camps, those the little man could actually remember. "Yes, they are not enough, not nearly enough," said the Doctor quickly reading his mind. "I must have the records from the Jewish places in America. It must be easy for you to get these things; without them my task is impossible." He petulantly threw down his pen.

Nothing is ever bloody good enough, thought Harry. He picked up a clamp which had been used in the experiments the Doctor had performed on various kinds of snake and pretended to examine it. "Mr Chambers has gone to Asunción where presumably it will be decided if we need to modify our long-term security arrangements in any way, and just how we are going to approach this letter-writing project of yours." He paused and then added: "If, of course, they allow you to continue with it."

"Allow? *Allow?*" The old psychosis seemed to be breaking through the Christian veil and now standing before Harry was the irritating man he had protected for years, a man so petty and self-centred his diaries were full of his fears concerning promotion. "Allow? It is not for you to order me what to do. If I want to I can see you all in hell, in particular you, Major. I will write to the survivors and the relatives. That is my right, or you can let me go to stand trial. The choice is yours. I think I have to see Von Hofmannstahl and his fawning acolytes soon. Should I tell them to release the documents?" Josef's voice was quiet now. "Even you as a military man, you must see I need help in getting this job done. I do need secretaries. You will not understand this, I cannot expect you to understand it, but I have made my bargain with Almighty God and must carry out my promise . . . efficiently. Just what would you do if you had such a weight on your conscience? You would do the same thing. I must explain that I was doing these awful things before I saw the light, I was like a man blind. Now I can see and want to apologize properly. Surely your government must understand the difficulty I have writing these letters! How, for example, am I supposed to track down all the gipsies and travelling people whose relatives passed through the camp? What exactly does one write to the relatives of a homosexual or a communist, and a lot were both; they might even be offended at learning such a thing, not everyone is broad-minded. Or what happens if I confuse a Jew with a dissenting German? The German family might be less than amused to get such a letter. Then I must have confirmation that all these letters have been received. How do you propose to do that?"

"You don't think you are stirring up memories people would rather forget?" Harry said, at which the Doctor jumped up and banged the table hard.

"I have explained this once to you, Major. I am not a man given to idle chatter and I've work to do and a right to apologize. God is guiding me."

Harry shuffled his feet. "We shall see what we can do. By the way, don't worry about any more air raids. The Yanks have brought all sorts of anti-aircraft wizardry, and I'm sure the good Lord looks after His own. I'll drop in later with some ink and paper from the house. Don't try and rush."

Harry left, resolving to do all he could to enlarge the Doctor's postal apology scheme and surely, before the thing got off the ground, for the letters could never possibly be sent, men in white coats would take the new convert off his hands.

When he got back to the house he found the two Americans sitting in the open-topped Land Rover, one in the back and Stebling next to the driver. In the back, too, was an inflatable rubber dinghy in case the Ukranian ferry service was not operating. It was their oldest boat, well patched and worn, but Stebling seemed not to be at all suspicious.

"Morning Major, we're all ready for the magical mystery tour. Is your sergeant up yet?"

"Yes, I suppose he's wrapping the Bible, the present I want you to give to Labuschagne. He's quite a civilized chap. Originally South African but felt hemmed in by the regime down there. He's the salt of the earth and I'm sure you can help clear up the misunderstanding and assure him we are quite neutral here. He'll listen to Uncle Sam. He's only got a bunch of *campesinos* helping him. It's just the helicopter that's the problem, and it's flown by two of your fellow countrymen. You might even know them."

Colonel Stebling puffed on his cigarette and serenely blew the smoke down his nose. "We are glad to be of service. Don't concern yourself, Major, this at least is what I'm trained for. We'll go in under the white flag which, being of Caucasian descent, he will respect. We were taught just how to do this at the special warfare centre. It's like a drill to us isn't it Sergeant?"

The marine did not give an answer, and Harry wondered what the laconic man had excelled in at the sinister-sounding centre, a section of Special Operations Command. He saw Hindle appear from the house, changed into civilian clothes, trying to carry the Bible casually. An almost imperceptible twitch of bushy black eyebrows told him all was well.

"Remember Ian, dinner is at seven sharp. It's a pleasant drive and don't be late. Please keep my man safe, Colonel. Labuschagne mustn't see him. He'll stay with the charabanc." Hindle passed the heavy package to Stebling. "Better take it out of its wrapping before giving it to the priest. He might think it is full of snakes."

The marine reached over, keeping Harry carefully in view, and tore off the brown paper wrapping from one corner, smiled and nodded. "Sorry Major, my sergeant is a suspicious sonofabitch," said the Colonel.

Hindle put the Land Rover into reverse. "Goodbye sir," he said and drove off. Harry was so nervous he waved until they were out of sight.

Chapter 14

The sun was going down. Harry watched the red sky from the veranda, listening out on the warm still air for the returning Land Rover. He had been gardening that day and a few times had fancied he heard an explosion but dismissed it as imagination. Hindle was late. He noticed an Indian guard by the flag-pole and wondered if against orders he was going to take down the Union Jack which had fluttered there since the battle with the helicopter, but he was only leaning against it watching the sunset, the crimsons blending into golds over the eerie landscape which tonight was more beautiful than ever. A rhythmic drumming started from the Aché village. A quick insistent beat backed by a more melancholy note on a drum made from an entire tree trunk; it was something to do with the tribe's funeral rites.

"Do you want to come in for dinner?" Maria asked.

He took her hand and squeezing it said, "You have not heard a squeak from the radio have you?" She shook her head and sat on the arm of the old club chair picking at a leaf. A tree frog started up nearby, joined by another and another. Soon the frogs were so loud that he did not at first hear the sound of an engine in the distance. Please God, let it be Hindle. I promise to be nicer to him in the future if he comes back, I really do.

But it was two engines not one and they were Jeeps. Both had Aché guards in them. The two white occupants of the first Jeep were civilians; the two in the second were in American military uniform, though they were not with the marines.

"Major?" said the thinner younger civilian, who had gold-rimmed glasses and a crew-cut. "Major Copeland-Smith? My name's Webster. Sorry we did not announce ourselves on the radio. Our people didn't think it wise until we ascertained the extent of the attack and if hostilities were still in progress. Luckily, we met your Mr Chambers on the way back and he was able to brief me. Oh, my credentials." He got down from the Jeep and handed Harry a letter and a CIA identity card. "I heard all about our conscience-stricken officer from Mr Chambers," he continued. "I will want to speak to him of course. No problem. I hear you sent him on a reconnaissance trip. No problem. We will want to screen the other soldiers too, although the marines usually do as they are told. Everyone has to be double-checked, as have my friends here. This rogue is Mark Wheatley and our role is just to keep Uncle Sam informed. We won't get in your hair and will be gone before you know it. These two men are engineers."

"Engineers," muttered Harry his mind on other things. "What do I need engineers for?"

The two men in uniform laughed. "Just to see if we can make the place a little more secure," said the plump Wheatley. "We have also brought a special scrambler, an amazing gizmo, you can talk to Mr Chambers on. Have no fear, the cavalry is here." They all grinned at him.

"Not the 7th Cavalry one hopes," Harry said before he could help himself and they guffawed. He asked them to come in and saw the plumper CIA man put two fingers over his top lip and give a Nazi salute to the picture of the Paraguayan dictator on the way into the drawing room. No doubt they would roll around the floor if he told them the shabby little mission he had sent Hindle on.

"It's a relief not to be met by Colonel Stebling," said Webster, who seemed to be one of those Americans with only a surname. "I expected to see him moping around with his tail between his legs. He is an idealist and forever lecturing us by the swimming pool." He laughed again and the others did too. "Forgive us, Major, Mark has heard some good news from home. His wife has had twins. He's still trying to count the days he has been down here to figure out if they are his." They all roared again. Harry stared stone-faced at the sniggering intelligence men and the more restrained engineers.

"Congratulations Mr Wheatley. Shall I break out the champagne? Or do you want to see Doctor Josef right away? He was an expert on twins you know."

Webster's face straightened in mid-smile. "I'm sorry Major," he said. "We were forgetting ourselves." Webster moved towards him. "Yes, Major, we would like to see the Doctor and we apologize for the levity. But wouldn't it be better in the morning? It's you we really want to see," he said with a public relations man's warmth.

Oh God, thought Harry, am I for the high jump? Where were Webster and his friend from?

"Been in Asunción long?" he said switching to a polite smile and concentrating on Mark, whose blue shirt did not match his brown jacket at all. He wondered how such an individual, who looked as if he would be more content managing a supermarket in Victorville, ever became a spy. But it was Webster who answered, a beanpole of a college boy who he felt instinctively was against him.

"Don't worry about that, Harry, don't worry at all. We ask the questions. Washington is very concerned to keep a lid on this one. Excuse me, we have some presents for you Harry, you don't mind if we call you Harry?" No reply was called for and in a flash Webster's 6ft 3ins was vanishing through the door with that rangy sinuousness which meant he had played for his college basketball team in between spying on student demonstrators. Harry sniffed, he didn't like the newcomers at all, even the engineers. They had a look in their eyes which meant they were sharing a joke he wasn't party to. Mark was showing one of the engineers a picture of his wife; perhaps they had just been drinking on the way down but he doubted it. The CIA may have cocked things up once but were not going to do it a second time; these boys were the pros from the coast, probably Santiago.

"Here we are." Webster was back, beaming like Father

Christmas. "Mark, you turkey, get the other things will you? Look at this Harry, for your personal use, a radio phone which will allow you to talk to Mr Chambers in Asunción." The tone of voice was helpful but patronizing, the sort one would use to a half-grown child or a partially lucid geriatric.

Agent Wheatley came staggering back into the room a few minutes later carrying two heavy batteries. They quickly linked the grey box to the batteries, as if Harry's electricity was somehow suspect. For a horrible moment he had a vision of a charred Colonel Stebling sploshing through his door, dripping and furious on his old silk rugs. The box was whistling now and they attached a microphone and something similar to the computer keyboard he had on the machine upstairs. He almost wished he had kept quiet about Labuschagne's raid.

"There you are Harry, the miracle of modern technology," said Webster looking at him intently through his round glasses. The speaker was connected and Mark inserted a pair of headphones as well, needlessly. He pressed a button, tapped something into the keyboard and the speaker gurgled and after an embarrassing half-minute an American voice answered, and suddenly he was talking to Chambers.

"Are you there Harry?" said the Fat Man in a quavering voice as if he were playing the spirit at a Victorian seance. "Are you there Harry Copeland-Smith?" Webster smiled proudly. "You are there Harry? Isn't this machine wonderful? I'm told it's quite secure."

"Nothing is secure in this bloody country," said Harry. "Or things have changed."

"Oh they have Harry," carried on the disembodied voice of the Fat Man. "Have you seen the old boy again? Is he stable?" Harry related as blandly as he could what he thought of Josef's mental state, turning the knife as he had planned, though he felt a little self-conscious with the two younger men leaning over his shoulder.

"He's realized the problem of writing all those letters he talked about." At this moment Harry could feel a frisson of mirth in the agents. "He's saying that he needs a staff, secretaries, that sort of thing, and accurate lists of the people involved. He's adamant about going through with this. Is there something I don't know about, Chambers?"

Chambers seemed to ignore the question at first. "It's been decided not to move the old devil for the time being. We're bringing in some clerks so we can have an excuse to send in more troops to guard the Doctor and them. The Americans want to set up an airstrip too. I protested at first saying it would lead to a greater number of security risks, but they promise everyone will be checked and some clerical personnel will be from London. Imagine that! We can have palm court dances in Paradiso, Harry. Really it's no use arguing. The Americans seem to have made up their minds." The wave of smugness in the room almost suffocated him.

He decided he might as well go for the jackpot, standing there holding the microphone, hoping he read the resigned note in Chambers' voice correctly. "Well, do you think it's time I packed my togs and decided to make a move myself? Back to England?" Webster stepped away from the radio and Agent Wheatley looked down. The mood of the room had changed as Chambers cleared his throat. "We feel it might alarm the Doctor at this point in time to be deprived of a familiar face and we do need a chance to give him a full psychological once-over. Also, there is another little matter the CIA boys want a word with you about. Not that anyone thinks you've been naughty, Harry. Just that damn fool Tough has been listening to gossip and made all sorts of allegations about you. The two chaps down there are just to clear things up. The sooner we can get all this sorted out the sooner you will be back in Blighty, miserable in the rain." The Fat Man had spoken; a reply was not deemed necessary by a bigger broom at the other end of the line and Harry was left staring at the microphone.

"Don't worry," said Webster. "Mr Chambers is coming down to join us soon. Things are really going to move around here."

Webster continued declaiming. Harry ignored him and sat down on the leather settee and filled his pipe slowly and elaborately from his tobacco pouch and began to puff on it, trying not to think about Hindle. What on earth had Tough told them? Obviously picked up some dog-end from his nasty friends Nabout and Rattucci, as Mabel's letter had said. And it had now become dark outside and there was no sign of the Land Rover; he felt the room closing in on him and even the furniture seemed to be party to the joke he was the butt of.

"Drinks?" he said quickly. "Sorry I was forgetting myself." He motioned to the maid standing by the door, waiting to see who was going to dine – and, indeed, if there was going to be a dinner. Through the door Harry thought he caught a glimpse of Maria trying to stay out of sight. Webster and Mark were engaged in a double act telling each other and the engineers how beautiful the countryside was, gentle but wild; it reminded Webster of Vietnam except the people were friendlier, but the greens were the same, which was strange because he had not seen any rice growing. "Oh they do that far to the west of here near Corrientes," said Harry. "I'm told by some Thais that live there that it looks just like Thailand. That's the beauty of Paraguay. You can make it into whatever you want it to be; you don't have to leave your country at home. So if you find this place a bit British it's because it's hard to say what's Paraguayan."

Webster nodded; he had read a state department briefing about lack of cultural identity in Paraguay. "So what do you do with your time when you're not actually dealing with Dr Josef? I'm sure I would find it a bit tedious. And I hope you appreciate how we have been ordered not to refer to him by his family name. Don't you have trouble filling your days?"

Harry wondered what he was fishing for. "No, not at all. Living in this part of the country with neighbours like Father Labuschagne, whom I'm sure Chambers briefed you about, is a full-time occupation, making sure that no one is going to creep up and murder me or try to lift the Doctor. I've always found it like one of those circus acts where someone keeps five plates in the air at the same time. Never a dull moment. We picked this place because it would be hard for a snatch group to operate here. And of course I grow roses. Put some new Arthur Askey bushes in for this year. Some of them are just coming out;

you'll see them tomorrow. Never a dull moment." He slapped his knees. Agent Wheatley glanced at Webster who had taken a pink coloured file from one of the boxes that his partner had brought in and was thumbing through it.

"You would have no objection if we put a few microphones in the Doctor's living quarters and the laboratory, which I understand are up in a jungle valley near here?" said Webster. "We might have to put a small concealed aerial on the lip of the valley but it will be camouflaged and we will be able to monitor things from here." He studied the pink file for a moment. "By the way, did you know what Mr Chambers was talking about when he said Plenipotentiary Tough had made allegations against you? It seemed, if you don't mind me saying so, as if you had prior knowledge."

Harry shrugged. "For some reason he's got it in his head that I'm living in clover here while he has to live in that sewer of a residence just outside town. His informants have been filling his head with all sorts of rubbish. I wouldn't believe a word of it."

Webster yawned. "Unfortunately Harry it's not quite as easy as that, because this operation to protect the Doctor effects US policy towards Paraguay as a whole. We have to look into one matter for our Drug Enforcement Agency. I didn't want to bother you with it tonight, but does the town Caagatu ring a bell? I believe it was first used by a man called Lorca. Your Sir Reginald Tough seems to have picked up rumours that you continued running with the ball when Lorca was taken out of the game a few years ago."

Harry looked at his profile in the mirror and noticed his hair was greying a little more at the temples than usual. There was not much wonder. He jutted his jaw and tried to look angry, all the time thinking of Hindle.

"Do I take it you are accusing me of smuggling? Is this some kind of interrogation? Am I under arrest? If you take the word of that half-wit Tough they should cart you off in a straitjacket to the nearest asylum. Have you read his file? The man's barking." He smiled sweetly. "Sorry gentlemen, I know you have to do a job, like I do. But what with the attack and then your Colonel Stebling turning out to be a fifth columnist so to speak and Josef's conversion to the Almighty, well it's more excitement than I've had in years, and I'm not getting any younger, you know. We never thought the old sod would live this long; that's why I chose such a nasty place for him." Harry looked at the men's faces; he mustn't overdo it. "In answer to your question, Señor Lorca was a good friend and came here many times for dinner, but I never inquired into the exact day-to-day nature of his business activities. And if I had tried to get involved in smuggling in this part of the world, I would not have lasted long. It may sound Irish to you, but the present trouble has arisen because Father Labuschagne wrongly suspects something along those lines."

Wheatley had written something down, and Webster thought for a while before turning to a page in the file. "I see," he said. "So Sir Reginald's allegations were mostly groundless. He even accused you of owning slaves."

"Oh but I do," said Harry quick as a flash before Webster could continue. I wonder what they will make of this he thought slyly; Americans were more sensitive than most about such matters. "Yes, all the Indios are slaves, bought and paid for. It was the custom when I came here and when in Rome, eh? The money was furnished partly by my government and partly by yours, with contributions from other interested parties. But if Tough says I mistreat them or deal in them he's wrong. They are very loyal."

The two men looked at him as if he had admitted molesting a child. Webster fidgeted with his papers.

"Well, we will leave that matter on the side as it sure is complicated. We all think you have done a swell job here, Harry. It's just we have to be careful that you could in no way have been compromised by an outsider. Please don't interrupt sir," he held up his hand as Harry was going to protest. "The thing is, Harry, that our Drug Enforcement Agency boys – who are very hot down here in Paraguay which tends to be a huge warehouse for every sort of drug, as you know – well they found that the entire female population of Caagatu formed a women's charity group and all applied for visas, ostensibly to visit Disneyworld in Florida. They were all granted visas by our office in Asunción on grounds of cultural exchange. No one thought there was anything suspicious at the time or noticed they were all from the same little town which only had a population of less than a thousand.

"Three hundred women applied for the visas over several months. The youngest was twelve and the oldest seventy-two. The DEA found that when these ladies stepped off the plane they had their wombs filled with cocaine; it was in knotted contraceptives. The cocaine went to Miami and most of the women ended up in New York, where the young and pretty ones became prostitutes. But the really interesting thing was the narcotic itself was found to be biologically contaminated due, it was said, to these Indian people's habit of chewing the coca leaf and spitting it out in the process of forming the drug base. Sir Reginald suggested you organized this smuggling operation, but he does not know about your prisoner. What we wondered was quite what the good Doctor was working on; he could not have tampered with a shipment of yours, could he?"

Harry was genuinely annoyed this time. "Mr Webster, if I smuggled drugs, which I do not, presumably I would want to keep my customers alive as long as possible. I would not stay long in the white-powder business in your hypochondriac middle-class market if the product was thought to be impregnated with some awful disease caught from my Indians, who, I may add, are in perfect health and chew coca leaves all the time. Nor do I go gallivanting about the countryside looking for towns who want to sell their women." Harry got to his feet and paced about the room. "As for Josef," he went on, waving his pipe in the direction of the valley, "he has never been allowed to have poisons in his lab, or experiment on animals, only snakes, which has proved fairly frustrating since his speciality was the study of racial purity. He did some terrible things but believe me, gentlemen, in all the years I have known him I have never noticed the strength of character or initiative required to actually commit a crime on his own. The whole theory is completely potty and could only have come from a nit like Sir Reginald."

Mark Wheatley was looking less happy. "Well if it's owning-up time," he said with a guilty little smile Harry didn't trust. "If it's owning-up time that theory was mine. But I'm telling you the cocaine was contaminated Major, and a couple of those women died. Our anti-drugs programme here is linked to our aid to the country. We don't want to be compromised."

Harry couldn't credit it. Narcotics, as they called it, was part and parcel of the government of the country and well they knew it. Surely they could not be so naïve. Yet they had been told to ask these questions. Webster seemed to be ticking points off a memo board. He braced himself for the next one, but just then Maria appeared in the doorway to say that dinner was served.

As they were going across the hall into the dining room, the large one with the dusty crystal chandelier, Maria drew Harry aside. He waved the others on.

"What's the matter?" He heard laughter from the Americans. Their high spirits had obviously returned.

"Sergeant Hindle, he is back," she whispered. "The chief came up to the house himself. He could not come in and tell you as he was in funeral gowns and it might have surprised the guests." You're not kidding, thought Harry. "The other two men are not with him from this morning and Sergeant Hindle wants to speak to you in the chief's hut. Chief said he used the words 'own goal', and this would mean something to you."

Harry gripped the girl's brown wrist. "Tell the chief to keep him down there. Under no circumstances is he to come up to the house tonight. I will slip away and come and see him later." He could imagine that Hindle would not be the most comfortable of souls in that wailing, drumming village at the moment, but he did not want a tired man questioned by the CIA. He wondered what on earth could have happened. From what Hindle said the bomb must have detonated prematurely. Own goal. It was some of Hindle's Irish slang. But had it killed the other two? The man couldn't even make a proper report. "Tell him I will slip away later," he repeated and went into the dining room.

Maria had organized things so the table was laid as if Harry had been expecting the four men for a week. As he sat down two maids emerged from the kitchen with a steaming cauldron of palm heart soup. A third poured the Argentinian wine. "Now gentlemen," Harry said, "what do you plan for Paradiso when you have decided that I am not the local representative for the Mafia?"

They all roared with laughter again and Webster spilled his soup.

"Come on, Harry! We're your friends. We were only asking you those questions because the DEA was anxious to ascertain your contacts in the area."

"We have some plans," said Wheatley, pausing theatrically. "We have plans to build, if it's feasible, a small airstrip here and to establish larger and more secure living quarters for your prisoner. Our government is treating this matter as top priority. The Doctor must be kept sweet. It will all start in a matter of days, sir. You will see the old place change before your very eyes."

The two engineers nodded in unison.

"The best place for an airstrip would be the football pitch I suppose," said Harry. "We don't really use it all that much although my sergeant will be most upset. I'm afraid you must excuse me in a second. I have to go down to the Indian village to witness the cremations. It's a ghastly affair but they think of me as part of the family, a cross between a father-figure and a district commissioner." More laughter threatened to break out on the cynical faces around the table, and as he stood up his napkin dropped to the floor. "Well you would not understand," he said huffily, "but I have to do my duty."

Webster raised his glass as he walked towards the door. "I'll drink to that Major!" and the titters started again. Harry felt like a Latin master unable to control his class or comprehend why the boys in 5b found the word "puer" so outrageously hilarious. Maria stopped him at the front door with a concerned look. "Tell me everything they say. Everything mind," he said.

He had taken four steps on the gravel outside the front door when she was beside him again, her light feet making no noise, and she thrust the heavy rubber torch into his hands.

He was challenged on the outskirts of the village. A youth shouted and two others, dressed only in loin cloths and necklaces and with bright red beetle stain on their bodies, formed his guard as he was led to the chief's hut. Not directly past the funeral pyre as he expected but a roundabout way and twice he stepped in watery pig dung.

He tried to question them about why he was not being taken past the school, the usual route, and for a moment felt a spasm of fear with three prehistorically attired boys, their hair entwined with feathers, shells from land snails and even in one case a small monkey skull. Harry calmed himself. They were his boys; they were simply still alarmed by the attack the other day. He could see the pyre now. It glinted on the boys' polished bows, each carried with two long arrows; bows for hunting, not making war.

The chief's hut faced a rectangular clearing at the other end of which the funeral pyre had been burning for some time. Out of his sight was the elaborately carved main door of the hut, but he was pushed through a small side entrance covered with a piece of canvas and almost fell down a step into the sunken well of the living quarters below. A transistor radio crackled a quiz programme from Argentina and the spell of what he had just experienced outside was immediately broken. His eyes rested first on the chief's older wife and then on the photograph of the Queen in her coronation robes that Harry had given to him more than twelve years ago. For some reason the chief found the picture arousing.

Hindle was at the opposite end of the hut.

"I thought it best to meet down here, sir, as the guards on the road told me you had more Yanks up at the house. I've been worried they were going to put me on the bonfire," he said in an attempt at a joke. The pyre was visible through a wooden arch partly covered by a blanket.

"What went wrong, Sergeant?"

Hindle bent his head. "The bomb went off too soon sir.

Didn't get Labuschagne. Stebling had the Bible on his knees in the front of the boat. His sergeant was in the back at the tiller when it suddenly went off right slap bang in the middle of the lake. Labuschagne had his boats out in a flash and I had to scarper. Stebling must have been blown to bits but I couldn't be a hundred per cent sure about the other man. I had no choice but to run."

Oh God, thought Harry. What if the sergeant survived? Having an American marine who had just been half murdered by the British would suit Labuschagne down to the ground. Cortez would not be at all pleased if Harry had played into the priest's hands, to say nothing of the Americans if they found out. He would have to make sure the man was dead, somehow. Outside in the night bamboo exploded and behind the blanket the corpses of the two *viejas* danced for the last time on the funeral pyre; then it began to rain.

"Bloody shambles," he said more to himself than Hindle and walked quickly out into the warm drizzle.

Chapter 15

"Perhaps I should take out another search party?" Harry said.

Wheatley smiled, shook his head and went on checking his reports. Harry pretended a fatherly concern for Stebling and his sergeant, who he secretly prayed were both safely fish bait. He had already sent out token Aché patrols but told them to go nowhere near Father Labuschagne's or Capitan Boda.

"I feel responsible," he went on. "When your man offered to do a bit of scouting it was not really necessary but we thought it would take his mind off things. He was quite upset about the nature of the mission here. You don't think he's deserted do you? He's not the sort of bloke to try and tell the world about old Josef, is he?"

"Now just hold it," said Wheatley, actually looking up from his reports for the first time and putting down his pen. "Hang loose, Harry. For a start Colonel Stebling is the kind of Holy Joe who takes the flag to bed with him. Second, Psy Ops are a law unto themselves and he might have decided to extend his reconnaissance; he might even be taking tea with your mad priest. Then there is his sergeant, a winner of a Silver Star and two Purple Hearts in Vietnam who I am sure is not going to let the colonel's conscience ruin his career. Lastly . . ." He picked up his papers again with the air of a barrister who has won his case. "Lastly, the matter of Colonel Stebling and his 'reluctance' to obey orders is being handled directly by Asunción. He's probably just delaying having to face the music."

Harry did not like the sound of things being handled from

Asunción. What he also found strange was that Wheatley did not seem to give a damn that Labuschagne could be flaying two Americans alive. Odd fellows, the Yanks.

They had interrogated him further on the war, his politics, and family background as if he were being vetted for the job all over again. At his time in life what he needed least was another job interview. Perhaps they were trying to assess if he would be a security risk afterwards; two arrogant young men held the power over a few years of happiness after he had served for a lifetime, and by their smiles these new *Mbareté* found the power amusing.

From Webster's arrival everything had started to change. The two engineers, busy now from dawn till dusk, were joined by others brought in trucks from Asunción with scores of marines and even more equipment. They started to build huts on the flat dry ground next to the football pitch and before long had a cookhouse making six flavours of ice cream. Compressors roared into life and a baby bulldozer, bought in Argentina, was slowly winning the battle at the end of the football pitch airstrip. More trucks unloaded civilians, right-wing Cuban exiles, *Los Maños Blancos*, "attached" to the Asunción embassy. Sullen-looking men in cruel and early middle age. To these overseers were added, much against Harry's advice, "trusted" Paraguayans and, finally, people who had heard the blasting and drifted up-river. The Cubans were meant to police these *vagabundos*. Soon a settlement was being built. His will was no longer respected; he stood and watched as a spectator. He felt he had been sent to Coventry.

Hindle kept to his own quarters, which had been repaired. He seemed beside himself with worry because of the business with Stebling. He would not listen to reason that Webster, Wheatley and the rest could not possibly have any knowledge of the plot.

Then they came to Harry again. He had put on his gardening clothes and decided to go and dead-head a few roses, and had taken the flat flower basket to bring some fresh ones for Maria.

"Ah, we've found you," said Webster. He was wearing a

fawn safari suit. It accentuated his height. He leered at Harry over a standard rose.

"What can I do for you?" he said, putting down his steel clippers.

"More and more people are going to be bussed in by helicopter in the next few days," Webster was saying. "I would like you to have a word with your Indians. Make sure they don't panic. I heard from one of our boys down here that there was nearly an ugly incident involving a flag when they first arrived. We don't want anyone getting hurt. Do they have their own private weapons except for bows and arrows and that sort of thing?"

"They only have weapons when they are issued," said Harry. "Mr Hindle sees to all that. The guards on the watch towers are armed with rifles and machine guns. Your men have taken over the anti-aircraft batteries so there is no fear of mine shooting anything down. They're not daft you know."

"I like 'daft'," said Webster. "It's a very English word, 'daft'. But, Harry, I would be grateful if you would make sure there are no little incidents." The man who was thirty years his junior had given him an order and expected him to obey it without question.

He wandered back to Hindle's hut and knocked on the door. "Will you come up to the Indian village with me, Sergeant? We've got a job to do. His nibs Mr Webster is in a flap because he thinks the Aché might start carving up the new arrivals. Might not be a bad idea, but I suppose we must humour him. Oh, and keep track of all the keys for the armoury. I don't want Webster poking around on our territory."

Hindle buckled on his webbing belt and put the two sets of keys in his pocket. Like Harry he now carried a pistol at all times.

The chief was sitting at the teacher's desk in the school, his bony knees sticking out at both sides and his gnarled hands holding a carved staff; he looked at them without surprise. Crammed onto the benches and desks were braves, and there was not a child to be seen anywhere. All the Indians were naked except for loin cloths, and Tatugi and two others were stained with red beetle dye. Some were wearing the traditional lip ornament, the *beta*, as proof of manhood. Only Jeronimo smiled as they came in.

The young men had been meeting to decide what to do. If Harry wasn't careful their feelings about Labuschagne would spill over onto the Americans; God help the first engineer wandering into the Aché village at night, blundering uninvited into a hut. Perhaps Webster's request made sense. He spoke to them against a background of silence.

"These people who are coming here are our guests and our friends. They are no danger to us. You have no need to worry. They know to respect you or they will be punished severely. But in case they forget themselves I suggest you post guards at night and not let your women walk through their encampments. If anyone molests you fetch me or Mr Hindle. Do not take the matter into your own hands. Do I make myself clear?"

The chief nodded, his brown eyes expressing no opinion. "What is to be done to Father Labuschagne?" he asked bluntly. "We Aché can tell the difference between our friends and our enemies. If we do not do something about this man he will come again. But you will not let us go near his village. Why not take him? We have the weapons."

Harry smiled. "Be patient for now, Chief. I know you want revenge on Labuschagne but at the moment the time is not right. Trust me. I will not let you down." He clasped the chief's hand. Shuffles and grunts of approval rumbled around the schoolhouse. But Harry sensed a growing anger among the younger men, an anger that would be hard soon to contain.

None of the Indians were anywhere near the football pitch as the Chinook twin-bladed helicopter circled in the dusk as if uncertain it could land. When the pilot finally brought the heavy machine in he did it at a gallop, and the craft was unloading almost as he touched the ground. First came sacks and boxes, and then a sight that made Harry's jaw drop. Onto the grass of the football pitch stepped middle-aged ladies, dressed in sensible two-piece suits. One even had a hint of coloured rinse in her hair, and already Harry could smell eau-de-Cologne and face-powder.

He gaped in amazement. The powers that be in Whitehall had evidently decided to send only their most experienced dragons to help in this operation, women who would cheerfully commit suicide if their head of security told them to, after making sure all the plants were watered. His eyes caught the unsteady figure of Chambers wrestling himself free of the narrow door and tumbling onto the grass under the spinning blades. He was the last one out. Fresh paper in bundles was thrown from the craft onto the ground, and without further ceremony the helicopter was off, banking sharply and turning north west, heading directly into the sunset for Asunción. Little groups of dazed ladies on the ground stared at Harry in anticipation.

"Don't worry," said Webster who had sneaked up behind them under cover of the rotors. "They will not be billeted in the house. One of those old hulks is to be the Doctor's personal assistant. Will you do the introductions?"

He handed over a file and was gone before Harry could protest. In his hands was the file of Agnes Garnett (Miss). A picture of the matronly lady in the top right-hand corner stared at him. The forty-seven-year-old had worked for everybody that was anybody in the security services. She lived in Berkhamsted and her only hobbies were knitting and reading romantic fiction. Whatever momentous decisions had passed through her hands, her life had been completely banal, ministering to a sick and domineering mother who passed away a year ago. She sounded frighteningly efficient.

He walked over to the women who were smoothing down their clothes and trying to adjust to the culture-shock of a clearing in southern Paraguay where dusky workers winked at them – something which, in most cases, had not happened for years, if ever. A discreet twittering like the faint start of the dawn chorus told Harry their spirits must be returning as they looked around for living quarters and beamed at him, obviously an Englishman. Despite himself he was drawn towards them. Hindle followed reluctantly.

"Welcome ladies, welcome to Paradiso." A Cuban worker nearby laughed. "Can you please tell me which of you is Miss Agnes Garnett? Will she come over here and please follow us? Miss Garnett?" He caught sight of a small posse of CIA who seemed to be waiting to take the ladies to quarters by the river. They did not appear to have much luggage. "These gentlemen will look after the rest of you."

He peered through the gloom for a few seconds into the face of Agnes, who seemed cooler than the others in a blue lightweight two-piece and a shawl which looked as if it had been bought on a Greek cruise.

"Major," she said, sounding incredibly fresh and ready for work. She shook his hand briskly. "You don't have to say anything, Major. I have been fully briefed by a dear Foreign Office man, Mr Chambers."

Harry looked for Chambers and saw him emerging from behind a hut. The helicopter ride had been too much for him.

"I say, Harry," he called and they halted as he puffed over. "Gosh, that was torture, sheer torture. Are you intending to introduce Agnes here to the Doctor now or in the morning?"

Harry found it hard to focus. He felt weak, it was all too bloody much.

"Now, I think," he said eventually.

The valley had lost a lot of its mystery with the vegetation and thorn cut back to make a respectable path. But despite the taming of Josef's canyon Miss Agnes Garnett had to have several brief halts along the way.

"I have never seen what you call active service before Major," she gasped. "You really must excuse me. All I ever do in terms of exercise is to go for a stroll towards Ashridge park, but I rarely get beyond the gates. Do you know Berkhamsted Major? Such a nice quiet place. I would have liked to have gone out East, such a lot to see and such a lot to buy. Have you ever been out East Major? Not that I can speak a word of a foreign language, but it doesn't hold you back really does it, I have never thought so. Are you married Major? It must be so lonely out here in the jungle with not another living soul for miles."

Her voice penetrated the gloom, the tones of lower middle-class Hertfordshire blocking out the sounds of compressors and pumps. As they came into the clearing, where the huts were now lit with electric lights strung from trees and no doubt visible for miles, he caught Chambers' rheumy eye. The man had obviously had an overdose of the dreadful woman on the helicopter.

"Oh what a charming little hideaway. To think we are right on the other side of the globe. My mother always said I would travel. She was quite gifted like that. She could always tell before she had to go in for another operation. Mother would say: 'Now Doctor I knows you know,' and would give her sly little smile. All the doctors and nurses loved her; she died under the anaesthetic. Listen to me, I really do go on."

A group of workers under supervision of marines were finishing off another smarter pre-fab.

"What on earth are those *chanchos* doing up here?" asked Harry.

No one gave him an answer. Oh well, he thought, every rogue along the Paraná river must now know of the American construction project. Well, the Yanks had taken control, they could bloody well take the responsibility for lighting the place up.

The Doctor was in the lab hard at work with a Dictaphone while several military secretaries bashed away at typewriters. In the middle of the marble-topped table and around the walls piles of paper were quickly being converted into letters under the yellowy electric lights slung from the ceiling.

Josef bowed. "Welcome, Major. I'm making a start; these men have now got into the rhythm but we need more, many more. Good evening madam. Excuse my manners."

Harry, for one astonished minute, thought he was going to kiss the woman's hand. Agnes looked deeply and inquiringly into his eyes.

"My name is Agnes. I know yours, no names no pack drill and all that. Don't worry, my girls and I will soon get all this mess sorted out for you."

Harry averted his eyes and waited for the reaction. When it

came it was totally unexpected. The Doctor looked around, and then, seeing there was no spare chair, wrestled one from underneath a typing clerk, causing the man to fall to the floor with a bump and the clattering of keys to come to an astonished halt.

"We are forgetting our manners," said Josef regally as if a film star, not the dumpy, ordinary Agnes had come into the room. She had sparked off something in him that Harry had never seen before; it was a look almost of affection.

"I mustn't interrupt your work sir, but I think you should stop for a while. These lights will strain your eyes and we cannot have you laid off. You'll do twice as much nice and fresh in the morning. Me and my girls will see to that. And what about cleaning up this dreadful place Major? Surely one cannot be expected to work, let alone live in a pig sty like this! If you don't mind me saying so it just isn't clean. We are used to far better in our Civil Service grade and Mr Josef is a very important man. Yes, the first thing we shall do is clean this place up. Look at that disgusting mould!"

The Doctor gazed at her with a mixture of wonder and admiration and murmured something. Agnes went over to the sink, took hold of a cloth and then screamed as it disintegrated in her hand and small crawling things ran up her arm. Josef leapt to her aid and as he exterminated every beetle from wrist to elbow Harry could see, between winces as the insects were trapped, a dreamy look in her eyes. Harry felt in need of some air. He had never believed in love at first sight before that night and was hardly sure now. Given one of the individuals involved it did not bear thinking about.

"Mr Chambers and myself have to go to the house, Miss Garnett. You have been billeted in the new cottage next door to the Doctor. I shall send some servants up to make sure it's clean and give this place the once over. I'm sorry it's in such a mess but we have always been more concerned about the Doctor's security. And the Indians who are my servants, in particular the women, always thought this valley a queer sort of place and didn't like coming up here. And then there are the snakes the Doctor used to keep – for his work of course."

There was a growing alarm on Agnes's face. "Snakes?" she said. "They didn't tell me about snakes. Poisonous snakes?" Harry sighed but Josef was on the problem in a flash.

"Don't worry," he said taking her hand and patting it. "We killed all the snakes in the valley. Every single one. Before I stopped my experiments and turned to the Lord. I will clear the place up myself. I'm a messy old bachelor."

And a liar, thought Harry, knowing Frau Josef was still alive and well and living near Zurich airport.

On the way back to the house they came upon a group of workers camping on a rock ledge. Chambers peered at them.

"Look at those chaps. Fishing I suppose. No by God, they are at their devotions."

In a little pit of sediment on the top of the rock the crouching men had lit three candles and by these lay a bunch of roses taken from Harry's garden. The man nearest the candles was chanting rhythmically and threw the flowers into the stream. Another at the rear of the band turned and grinned into the beam of Chambers' torch.

"*Buenas noches*," said the Fat Man but there was no reply.

"They're Brazilian, from up your way," said Harry as they walked back to the easier path. He noticed, to his intense irritation, that some of the Americans were holding a barbecue near Hindle's hut. "Those men are sacrificing to Iemanjá, Queen of the Water and I doubt if they are asking her to forgive the trespasses of their enemies. My Indians have a similar system of beliefs which they retreat to when there's great upheaval all around." He gestured down at the flickering lights which followed the river. "They know that all this is not right. What are the Yanks up to, Chambers? They must know they will have to move the Doctor after this. Are they trying to ruin what I've done all these years in order to score a few diplomatic points? If they are you can send me home now. I have had just about enough of it all, especially that insufferable Webster. He's virtually taken over the place and has been accusing me of smuggling and all sorts of skulduggery."

Harry stopped and saw Chambers was puffing at least two yards behind him. "Hang on old boy," said the Fat Man. "Just hang on. Let them play their games. I agree they will have to move you but the orders about letting the Doctor say he's sorry come right from the top. It looks to me like someone up there has got a bad dose of idealism, but it's not for us to reason why Harry. Just keep your nose to the grindstone for another week or two. We want to make sure Agnes and her dragons settle in. After that I'm sure we can both go home and then the Americans can canonize the old boy if they want to. I think Whitehall is anxious to get rid of this one."

Harry was only sure of one thing: very much more of this and he would be first in line burning black tallow and throwing his prize Arthur Askey roses into the phosphorescent moonlit creek, murmuring all the awful things that the Queen of the Water could do to Webster and the rest of them.

"I need a rather large snort," he said.

The Fat Man gratefully echoed his sentiments.

Chapter 16

Perhaps it was old fashioned but Harry was not sure if he totally approved of what had commonly come to be known as "bugging" after poor Mr Nixon had been discovered listening in to the opposition. He had always called it surveillance, but it was something one did to enemies, not to people one knew quite well. To the CIA and newly arrived Foreign Office men it was second nature.

"Here is the volume button," said Wheatley, smiling as usual. There was a cold sore on his lower lip. "But this is really interesting. Using this little joystick you can follow the man round the room or from building to building. You can see where the microphones are on that computer screen. Some technology, huh?" Harry reluctantly took the joystick and put on the headphones, immediately having to turn down the volume. Miss Agnes Garnett was in full cry to some of her underlings, laying down the right way to set out the Doctor's letters and insisting that the entire previous day's batch be redone on the new typewriters they had brought in. Every letter was to be original and anyone caught duplicating material would be disciplined.

"What are those large holes at the north of the airstrip?" asked Harry. "I went for a walk up there this morning and a digger was excavating them. They're not sewage ditches are they? What are they for?"

Wheatley looked at one of the other men in the room. Then he glanced down at his checkboard.

"Rubbish," he said. "Rubbish," he repeated, cheerfully satisfied with the explanation and slapped Harry on the back. "We can bury the Doc's letters there if we can't get them out fast enough by helicopter I suppose. The original plan was to shred them down here and then burn them, but we thought he might catch on to that. Instead we are dropping them several hundred miles out in the Atlantic. How's that for efficiency?"

"But how long are you going to play along with him?" said Harry. "If you don't mind me saying so, aren't things getting a little out of hand? Did you see that list, the computer print-out that Chambers brought with him? There are millions of names on that list."

Wheatley looked at him, his face expressionless. "If it was easy Major, they wouldn't pay us for it."

"And what about the answers?" Harry persisted. "He is going to expect at least some reaction in the world's press."

Wheatley smugly said they had seen to that, having a computer, or so Webster had told him, employed on the project.

"We have got every avenue sewn up Major, and tapes of the Doctor's conversations are even being sent to the States for psychological analysis. They seem to be confirming that your man's conversion is totally genuine. Don't worry, we've got the lid on things all right. There is no danger of disclosure. I think we are doing a good job but you led the way, Harry. Now could you see there are no hitches between the Doctor and the British secretaries?"

Only the desire to get home, to be able to snuggle down in an English armchair behind a paper after a roast lamb lunch and read an amusing little story about a scoutmaster, made Harry bite his tongue and not remark that the security of the entire operation as far as he was concerned was lax, sloppy and full of holes. These people did not seem to care a damn that the place was crawling with all sorts of undesirables.

Miss Agnes Garnett, or to be more accurate her disembodied voice on the other end of a pair of earphones, kept Harry sane in the days that followed. Sitting by the little box of tricks the technical aides had installed to eavesdrop on the Doctor, Harry could completely lose himself in Agnes's voice: those clear comfortable tones of the Home Counties transported him. She had absolutely no understanding of why she should be in the heart of the jungle as the office manager of a wanted war criminal, taking his dictation and organizing his secretaries. Her lack of knowledge was formidable. She had the middle-class talent of elevating ignorance and absence of a coherent moral view of what she was doing into a positive virtue. Harry was fascinated, like a burglar who lingers too long in a neat parlour because it reminds him of his mother.

"I like the Major," she was saying at the moment against a background noise of a shuffling of papers and a rough bump-bump sound that Harry finally decided must be the Doctor bouncing back and forth in his rocking chair. His spirits seemed to have been lifted by Miss Garnett's presence. Harry had never known him use the rocking chair before, but Agnes had changed all that, a veritable archangel of life's little pleasures. "I like the Major. To think he looked after you all these years on his own. You poor man, Doctor Josef, you must have been through such a lot, my heart goes out to you, really it does. To be cut off from your work. . . . "

The Doctor at this point obviously looked as if he was going to get up, say something or start work again. Agnes was not having any of it.

"Now you sit down in that chair like a good boy. There's nothing you can do. We took all the dictation this morning. Now I just have to sort out this rota. There I go. I hope you don't mind me rabbiting on, I mean talking?"

The Doctor cleared his throat. "Not in the slightest, dear Miss Garnett – may I call you Agnes perhaps? Your presence here is a comfort. You have no idea how your conversation cheers me."

And me, thought Harry.

"Well, I used to talk to my mother a lot when she was ill, very poorly indeed. Cancer is a terrible thing. You'd have thought they would have done something about it by now instead of giving away money to all those blacks. They've even come to Berkhamsted now and I suppose it's just the same in Germany."

"My friend Willy has been taken ill," said the Doctor ignoring her last remark. "I am a doctor and could do nothing. I felt so helpless. He has been with me for many, many years. They have taken him to Asunción. . . . "

And from the appearance of him he wouldn't be coming back. Burst ulcer, according to Webster. Whatever it was Willy had looked extremely ill.

"Please don't be shy about telling me all your troubles," Miss Garnett's voice went on. "Talk to me like a true friend. My men, I mean the gentlemen I worked for, always liked to tell me all their little problems. Everything from East of Suez to lipstick on their collars. I'm as safe as houses. I have signed the Official Secrets Act and I'm sure that includes talking to you even though you are a German. Oh I'm sorry, I hope you weren't offended."

"Do not give it a second thought," said the Doctor warmly.

"Don't worry, Doctor Josef, I do not judge, not ever. Whatever you did in your professional life is nothing to do with me, just goes in one ear and out the other. You wouldn't credit some of the things my gentlemen got up to, all in the line of duty of course and doing it for Queen and country. Politics makes me giddy anyway, although I did used to go to the Little Gaddesden Young Conservatives dances. Wonderful spectacular occasions they were."

Harry heard a strangled gargling noise.

"Thank you, thank you so much. God has obviously sent you to me as a good friend, a ray of sunshine to help me with my work. I have always . . . I have always found it difficult to express my feelings. I hardly know how to write these letters. To merely say I am sorry does not appear very elegant. Perhaps you can teach an old scientist to see things differently?"

There was a clicking sound; Josef must have stood up and saluted Agnes. Harry longed for a television screen.

"You don't need to do that Doctor Josef." She positively blushed down the wires. "There's no need to stand on ceremony with Agnes Garnett."

The following morning Agnes told the story of how she had come to Paradiso: "Every day," she was saying to the Doctor, "every day I leave my little house and walk down the hill across the main road to Berkhamsted station to wait for the early train. I like to get in early, no use moping about the house. But I always say hello to Mr Polly Parrot in the pet shop. It may sound silly but I say it out loud and I think he can hear me through the glass as he lifts his claw and cocks his head to one side. He's a very old parrot and all the feathers on his breast have dropped out making him look like an old gentleman who's forgotten to put his shirt on. We've never actually met face to face, in the flesh as it were, because I'm never there when the shop is open but I think he still knows me.

"'Hello Mr Polly Parrot' I say."

Harry felt a touch on his shoulder. He switched off the radio and became conscious that he had been laughing out loud. One of the radio operators was looking at him as if there was something very wrong. He put the headphones back on again. The strange relationship between Miss Agnes Garnett (spinster) and Mr Polly Parrot was not something one could easily explain to anyone.

" . . . I'll cry when he dies," said Agnes, presumably still talking about Mr Polly. "He seemed to have a different expression on his face the day they sent me here. He must have known I was going away. He looked quizzical as much as to say 'Where are you going my girl?' and of course I couldn't tell him because I didn't know. And if I did know I wouldn't have breathed a word. Parrots could lead to breaches of security even through plate glass."

Tears were beginning to form in the corners of Harry's eyes. What on earth was "Doctor Josef" making of Agnes's monologue?

"I knew I would be off and going away somewhere when they called me into one of the High Ups' offices with all these other important men sitting around. Did I like gipsies? they asked. You come to recognize trick questions when you work with gentlemen like I have, and I said I have no strong feelings on the matter, even though I cannot stand them. I don't mind any race if they're clean and you should see the mess they make up Cherry Tree Lane. But they were testing me. They really wanted to see if I hated dagos and the people who live abroad. My mother always counselled me to keep my brain nimble and most evenings we played Scrabble to expand the mind. I'm not boring you am I, Doctor Josef?"

The Doctor rustled his papers. "Not at all Fraulein, go on, go on." He seemed genuinely interested in the story. Probably the mention of gipsies, thought Harry.

"They then asked me if I had ever had any lovers from other races," said Agnes lowering her voice. Harry had to turn up the volume. "No time to beat about the bush, they said. But had I ever been to bed with any Negroes, Slavs or perhaps the odd gipsy? Another young man asked if I had any Jewish blood. In my veins. I very nearly lost my composure. But my mother always said when you feel angry just look straight ahead and slowly draw an imaginary figure of eight with your nose in the air. After that you will be completely calm. I asked them what kind of place they thought Berkhamsted was and remarked in passing, to show them where I really stood in a subtle sense, that I was a member of the Church Flower Committee that had stopped the gipsies from using the cemetery standpipe to fill their water bottles. Once they get a hold in a place they're like moss. You can never get rid of moss from a lawn. That's what my mother always said, God rest her soul.

"I told them I had been on the Security Service self-defence course seven times. I like the nice house near Cheam that it's always held in and you meet such nice people. I asked them to take the marks I had got at Cheam, especially for 'Aggression', into consideration. It seemed to satisfy them. The next thing I knew I was in a green bus heading with the rest of the ladies to a little airport near that Polish war memorial. I do like the Poles and of course Germans like yourself. No one could help the war, could they? Then we were on a plane, then another, then another, then a helicopter and here I am. I bet even Mr Polly Parrot could not guess where!" Both she and the Doctor laughed indulgently at what Agnes would have called the fickle ways of fate.

In the days that followed they grew closer together until it was like listening to a happily-married couple. The old German seemed to want to squeeze his intellect into Miss Garnett's mental corsets and something else entirely into her real ones.

"Do you know Agnes," he said one day, "I am growing very fond of you. Very fond indeed. Mine has been a lonely life devoted to science and now I must devote it to the Almighty. I am sure He has sent you to show me how. And in all my life, and I have considerable experience, I have never seen anyone organize people like you do. You even manage to organize me!"

Cupid's dart had struck and was embedded in what Josef might have called his heart. It was altogether too much. Harry put down the headphones and decided he needed a large whisky.

Webster was in the drawing room with Chambers. He poured Harry a drink. "Have you heard Chambers' idea to bring us all into line? He wants to hold a dance, don't you Mr Chambers? If you don't think we are turning the place into a Caesar's Palace, we would like to hold it here Major."

Harry looked at Chambers with mounting incredulity. "Fine by me." The words came from his lips in a growl. "As long as you don't expect me to arrange the tombola."

Chapter 17

Even the cracks in the wall of his bedroom seemed threatening as Harry leapt out of bed grabbing the Webley from the dressing table with a scream on his lips and came as close as he ever had done to putting a bullet in his electric trouser press.

Maria moaned in her sleep but didn't wake, having taken on board an alarming amount of Amontillado, poor thing. She had seemed uncharacteristically on edge lately, drinking sherry, she said, so she could sleep. He looked down at the gun barrel, lit by the moonlight dancing in through the curtains, and for a moment he almost began to turn it towards himself. He sat down with a bump on the bed and Maria moaned again. But if he blew his brains out that might be just what they would want: a loose end neatly tied up, and he wasn't going to do them any favours. He laughed out loud, wondering self consciously if Webster had bugged this room too; he didn't really care all that much any more.

He could still feel his heart pounding in his chest. It was the meeting in the garden that had disturbed him. He had gone out to prune his roses, which he had neglected of late and some of the bushes were in a terrible condition. He had set to work and was soon lost in the snipping and clipping. Until he saw the man watching him. He was an ugly looking brute and was staring straight at him, unblinkingly. By the look of his clothes he was one of the Cuban exile overseers. He had a crooked little smile on his face.

"Go away! This is my private garden. Go away, get back to

work!" Harry had shouted, but the man did not answer and merely continued smiling and staring, half concealed by a tangle of cinnamon bushes.

"Bloody hell," Harry had said, more to himself than the interloper, and, throwing down his clippers, strode angrily over, his hand on the Webley's leather holster. "Just what's your game?"

The man's hand was in his pockets in a flash and Harry thought for an awful moment he was going to pull out a knife. Instead he found himself looking at a St Christopher medallion. The medallion he had been wearing when detained at Napoleon Cortez's pleasure and the only possession not returned to him. He reached out for the trinket in the dirty hand but the fat fingers shut.

"I have come from Señor Cortez. We do not have much time. It is dangerous. The men who came here before me to talk with you have not returned. Señor Cortez is very angry. Pay attention. I must talk quickly or suspicion will be aroused. Do not ask questions."

Harry had stood there with his mouth gaping open. The messenger's eyes darted from side to side as he said his piece. He literally stank with fear, and he raised his hand every time Harry tried to interrupt.

Cortez, it seemed, was eager to conclude his fight with Labuschagne. He had a force ready to come south but the presence of the Americans made this impossible. The only thing for it was if Harry sent in his Aché guards against Labuschagne. Then Cortez would be justified in leading his troops in defence of proud Indians who were part of the country's heritage. Cortez left it up to his own imagination, said the man, if he did not do as he was told and reinforced the point by running a finger across his throat. Harry did not doubt the threat for a moment or the efficiency with which Cortez could have it carried out. The messenger could easily have killed him as he rummaged among his roses.

But something else was becoming clear. Cortez was livid because he did not really know what was going on in Paradiso, except it had something to do with a paper shortage throughout the country. He was concerned about how gringos had taken over all the warehouses in Asunción and more or less brought smuggling to a halt. Then the man repeated how spies who had come before him had all disappeared, presumed dead, killed by the gringos.

Harry was about to protest when he saw a marine guard pacing down the lawn towards them. When he turned to look at the messenger again he was gone, back in the direction of his master. At his feet was the medallion. He bent down and picked it up. If he was going to lead the Aché against Labuschagne he would need it.

The Aché themselves did not need any persuading.

"I come as I promised to tell you we will lead a raiding party against Labuschagne's fortress together and avenge all he killed and more," he had said and the chief hugged him, a grinning muscular hug. The drumming had started immediately and he left them in the village to their spirits, shamans and spells as they prepared for the ordeal. He was glad he did not have to stay and take their oaths as he was a Catholic, or so they thought. A shaman might have seen into his heart.

Harry was almost grateful to see the young commercial attaché who had popped down from the British embassy in Asunción. Sir Reggie, it seemed, had heard about a secret project in Paradiso from the Americans and had suggested his aide take down a few creature comforts to the British and Americans working there. Webster took a dim view of the young man's arrival with a lorry-load of perfume, soaps and chocolate and obviously decided he was Tough's spy.

As it turned out he was anything but.

"Mabel and I have split up. I thought you should know. She really goes a bundle on you," he said dismally, handing Harry a note right in front of Webster. How naïve could one get? But it was too late. The CIA man had seen the envelope pass into his hand. Harry took it and walked from the front of his house, where they stood, out into the comparative privacy of the garden.

Mabel's letter said she had broken up with "the boy". Harry was quite surprised to learn they had been engaged. He read on:

But I have always loved you really my darling, it is just that we have never said it to each other. I am writing this to you because I believe you are in very great danger, very great danger indeed. It is more of a feeling I have than anything I can put on paper, and it would not do to write anything down in any case. But please, please Harry remember we are more than friends and if you have to run anywhere run towards me.

She went on to give a sketch of how the gangsters of Asunción had begun to fight among themselves. The expansive Rattucci and his Fancy Mouse Club were locked in mortal combat with Nabout and his men. The Lebanese and the Italian families were fighting each other. Cortez would be livid. The joking had come to an end.

In the middle of all this, she remarked with disgust that Plenipotentiary Tough had taken up his old hobby of taxidermy again, and had even done the honours on Nero, Rattucci's favourite rat, when the beast passed away from old age. Harry was beginning to wonder if it was not time to make a dash for a safe Argentinian garrison town and think about the consequences from a position of safety while the factions wiped each other out. He would like to be on a plane somewhere, anywhere with Mabel this very minute. She had made him a tempting offer that he could not get out of his mind. But what about Maria? He burnt Mabel's letter later, as Webster had seen it. He almost kept it. Was he slipping?

When Webster called for him the next day he thought it must be more questions. Or was it Mabel's letter which he had seen the young commercial attaché hand over? The poor man hadn't been in for dinner last night and was obviously on the carpet too. He found the American leaning against a long table in the dining room where rugs had been removed and the floor was being polished, as secretaries excused duty for a day weaved and dyed paper decorations, laughing to themselves like schoolgirls and passing round a tray of hefty cheese sandwiches. The problem of the band had been solved by a gramophone and a collection of 78s.

"These are incredible, really incredible," one of Webster's

men was saying. "I wonder if anyone realizes what these are worth. Priceless, really priceless; it's a museum of the roots of popular music in the twentieth century."

They found a quiet corner. "First of all," said Webster, "Miss Garnett is bringing You Know Who to the ball. Everyone has been briefed not to call him by his full name but we want to avoid any little incidents. So the dance has to be for Americans and English only, no coloureds I'm afraid, or Indians."

"If Maria's not coming you can count me out," said Harry quickly. "We'll hold a rival knees-up."

The long, rangy American sighed. "Naturally I didn't mean to include Maria or any of your maids in the ban. Of course she can come, only please try to keep her from getting too plastered. These are respectable folks and I want them to feel secure. But that's not the problem."

He motioned for Harry to follow him and they went out through the French windows, walking at Webster's fast pace through the garden under the hot summery sun which already was taking a toll of the roses, as the house could no longer spare the water. The smaller varieties were bearing up, Harry noticed with relief. Out of nowhere a small guard of marines had joined them and they were all heading towards the Aché village. They stopped near the armoury. By the river Harry saw two bald heads shining above almost identical safari suits; one of the men wore a large and extremely hot-looking pair of climbing boots and round his neck was a pair of binoculars. Both had that nervous diffident look of British civil servants abroad.

"Major Copeland-Smith?" said the man with binoculars. "I'm Tapster, this is Jones. We're from Records. As luck would have it we both have a consuming interest in wild cats." Harry glanced at Webster. There was not a trace of a smile on the American's face.

"We were searching for droppings," said Jones, wrinkling his nose slightly. "I don't know if you realize, Major, but this area is a treasure house of rare cats. We found what we thought were some Geoffroy's Cats and were terribly excited weren't we, George? Then we found that dreadful thing." He waved towards the armoury. "Whoever did that must be insane. For two pins . . ." There was a plaintive whimper from the side of the armoury and then a hiss. "My God, it's still alive."

A marine poked first his M-16 carbine and then his head around the side of the armoury and drew quickly back. "Excuse me sir," he said in the direction of Webster and was sick into the bushes by the river. Harry had a good idea what they had found.

"You will tell no one of this, any of you," he said with some of his old authority. "You've taken a look?" he said to Webster. The younger man nodded. Harry slipped the pistol from its holster.

The side of the armoury was in deep shade and at first he had to squint to make out the animal, a large domestic cat as the Aché had not been able to capture a wild one, nailed expertly to the wooden planking that surrounded the brick walls of the armoury hut. The eyes were glazed and the teeth bared. The animal had been ritually slit about the face and feathers inserted in the wounds; on its head was a crown of jungle thorns. For some reason, to the Aché the Tigre represented Jesus who formed a trisagion of magic with the Fish Man and the Alligator. The Aché had borrowed extensively from Christian religion, finding a use for almost everything except the doctrine of forgiveness. This ritual was performed to change their present condition, and although Harry had heard of it from Indian hunters he had never witnessed one before. It was difficult to imagine young Jeronimo and a few others crouching by the hut in the dead of night and doing these abominable things to this animal, as through its pain they made themselves strong – strong enough to overthrow Labuschagne. Mindful of the possible ricochet, Harry squeezed the trigger and blew the creature's head away, sending a stream of blood and urine down the wall which put out a tallow candle by a holy picture of St Peter from the chief's hut.

The hideous corpse quivered again even though it had no head, and the breath whistled from the lungs. It reminded him of Duarte. A cloud of flies enveloped him and something rustled in the grass beside the candle and rushed, with some difficulty, away, the head of the cat in its jaws. Harry stepped back.

"That was the work of your Indios, right?" said Webster. "They are not going to be any trouble are they?"

Harry walked Webster away from his soldiers. "Look," he said, "that must seem revolting to you but it's part of their beliefs and it means they are planning to have a go at Labuschagne for what he did to us. Let me go with them. I'm only in your way here. I could take Hindle as well and perhaps find out what has happened to Stebling and his sergeant. Labuschagne might be holding them. Believe me, Webster, short of tying them all up there is probably no way you will stop them. What better way of getting rid of Labuschagne's threat to this place than by letting a band of hostile Indians destroy him?"

Webster pondered the idea. "Would they do that to him?" He gestured towards the buzzing side of the hut.

"They might," said Harry, truthfully. "That's what I want to go along and prevent. Labuschagne *must* be up to something. We haven't heard a peep out of him. Have you?"

Webster shrugged his shoulders and thought for a moment. "If you do it," he said finally. "You do it on your own and on the following condition: that the Indios clear out of here for good. You find them somewhere else. One, I don't like the fact they are slaves; two, having them armed makes me nervous; and three, things like this scare the shit out of my men. But could they cope with Labuschagne? I thought you told me he had a little army of his own. Oh, and another thing; I will explain to your Mr Chambers that I don't want it going all the way back to Washington and London, okay?" He looked at the ground. "How on earth do you live with savages who would do that to a dumb animal? You're a strange one, Harry."

I'm not half as strange as you, thought Harry to himself as he went off to fix the time of the raid. Hindle would be relieved and he bet the chief would be delighted. They would go the night after the ball.

He walked up alone towards the children's school and watched a snake sunning itself on a log. If the Aché chief was in agreement he could move his people quickly – the beauty of having few or no possessions – and after they visited Labuschagne he would find them somewhere secure, and see to it that the Americans helped. There was no choice.

The snake moved slowly off the log as a girl walked by on her way to draw some water from the well. A construction worker in a hard hat whistled as she passed. She made a smacking noise with her lips, which was an insult. Webster was right; the two cultures could not live together.

When he returned from Labuschagne's what alternative would they have but to send him home? He was not going to stay with Webster for the rest of his life and Josef seemed to be more than well taken care of. He filled his lungs with pure air and slapped his chest with his hands. And he would take Maria with him. "Promise you not leave me," she whispered in her sleep. She had said that to him on their first night.

But it was easy to talk of tackling Labuschagne in that still peaceful spot, a cool hint of a breeze siphoning up from the river and touching his face, spiriting away the smell of diesel from the compressors and lifting the complex blooms of the passion flowers which tangled over what the workmen had left of cinnamon bush and thorn. He flexed his bad knee. Would he hold up? He had never really faced up to being old and the last of the seven ages of man seemed a long way off. Or was it? The mornings were not easy any more.

The woman came walking back from the well, the hot sun beating on her body. She was wearing a torn cotton dress, garish flowers on crimson, and she smiled at him. Perhaps he wasn't losing his grip after all.

Chapter 18

Final preparations were being made for the ball. Plump agent Wheatley had gone about explaining to everyone why the dance had to be a whites-only event. The Americans made extravagant gestures of agreement while the British looked slightly confused. Surely, said one lady helping with the gramophone records, surely there had never been any question of the people from the town coming to a private function? Anyway there was security to consider. Permed heads nodded in unison and Wheatley scurried away and pounced on an agent by the door, who had just arrived with an armful of riot guns.

"They must be expecting trouble," said Harry impishly to a jelly-bosomed lady who wobbled the tidings to her mate for the evening. The man, no doubt a colleague of the cat-lovers in Records, sneaked a look as the agent struggled through the hall under the weight of the buttless shotguns. Wheatley was admonishing him. "You haven't the sense of a dead jack-rabbit. Dumbo."

"I expect they are the prizes for the tombola," Harry said to jelly-bosom and left her in a quivering haze of face-powder as he went to broach a bottle of champagne in his room. The arrangements with the Aché were complete and he felt he needed a drink.

The bottle of Krug was where he had left it chilling among huge pieces of ice in a champagne bucket which belonged to the house's previous owners and was meant for several bottles or a jeroboam rather than just one. As he loosened the cork he recalled the days in the war when he always had a bottle of bubbly with a friend before going out and had never touched anything else. Old Morgan had the habit of putting his large thumb over the end of the bottle so as not to let a drop escape. Morgan had been a good servant in those quarters near Welwyn. They had called him "Thumbs". Harry preferred it to spill a little. There was no fun in champagne if one couldn't be just a little wasteful once in a while. No doubt "Thumbs" had lived to a miserable old age. He poured himself a glass and looked for the light under Maria's dressing room door but decided not to disturb her; she had been hard at work with the refreshments and could not decide which dress to wear. Her favourite was a white lace confection but she was ashamed it would draw attention to her dark skin. Harry had told her not to be so silly.

The engine of a Land Rover started up. Christ, they mustn't take his. That was the only way he and Hindle would catch up with the chief on the shores of the lake tomorrow. He ran to the window of his bedroom, spilling some champagne on his lapel. Through the dusk he saw it was not his vehicle but one full of marines with a figure in the back, handcuffed between two guards and looking very sorry for himself. The figure was unmistakably the careless commercial. Webster and his merry men had decided he represented a threat to security, which he most certainly did, poor thing. Harry raised his glass as they drove off.

Bit of a shame, though, the young man was always such fun at parties. But he would be a lot better off cooling his heels in Asunción than getting mixed up in things down here.

"Maria!" he shouted, and refilled his glass. "Maria, I hope you're not going to be all night." He heard a few cold Indian insults from inside and the staccato chatter of Ramona, the *mestizo* maid who was trying to dress her, and then the monosyllabic insults again. He went back and poured himself a third glass and spun the bottle round amid the little icebergs.

He must be in for a fair whack of pension when he got home to say nothing of the money he had left for the brokers to invest for him. That was something he must ask Chambers about. He would be entitled to at least the same treatment as an ambassador by his own reckoning, enough to allow him to live comfortably in the country and have a little place in town. They might also give him a Silver Rail Card, all ex FO high flyers got those; or even have a car at his disposal because of ill-defined "security reasons". He chuckled. Lost in plans he nodded off into a shallow, gliding doze on the rustling counterpane.

The half-waking dream that followed was of Labuschagne's fortress, set in the rolling Paraguayan countryside of further downstream, bathed in luminous evening light but with nothing moving, everything flat, as if he were looking at a medievalist painting. Over the lake, a white lake without a ripple as if it were full of milk, towered a black hand which vanished beneath the surface with a plop only to reappear somewhere else. People were calling to him from the far bank and he felt he should be frightened. At the top of the ziggurat chests of treasure had been upset on the steps and a ruby bounced down and fell at his feet, while overhead a helicopter hovered and played his song, "Wild About Harry".

The song was playing on the old gramophone as he woke with the peculiar notion that he was sitting in the cusp of the black hand. In front of him stood Maria, her dark hair swept up in a Spanish mantilla and the soft flat lines of her Indian face made harder by skilfully applied make-up. She drew herself up haughtily but her eyes were full of tears and fear above an ocean of black lace, as black as the hand in his dream, with a red paper flower on the bodice. "You think it's awful?" she said, ready to cry.

"I think you are a princess." He was truthful. "You will come to England and live with me, my princess. We will go soon." Inexplicably Maria burst into tears and ran headlong for her dressing room.

But when she came out half an hour later her face was serene, and if Harry had not known her origins he might have hazarded that she was a rich farmer's daughter. She looked lovely. As she kissed him he thought he caught the taste of coca on her lips. "I love you Maria," he said. She threw her head back and laughed and they went down, proud of each other, descending the staircase with the regal disdain of its original owners for the gaggle of civil servants, agents and substantial ladies in the chequered black-and-white marble hall. One American was wearing a blue tuxedo with matching tie, and Harry pointed this out to Maria who giggled attractively. "And look at Señor Webster," she said. "*Madre de Dios*, he looks like an undertaker."

Maria had just recovered her poise when they were announced: "Major Harry Copeland-Smith and Doña Maria de Rodriguez y Castro." She looked every inch of her new name, thought Harry, and a secretary more used to the suburbs started to clap. "Take your partners ladies and gentlemen for a rumba," said the agent in heavy rimmed black glasses in charge of the gramophone.

Harry stepped onto the dance floor with Maria, who he knew was a practised dancer. Ramona, who was passing around the canapés, smiled at her handiwork. Two other American couples, the girl telex operators and much more glamorous than the dragons of Whitehall, joined them while most of the men stood rigidly against the wall talking about sport, drinking as much as they could and trying not to catch the eyes of the predatory spinsters. After the third dance Harry sat down and Maria was whisked onto the floor again by one of the Americans. He told her about his wife and children back home and how he still liked to go game shooting with his father. He fancied himself and swung his hips.

Webster stood near the microphone; Harry almost expected him to have a clipboard. Tonight he looked like a curly-haired, bespectacled Abraham Lincoln. There was that same gaunt ugliness about him. A toad-like woman said something sharply to another woman who scowled and grumpily got to her feet, and the odd couple began to waltz together in a slow dignified way.

"Come on now gentlemen, leave the bourbon. We want a few more of these ladies on their feet and dancing, and not with each other." A bald-headed man bowed to a woman in a two-piece suit and pearls and was brusquely turned down. He backed away into a waitress, smashing a glass. "Better luck next year sir," quipped the man with the mike.

Harry danced with Maria again, and they were drawing the tombola as he walked her out onto the terrace and kissed her lightly on the lips so as not to smudge her make-up.

"What was there to be scared of? You see they are all nice people. Before you know it we will be in England and I will buy you many pretty dresses."

She thought for a moment, alcohol and coca leaves making it a difficult process. "You do like my dress? It does not look too much like a funeral? Too many people in black. We all look as if we go to see the city of the dead," she laughed nervously. It was the Indian phrase for a European cemetery, something which they found absurd and amusing. Harry found it chilling.

"I like your dress very much Maria. But I would rather go to a fiesta with you than a funeral. Let's go back in."

The night seemed suddenly cold and a bawdy shouted song was coming from the construction workers' camp. By now his Indios would have split their people into two columns, carrying everything with them, making their way round the village and onto the road, hoping that the slight moon would soon be hidden behind clouds, padding on bare soundless feet with the weapons Hindle had provided from the armoury. He tried to put the thought of tomorrow's attack on Labuschagne from his mind and took another glass of champagne from a silver tray.

"Hello Major, we met by the river," said a voice. "Don't you remember, the cat?" Harry turned round and two flushed faces beamed at him.

"Good evening. What do you think of Paradiso gentlemen? Longing to be back with your wives, I bet. What?"

"No, not for the moment," said Tapster, a certain gleam in his bloodshot eyes. "It's the only adventure I've ever had and am likely to get. Thank you for the hospitality." Two bald heads bowed in deference to Harry.

"I must say I was surprised by Doctor Josef," said Jones. "I thought we all might have a little adjustment to make working with him but he is charming, a true gentleman, not like that dreadful Wheatley who chews gum. I think our Agnes, spinster of Berkhamsted, is quite taken with the Doctor and vice versa." He stopped and gazed around. "Smith, the computer boffin, burst in like those boys do the other day and found the old Doctor on his knees. He and Agnes together. They were holding hands."

The assembled company quaffed champagne and held out their glasses for more. The noise level in the room rose as shrill Surrey soprano joined the bass voices of Balham and Boston.

"Have you got a moment?" said Webster. With him the phrase was always an order of sorts and, excusing himself from his partner, Harry went through into the quieter drawing room where Chambers was drinking whisky by the fireplace, his back to Agnes Garnett who was trying to sit daintily on the arm of a chair next to the Doctor. He was wearing an immaculate white silk jacket.

"Doesn't he look a picture?" said Agnes. Josef did not smile; he seemed to have taken the news of Willy's death very calmly.

"We have a surprise," said Josef, the hard brow softening for a moment. "I want to tell you in private as it were. You have kept our bargain well over the years, and although we may never be friends I feel we do mean something special to each other, Major. I am engaged to be married to Agnes." Harry coughed and saw Chambers and Webster were looking at him hard; he was expected to behave and not mention anything about the wife the Doctor already had. "And Agnes has persuaded me to go into the ministry, to become a priest. To take the word of God to the people. She says I cannot stay and rot, apologizing for my sins all my life. God has other work for me."

Good Lord! How, and where, on earth were the Americans going to swing that one? But Harry was not going to be a killjoy. He had watched the romance bloom even though he found it hard to take seriously. The other matters were out of his hands.

"Congratulations," he said and took Agnes's hand and kissed it. She grabbed him round the neck in a grip worthy of a wrestler and planted a sloppy kiss on the side of his face, her blue eyes twinkling. "I've been wanting to do that," she said darkly. "You want to watch that no one pinches him," she added to Maria who was standing like a statue in the doorway, narcotically divorced from the grim proceedings around her. "Are you all right, dear?"

"It's the champagne," said Harry. "Always goes to her Indian head. Webster, I think you should announce it; it's your show now."

The American looked decidedly sheepish about the task.

"What about Mr Chambers?" said Agnes in the direction of the skulking Fat Man. "He has such a lovely voice." A curious gloom, Harry noticed, had descended over Chambers.

"Must I?" he said with all the enthusiasm of a Christian stepping into the amphitheatre. "Well, if I must." He managed a smile.

"He is a one," said Agnes.

They crossed the hall into the other room. Chambers waddled up to the microphone as the twirling dancers stopped to stare at the man they had come all that way to serve and mostly had not seen. There was a whisper of admiration and awe around the room.

"Ladies and gentlemen. I have an announcement to make," boomed Chambers into the microphone. "Do settle down dear," he said to a man at the back who was waving a bottle of champagne and singing "Rule Britannia". "Settle down, children," continued the Fat Man. "What I have to announce is happy news indeed. Our own Doctor Josef has been stolen from us by that temptress from the Home Counties, that Jezebel from Berkhamsted, Miss Agnes Garnett. The couple have asked me to announce they intend to be married and we can do no less than wish them all happiness, especially as it will be an excuse for another party, eh Mr Webster?"

There was a roar from the throng on the dance floor and for a moment it looked as if the Doctor was to be carried shoulder high. Many hands stretched out to clasp his, more than one thumb probing to see if he was a Freemason. He was smiling. In an undulating tide of Official Secrets Act signatories he felt sorry for Josef as that stern face was clasped deep into the bosom of his intended like a favourite doll. I would rather be hung by the Israelis than marry Agnes, thought Harry. What astonished him was the speed of official approval. Something was afoot.

But he had no desire to nudge the arms that were offering Josef Argentinian pink champagne to celebrate his coming nuptials. They would almost certainly move him now and Major Harry Copeland-Smith would be quietly retired before the ghastly spectacle occurred. Some remote little West Indian island under the American flag would be perfect for the newly-weds; the Doctor could convert the natives and Webster's men could see there were no boats calling to breach security.

"Did you know Hitler?" someone was asking in a friendly voice.

"We met many times in the early years, but I don't think I could ever count myself as a close friend," Josef replied cautiously, and then leaped onto the safer ice floes of the Russian Front and Stalin.

"Yes, Stalin was the real enemy. We're both the same sort of people really," declared a secretary who had had too much, pausing for emphasis as if she had said something momentous.

The Angel of Death took her hand and gently kissed it and the spell was only broken when he looked up and met Harry's eyes. You deceitful old bastard, thought Harry. They were parted by the crush as if the Doctor was some star of popular music. A maid had to be taken into the kitchens with a twisted ankle and one of the secretaries became dangerously hysterical; the gramophone played "In The Mood". "My favourite," said Josef, lying effortlessly. He beamed. People didn't seem to want him to apologize any more. He had been forgiven just like God had said. Harry saw it in his eyes.

Chapter 19

Harry took the brass cartridge bullets out of his Webley, shaking them nervously into his hand, and then started to put them back in again, click, click, click. They went over a bump and he saw Hindle give the operation a sideways glance. It was irritating him.

"Sorry old man, just a little bit jumpy," he said fingering the safety catch and putting the gun back into its holster. The sergeant grunted. He seemed to be on edge, too, and had hardly said a word since they set off at mid-afternoon. Both Chambers and Webster had come to see them on their way.

"Don't get mixed up in any bang-bangs Harry," Chambers had warned, wagging his finger. Webster had said nothing but gave him a knowing look, possibly recalling the tortured animal by the stream. They had both made it clear to him that whatever he did he was on his own, and they could not help if he got into hot water. Father Labuschagne's palace was not to be stormed under the banner of the Union Jack or the Stars and Stripes.

"If you have any sense you'll watch the proceedings from a rowing boat with a picnic basket," was Chambers' parting shot.

He reached for his pipe. "Do you think we can do it Ian?" he said spilling tobacco on his camouflage trousers.

The sergeant pursed his lips. "As long as it's at night and as long as they don't see us coming . . . As long as the helicopter is not there and most of the guards are in the village . . . Don't worry, Mr Chambers has told me to make sure you get out in one piece if things get nasty, sir. I can't abide that Webster. I don't trust him sir. He has completely taken over with his blasted waste-paper factory." The road collapsed into a track beneath the vehicle and for a few moments the bumps were so severe they couldn't speak. Harry dropped his pipe and retrieved it from the buffeting floor.

"I wouldn't be too worried about Webster. The German guarantors of Josef's agreement, or at least one of them, is being flown down so it may not be too long before you can get the hell out of here. It worked quite well encouraging the old brute to write letters; they can't leave him here now and we may as well go home to enjoy a substantial pension. What will you do, Sergeant?"

Hindle thought for a moment. "I might go to Australia and start a business. Somewhere by the sea. I'm bloody sick of all this green. I might even settle down." He looked at Harry and actually smiled. "What are your plans sir? Though my old mum would say we were counting our chickens in the circumstances."

Yes, thought Harry, better keep the old head down as Chambers advised. All he had to do was make sure that Stebling and his sergeant were not being held prisoner and let his Indios shoot up the place a bit. He pondered how strange it was that the Aché's wishes concurred with those of Webster and Cortez. The locals would be hard on the tribe if they lost. They would be hounded, probably all the way back to the Chaco, in little bloody bands seeking food at unfriendly missions and finally being herded into a living death on the government reservations. But again if he had not parted with British government money all those years ago the small tribe would not exist. Surely he was doing all he could. The Land Rover bumped on; his conscience and the road were clear.

The sun was setting and the lake had turned to gold as they gingerly rolled the Land Rover, motor off, down the incline towards the jetty. A figure flitted towards them from the trees to the right. For a moment Harry thought it might be a

Ukranian guard and his pistol was in his hand, but Hindle put a hairy paw over his and in the gathering darkness he saw it was Jeronimo.

"I thought it was better they wore uniforms, without badges of course. For once they didn't seem to mind. Saw the sense. Could hardly clip water-bottles and grenades onto their ding-a-lings," said the sergeant gruffly. Even so, Jeronimo was still every inch a parade ground nightmare.

"No one is here. We watch all day," said the Indian. "No one crossed." Harry looked across the strip of water to where the building rose among the trees. He spotted two Ukranians by the water on the opposite bank, both men wearing gleaming white shirts, but no light twinkled in Labuschagne's quarters yet. They were in luck: the helicopter was not there.

"When I came with Mr Stebling I was in the bushes over to the left," said Hindle, careful not to say much in front of Jeronimo. "It went up right in the middle. I don't think there was any chance of survivors."

They found the chief on the bank several hundred yards from the jetty, examining the ziggurat minutely with his Army-issue binoculars. He was bare-chested and anyone seeing him from the island would have thought he was a fisherman. Except for the splash of feeding fish jumping at the legions of mosquitoes in the shallows there wasn't a sound: no rasping motor-boat engine heralding the approach of shore-line patrols as they expected. The ziggurat itself looked like a tomb and was as silent, silhouetted against the red sky.

"The others are here," the Indian said pointing towards the pitch-black shadows of the trees. "Thirty. The rest are with the women. We cross in canoes, Major, I hope it will be easy."

Harry scanned the island again. The guards hadn't moved and the windows were still not showing a light even though the sun had all but set and the moon was out. Half an hour passed as he and Hindle fidgeted on the bank. The Indian did not move a muscle, except for the occasional raising of the field-glasses. He was being as patient and careful as a cat, letting those guards doze right off to sleep. If he made a mistake it might mean the death of his people yet there was not an iota of worry in that flat, lined face. Only watchfulness. Harry envied him.

Satisfied with the darkness at last, the chief raised his hand and in a moment Tatugi and Jeronimo were at his side, black streaks of camouflage paint on their brown faces still just visible, and bandoliers of bullets encompassing army denim tops. They were a fearsome sight. Then he heard a faint dragging sound.

The canoes were not the light, flimsy bark constructions, craft built for speed which one could easily put one's foot through, but heavy boats for fishing and negotiating the rapids of the fast tributaries flowing into the Paraná, where submerged rocks could rip the bottom out of a boat in an instant, leaving the occupants to the mercy of the waters, if they were lucky, or to the voracious little fish that lived in them if they were not.

It seemed to make an awful noise as the three canoes were pushed and heaved through the low bush, across the strip of grass and through the straggling rushes into the water. Yet the natural sounds of the lake and forest hid them: the chorus of tree-frog and cicada, a rising humming tide of sound that meant one could only hear the grating of keels or the clanking of cartridge cases if one listened for it. Soon the band was assembled in the boats and at a wave from the shore party they took out the paddles and very slowly began to inch through the mist forming on the lake, obscuring the surface and making it seem possible to walk to the island, as if the god of the ziggurat was trying to deceive them, changing water to dry land in the flickering moonlight which made the construction itself look even more evil. If they were careful, very careful, Father Labuschagne was going to get the shock of his life.

The crossing of the lake seemed to take an hour; the chief insisted there was to be no rushing and if they hovered like demons in the mist they would not be seen. Over the years he had become, unknown to Harry, an expert poacher of fish and knew the lake. He proudly sat in the prow of the boat listening for the slightest sound from the island.

They crossed to the western tip where a cliff of clay and

rocks tumbled into the lake and trees which had become too heavy for the rim of the island had come crashing down, bringing a tangle of vegetation with them, alive with noise and flies. Here they hid painfully, watching the fruit bats loop overhead in the cooler night air, until the chief was satisfied they could safely move again. In the preparations for the raid Harry had expected to assume command – that would be only natural – but there were no verbal orders. Only the occasional gesture of the hand and the operation went ahead like clockwork. He could sense Hindle's admiration, but the fact remained that the Aché were now under no one's control but their own. Ironically this business with Labuschagne, a quarrel which the Aché would never understand even if he explained it to them for a hundred years, had tonight freed the tribe. Nothing had been said, but he was no longer their master. Harry was also sure that this decision to take revenge would eventually bring annihilation, as it had done hundreds of years before when the Jesuits armed the Guaraní on the *reducciones* and reduced them to a faded memory on a bank-note. Under the umbrellas of ferns by the rotting stillness of the island's western point it was much easier to believe in his own destruction than worry about the proud, doomed tribe. The boats started to move again. Theirs slipped in front of the other two and after ten minutes of interminable painstaking paddling, so slow it made you want to shout and Harry fancied he could hear the heartbeat of the man behind him, they bumped gently into the reeds near the first guard post.

The man was less than forty feet away, hunched on a wooden stool.

Although Harry could not see it he knew from his previous visits that there was a bell in the guard house to set off a series of alarms. Then the chief turned, rocking the heavy boat. He produced a six-foot bow from the bottom of the canoe, stringing it as if it were a child's toy and fitting a spear-like arrow. He lay flat on his back on a wooden chest holding the belts of ammunition. With one foot he jammed the weapon against the craft's prow, hooking the other foot around the bow and steadying it with his leg muscles, pulling the string back under his chin. The entire boat held its breath. Harry thought he would choke as an eddy threatened to shift them and the chief moved slightly to compensate, looking down the silvery length of his own body in the moonlight, correcting his aim. Then he let the arrow go with a buzz and a hiss and the boat shuddered. Everyone had been looking at the archer; no one at the target which had disappeared except for a hand and a boot sticking up over a ditch. Between the two the steely arrow was straight as a reed. The only sound had been that of the man and the stool falling into the ditch. No other guards appeared, no alarm bells rang.

They landed, and despite Hindle pulling him back he went up to look at the crumpled body, getting within three paces before the foul smell hit him. At first he thought it was a latrine pit and forced himself on, picking up a stout stick the guard had apparently been whittling, and drawing his revolver. He poked the corpse in the chest and something gave, adding to the smell of putrefaction.

The man had been long dead. His eyes had gone and the face was swimming from within, alive again with its own decay. He had been there for days and a rope showed he had been tied to the stool. They had just expertly executed a corpse.

Men from the other canoes had landed further down the island and overrun another guard post on their way. He could hear muffled excited chatter, but could not make out the words. Then on they went. He moved behind Hindle. He was not planning to get himself killed.

"Psst Ian . . . The guard, the guard was dead. He was dead."

Hindle did not answer at first. "It could be a trick," he said eventually. "They used to do it in Ireland. The other boys probably found the same. Some poor bastard from a village they didn't like. To put us off our stride."

They moved gingerly over the helicopter landing-pad onto the first level of the strange pyramidal structure. They met no opposition, no one challenged them. Up ahead Harry could see the two columns of Indians clearly in the moonlight, edging forward, now dodging behind the low wall of the second terrace with its potted palms. He could hear weapons being cocked, hoping all the time it was his own men, the Aché, and not someone on the levels above, someone with a machine gun and the switch for the floodlights. But there were no shots, just the usual night sounds of the jungle. Two stairways led up the terraces on that side of the island. Any moment all hell would be let loose.

They inched slowly up the staircase, Harry lagging in the rear guard. Where were the bastards hiding in that darkness with those long machetes that they had used on Petroni? The thirty Aché had overrun every level, but what of the warren of darkness inside the building where a small number of men could hold off for days? Where hidden wires, micro-switches and booby traps could decimate their numbers until the island's owner rowed back in the morning, with fresh men who had slept and breakfasted well, and set about the serious business of murdering them all. Yet, such a finesse would be beyond Labuschagne. Harry would have almost been comforted so see the black-coated figure look from the door of the banqueting hall, now only twenty yards away up the steep stone steps. Every step he took he felt was going to be his last. Ahead of him Jeronimo disturbed a *cocrico*, a ground turkey which made a noise fit to wake the dead as it took off for the forest, and like many behind him he very nearly fired. The bird's laughing cry was repeated again and again in the trees and others joined in. The entire jungle seemed to be laughing at them stalking shadows. The heavy wooden door of the great hall was in front.

Aché braves flattened themselves against the walls to the left and the right as the chief turned the huge brass ring and pulled the door towards him. Gently, very gently. If people were hiding it would be here. The chief ran his hand slowly up and down the inside, feeling for the wire that might blow them all to kingdom come. But there was no wire. He went inside.

Men from behind him rushed forward in a wave, making Harry feel small and fragile in their violence. As he had become nervous of the place they had become more frustrated that the enemy they had prepared for was not there. The fears and inner searching and questioning of their own bravery in the cold hours of morning had all been for nothing. Their confessions of cowardice to friends, their feeling of sorrow for wrongs done that could not be righted had they been killed on the dreadful stone steps of Labuschagne's palace, swept as they believed it would be with gunfire and ruled by the deadly machine from the skies, seemed stupid. Lights went on in the hall behind the door, which had closed in front of Harry. First there was a crash then the sound of smashing, then shouting and then silence. Like soldiers in any army they had wanted to vent their spleen breaking up the place, only unlike other armies this chief would not let it happen. As Harry peeped round the door, the chief, his bare shoulders glistening with sweat, was standing over another twenty years his junior who Harry quite liked. The young brave was nursing a cut lip. The chief turned.

"He has gone, Major. There is no one to fight. The island is ours," he said simply.

And so it was, but how?

The chief was not about to question the magic of the Tigre sacrifice and set off with his men to make sure of the rest of the building. Harry collapsed into a chair, looking around the baronial hall with the raised podium at the end and the Ukranian national flag on one wall, giving the air of a shrine to the barn-like structure. The hall was out of place. It did not fit in with the rest of the ziggurat. Labuschagne must have added it later. Hindle marched in and came smartly to attention in front of Harry's chair.

"The place is empty, sir. The wee man must have done a runner."

Harry wandered over to a roll-top desk which stood in an alcove at the side of the hall. Papers fell out as he lifted the lid. In a writing case made of tanned leather there were letters in Afrikaans. Typical that the good Father left his personal possessions at the corner of the most public place, the pressed flower in a relation's letter kept private by the fear his servants had for him. Now some greater evil, something more frightening than Labuschagne had removed him, ruthlessly scrubbed him from the face of the earth.

"What do you make of it, Sergeant?"

Hindle examined the blade of his commando knife. "Looks as if he got the wind up when he thought he might get a battering. He heard about the Yanks and decided to get out while he could, in one piece."

Hindle was slicing the sandy red mud off his boot; he did not look up. In the corner of the room was a bar. Harry took off his own boots and padded over to it. On a shelf was a whole bottle of Glenfiddich.

"Fancy a wee dram Hindle? Might as well be comfortable, it's going to be a long night." His limbs felt limp with exhaustion, being so tense for so long and now this anti-climax. He did not want to sit down and figure out why Labuschagne wasn't there. He was just glad he wasn't. He did not wait for Hindle's answer or see the Scot leave as he poured a stiff one into a greasy glass, and then another. He took the bottle over to the chair and sat there watching the rippling moonlight on the lake below, playing king of the castle as the Aché ferreted in the rooms and tunnels underneath, some still convinced that Labuschagne was down there lurking.

"Major, Major," the voice called. Someone was shaking him. He had been asleep. When he opened his eyes no one smiled.

Hindle was there looking into the bottom of a glass, but he was drinking water not whisky. Ten or so of the untested warriors slumped moodily on the refectory tables. Harry's mouth was dry and he felt sick and a little giddy. A few of the streaked-faced men looked at him contemptuously as if he had arranged such an inglorious ending to their expectations, had betrayed them again as he did with the helicopter, leaving them without even an enemy, fidgeting like children.

"Let's have a drink Ian," he said feeling for the bottle. It had been removed. Morning was moving in washes of grey light on the lake and a flight of wild duck skimmed across the surface of the water. They handed him a glass of water. Bloody water. "You found no one. They are all gone. All run out on us. Ha, ha." It was the croaking laughter of an old man and it echoed through the hall, seeming to annoy Hindle the most.

"The village, Capitan Boda, is deserted too. There were some bodies. The guards here had been strangled. Oh, and we found Labuschagne's black hat but no body. I'm going to stay here for the moment with the Aché and organize their defences; they have asked me, if that's all the same to you."

Harry looked at him. Hindle wasn't meeting his eyes but he looked determined. All right, let it be my lad. Stay and rot in the bloody jungle. I'm going home.

Hindle did not come down to the landing stage, but the chief was there to see him off.

"We will make this place strong today, Major. You will see. You will always have a place here with my people. I will send one of my men with you to see you back safely."

Harry got into the boat. This was the first stage of his journey home. When he reached the far side of the lake he watched Aché moving up and down the ziggurat for some time before he turned round and saw something which changed his mood completely. There was a cloud of black smoke rising on the horizon, plumes of blackness which made his stomach ache. Oh my God, he thought, Paradiso is burning.

Chapter 20

The Indian, a man he did not know, escorted him to the Land Rover but refused to get in. Harry was in too much of a hurry to argue the toss, and nearly ran him down in his haste to get home, to see if Maria was all right. What on earth was Webster doing? Was this what Labuschagne had been up to last night or had Cortez's patience run out at last? The smoke hung in a huge question mark over the area as he bumped and buffeted back to the main road, cutting the usual time in half. As he raced into Paradiso he saw his own house on the hill, not the village as he first supposed, had more or less burnt to the ground. He stopped. What were they trying to do to him? Other smoke showed the Indian village had been set on fire as well, and the new pre-fabs. It had to be deliberate for no accidental fire could encompass that area. A shower of sparks went up hundreds of feet as the pillars of the big house finally fell in and there were several explosions. He started the Land Rover again. No one was in the main square. Paradiso was a ghost town.

It was the oldest trick in the book and he should not have fallen for it, but it soon became insignificant. There was a body stretched across the road near the *cantina*, the body of a woman, and he pulled up in front of it. A breeze rustled a fiesta poster on the wall and a blind swayed slightly. Everything else was still on that hot morning as he got out of the driver's seat, took his gun and went over to the corpse. The girl was about fifteen. Her full red lips were open and round her neck was a silver crucifix. She had been shot in the back of the head and dragged there. His tired brain formed the conclusion too late.

"Drop the weapon, Major."

The voice was Webster's and it seemed to come from inside the *cantina*; perhaps it wasn't the wind that was moving the hessian blind. He heard a disturbing click from the church across the square. There were heavy truck tracks round the statue of the Aryan woodman whom the giant land snails had not yet brought down from his rotting wooden pedestal. In the bright, hot sun the village looked much cleaner and tidier without people; only the dead girl and Harry littered the street. The usual piles of rubbish were gone, even the birds. He wasn't thinking clearly. He felt he needed to sit down; the sun was too strong on his bare head. He chuckled to himself, imagining Webster directing his soldiers to pick up every scrap of paper. That was what Webster was doing, cleaning up.

"Please drop the gun, Major."

And this time he did, letting the Webley slip from his grasp onto the red dust, and he stared at it where it had fallen. The moment of his retirement had come; this was going to be the equivalent of his gold watch presentation. He laughed, out loud this time, but the hollow sound stopped abruptly as he heard two volleys of automatic rifle fire followed by the zipping burst of a small modern machine gun. He was listening to a firing squad. He thought of the large holes to the north of the airstrip. He thought of Maria. What on earth were these people doing?

"Come in, Major. No heroics please."

Harry cried out in pain when he was grabbed by the neck as he was inching through the doorway of the once-cheerful bar into the cool dark interior. He was thrown so hard against the crumbling wall his mouth filled with dust as the man behind him kicked his legs apart, catching the insides of his shins with the rigid sole of his combat boot. Then expert hands ran up and down his body, probing the breast pocket of his uniform for his pipe, which the owner of the boots dropped on the floor and stamped on until the bowl was half driven into the rotten wood.

"I think the sergeant here would like to kill you," said Webster in a matter-of-fact voice. Harry kept looking at the wall, examining the tiny flecks of green on the plaster. He refused to believe this was happening. The sergeant was behind him waiting for the order – or was it the excuse? – to hit him.

"Why am I being treated like this? Is the Doctor safe? What has happened to Maria? Were you attacked?" He tried to get the questions out in a flood before the blow to his kidneys caused him to buckle and weep as he slipped slowly towards the floor.

"That will be enough," said Webster firmly and the boots moved away. "Get up Harry." He struggled to his feet, painfully straightening out his bad knee, and turned round. The owner of the boots was staring at him, a half smile on his face – the face Harry had last seen in the back of Hindle's Land Rover leaning forward to examine the contents of a parcel on his colonel's lap.

"I don't understand. . . ."

At a table was Colonel Stebling himself, holding the picture Harry had saved from the Jesuit Bible, the one he had found impossible to throw away.

"Thanks a lot, Harry, for saving this. I can never tell the story but it will sure mean a lot to me hung up in my den," said Stebling grinning from ear to ear. The sergeant did not say a thing. He did not like people who plotted to kill him.

"I want to see Mr Chambers," Harry said as firmly as he could. Webster seemed to be in no hurry to do anything, draped as he was on a chair with one boot on the table, dressed in a pair of light trousers and a T-shirt. The other Americans were in full military kit and there were packs by the door. They were ready to move.

"Your Mr Chambers went yesterday. He flew with all those nice ladies and gentlemen to Puerto Stroessner where they boarded a bus and were taken to those splendid waterfalls at Iguazú and are now on their way to Rio. One of the ladies slipped on the steps down to the falls, terrible business, twisted her ankle. But she will be all right in a few days. Your Sir

Reginald Tough came down to see them off. He was in a very good mood. He's taking over your Paris embassy. Quite a plum job. He seems to be very pleased." Harry held onto the side of a table. "He seemed very taken with Miss Garnett and her fiancé. Promised to go to their wedding."

"The Doctor isn't here?" stammered Harry. "You have moved him?"

Webster slowly lit a cigarette. "The Doctor is here; you are the Doctor. Come and look at these."

A chuckle went round the room and he approached the table cautiously, like a third former being bullied at school. He looked at Stebling who had so completely taken him in.

"I was only doing my job. It was for the good of the operation," he announced bleakly.

What he said brought a further ripple of laughter. On the table in front of him were documents, fingerprints and files, copies of a Jewish newspaper and a Brazilian one. His picture appeared on all of them and a headline screamed in an Argentinian magazine called *Hoy*: "The Angel of Death: New Pictures" and the pictures were of him. But still the obvious did not dawn on him.

"Your man Hindle came up with the idea," said Webster. "You really should have treated him better. He's a good man, going to be working for us in the future. The problem was to put Josef back in Europe where we can keep a closer eye on him, but he needed a background that kept him out of the country for twenty-odd years. Yours was perfect. Miss Garnett is to marry Major Harry Copeland-Smith, a man who has done saintly work among the German missions of southern Paraguay. I understand the Major fully intends to be ordained as a priest and seek a living near Berk-ham-sted. I think I've got that right? We felt this was a better way for you to do your job Harry. Killing people is wrong."

Harry sat down, feeling winded. "But I've just left Hindle," he said. Webster smiled.

"Your Mr Hindle and a few of your Indians helped us remove Father Labuschagne some time ago. Our drugs people had their eye on him. Most of his band fled to Argentina but the good priest is with his maker." Webster paused. "You see we had just set up a new section of the Company in Santiago when the Somoza business happened. Plenipotentiary Tough drew attention to you and this place. At first we thought it was someone taking us for rookies, having some kind of joke. The more we found out . . . Hell! I don't think you appreciate what this mess looked like from the outside. It was a time-bomb, and you know all about bombs, Major. But I shall have to get used to calling you 'Doctor'. The business of Labuschagne's attack and Josef's conversion gave us the excuse we needed to move in and set up a big operation, which naturally went over budget. It was easy to convince your government to try something new; they really are a bunch of skinflints and the German guarantors liked the idea too. We all thought you were going to smell a rat, but then I suppose you are used to people doing what you say."

"Maria?" Harry said. "What about Maria?"

Webster shook his head. "Just another Indian, wasn't she Harry? Not quite good enough, eh? She really liked you, Harry. It was hard to get her to come over to us but she did, doped up to the eyeballs. Pretty young thing . . . She'll be working for us in Santiago. Your servants have been taken over by your embassy in Asunción."

Maria had deserted him? Harry didn't believe it. Two rifle shots in the distance added to his confusion.

"But I served my country, spent my whole life here," he said. "Doesn't that count for something? I did my duty. I did it bloody well." He felt a tear start to roll down his cheek.

Stebling replied in his dull cultured tones.

"From what I have in this file you maintained a slave plantation, protected a known mass-murderer, killed everyone that came near him, lived in colonial luxury and acted as an agent in the service of Napoleon Cortez, perhaps the most corrupt individual in Latin America . . . When it was decided to get Josef out of Europe and sit on him down here, the Allies never intended anything like this. You encouraged him in that absurd letter-writing business which in its turn engineered your own downfall. It was only a matter of time before someone exposed your extremely eccentric interpretation of orders, and that would have left us all with egg on our faces. You were a danger to the operation. We set a trap for you and you fell right into it. In my book you are just as bad as the man you were sent out here to protect."

Harry looked around the room. "How can you accuse me? The girl outside . . . Look what you are doing! How many completely innocent people have you killed up there?" He pointed out of the window at where his house had been.

Webster smiled. "You did that Harry, we didn't. The British insisted no one who didn't have security clearance . . . Well, you know the score. We are only continuing what you started, Harry – or should I say Doctor? Just look at this."

On the grubby table was a poster, a small handbill such as graced the post offices and saloons of the wild west, and his face was on it. The writing underneath said he was wanted dead or alive and offered two hundred dollars reward; it somehow did not seem very much.

"And don't expect any help from Cortez," said Webster. "He was coming south with his tin soldiers but unfortunately had to go back to Asunción. A delegation of our congressmen arrived questioning him on that sewage project of his. Do you know he was planning to charge one town a hundred dollars a metre? Our people told him it was you who complained. Strange, Harry. You don't seem to have made a lot of friends down here."

Why didn't they just bloody shoot him and get it over with?

"Bastards," he suddenly said out loud. "I'm going to tell every bugger about this, just you wait. I will, you see, you can push someone only so far. . . . "

Stebling stood up, put two fingers under his nose in a mock Hitler moustache, as Harry remembered Wheatley doing, and clicked his heels.

"And who on earth is going to believe you, Major? We do seem to hold all the cards and if you are worried about that," he gestured towards the smoke, "no one is going to miss a few *chanchos*. Those right-wing Cubans, *Maños Blancos*, get a bit over-enthusiastic, but if there is any blame it will fall fairly and squarely on you. Your old smuggling friends will even turn against you."

Were they really killing people by those huge holes near the airstrip gouged by the digger? Or was this yet another trick? Were they just trying to frighten him, to make him running scared? He examined the impassive faces. Surely these men could not do such things? The girl outside on the street was dead, he was certain of that. His head ached. He wondered if he could make a dash for the door, get the pistol growing hot in the sun in the deserted street and take off in the Land Rover.

"If you are thinking about certain documents becoming public knowledge, forget it," said Webster. "Your own people got to those and had them destroyed. Amazing what the old-boy network can do. Not that they mattered very much. There is only one safe place for you and that's Capitan Boda. The legend of Labuschagne will become fused in rumour with the legend of the Angel of Death living in his strange fortress surrounded by a machine-gun-toting tribe of Indians. By the way, the chief will find that the heavy weapons do not work. I have arranged for a pension to be paid to him and his tribe, through the Swedish embassy. They think it is for humanitarian reasons. All you have to do is to beg them to take you back." One of the marines by the bar sniggered. It was all so desperately unfair.

"Look here," Harry said from the stool he had sat down on. "I'm not going along with this. I want to see your boss. I demand to speak to Chambers."

Webster smiled. "Our boss has been moved," he said simply. "They've sent him up to Central America. That's where the trouble is going to be from now on. We are probably all going up there. No, you are not going to see or speak to anyone. And consider: if you ever did find someone to believe your story, what would be the point? You would only succeed in looking even more stupid and pathetic than you are at the moment."

The man is so bloody sure of himself. I'll show the bastard. Harry measured the distance to the door.

"I would like a drink," he said. "You seem to want to

destroy my life entirely but if you are not going to kill me I would like a drink. I really don't see why you have to be so bloody beastly."

Stebling offered an answer as he played with the top of his clipboard.

"We don't like unknown quantities any more, Harry. We don't like crazy half-assed individuals lousing things up for us. This operation out here was funded and thought up in Great Britain by people who had been at Oxford and Cambridge with known Soviet agents. Spies, Harry. It was their idea you came down here with that madman. Do you follow what I am saying? How can we be sure of you Harry?"

Right, thought Harry, that's bloody well it. They can accuse me of more or less everything else, but I have not betrayed my country. What was the use of talking to them? He flung himself towards the door, rolling on his bad leg past the sergeant and out into the bright sunlight. He wasn't going to play bloody silly games. And then he stopped.

The street was even emptier than before, although his Land Rover was still there. The body was gone and so was his pistol. He stood looking around him, smelling the smoke from the hillside. Someone had taken the girl away. Even the bloodstains were gone. When he first looked at her body there had been bloodstains from her head near the boardwalk. Had he imagined it all? If he went back into the room would he find no one there? The street was as hot as an oven and it baked in waves from the red earth up into the vast blue sky over the violent green of the hills beyond and the black smoke where his house had been. He thought numbly about his roses and about Maria and Hindle. How could she be so bloody disloyal? The engine of a truck started up on the other side of the *cantina*. Was he to spend the rest of his life begging from the Aché, people who had once been his slaves?

The truck turned into the main street, followed by a Jeep, full of American civilians he did not recognize. Three men and a woman. The woman was expensively dressed in a cream silk jacket and was holding a posy of roses. His roses from the house. She turned towards him.

"Maria!" he shouted. He could not help himself. He took a step towards the Jeep but the driver changed down and accelerated. She looked away, covering her face with her hand. "Maria how could you . . . ?" He was going to follow her in the Land Rover and had taken a step towards it when a blow caught him from behind. All he saw was a flash and the ground rushing up to meet him.

He was surprised to be alive as he woke. His watch had stopped but it was light outside. He supposed it was the morning of the next day. They must have drugged him as well as trying to bash in his skull. Now he was shackled by the legs in the little church to a long chain looped through the hole where the grille had been in the confessional box. It was made of heavy hardwood and impossible to move. He was at the back of the church but could see occasional stirrings on the street through a crack in the old door. In one group he caught sight of the unmistakable figure of Hindle, proud as a fighting cock strutting along the street, pausing for a moment to look at the church and then mercifully walking on, into a new life with new and deadly friends. Later they sent in a guard, a young American who placed Harry's Land Rover keys on the pew beside him.

"So you're the famous Doctor?"

"Yes, I'm the famous Doctor."

There didn't seem to be any point in the truth. He noticed someone had taken the Black Madonna from the altar along with the other trappings which made the building a church. Why couldn't he be more like Josef, that calm old German who felt no remorse? Harry shifted the chain. What had he done that was so wrong? If there was guilt in his mind it was for the things he hadn't done, for the choices he failed to make. All he had wanted to do was get home for a few years of peace and quiet, and what had started as a whim after years of drifting with the tide had led to all this: to the death of Petroni, to his plotting murder, to his house being burnt and the shooting and sinister holes near the airstrip. He would have sent the Aché to their deaths just to get away – and, indeed, by encouraging them to attack Labuschagne, he had done just that. He had, after all, expected them to come under machine-gun fire while he skulked at the rear. Was there really any difference between him and the Doctor?

He was glad they had taken the Madonna and her gentle accusing stare. They did not need to chain him, really: he had made his own. The American rolled fat cigarettes from acrid pipe tobacco and gave him one, and later brought him a hamburger and can of Coca-Cola. As the sun started to go down, he came over and undid the chain, placing the Land Rover keys in Harry's hand.

"I have orders to give these to you, Doctor. Your vehicle is gassed up and I'm to tell you to join the Aché. Mr Webster says the alternative risks have been explained to you." The fair-haired man smiled. He could have been explaining the rules of golf.

"Thank you very much. And for the cigarette."

"Thank you, Doctor. Goodbye. Safe journey now."

He walked slowly towards his Land Rover. He heard the young man's Jeep start behind him and roar away. He was the last to leave. He looked at his grimy face in the mirror, his eyes red from crying. Webster obviously didn't think he would do anything but go to Capitan Boda, that he was drained of energy. He started the engine, toying with the idea of going up to the house for a last look. But they had destroyed it as they had him; his roses would go back to the wild. He reached the fork in the road for Capitan Boda and the Aché. The other road led to Asunción. What, he wondered, would Josef do in his position? Yes, what would the old fox do?

Damn the consequences he thought and turned up the Asunción road in the gathering dusk. His mind, battered as it was, began to focus on the kind face of Mabel. Hadn't she said run to her if there was trouble? She knew plenty of Germans in Brazil who would assist them, who would help an old Nazi. The photographs Webster and Co. had released to the papers were an advantage now, for who would question his identity? His German was not bad. He would say he hadn't had much opportunity to speak it in recent years. They needn't know about Willy. Harry's mind was racing now. He had kept Josef hidden all these years by deceits and trickery. All he had to do was step into his shoes. It was about time he stopped obeying orders and thought for himself.

The words of the young American echoed in his brain.

"So you're the famous Doctor?"

"Yes, I'm the famous Doctor," he repeated out loud to the setting sun, smiling to himself. "Yes, I'm the famous Doctor."

Epilogue

On a cold day in October the Reverend Copeland-Smith of St Mary's Church, Berkhamsted was greeting his parishioners out of the fine Norman structure where he had just given a rousing sermon on the whole perplexing question of morality in international relations. By his side stood Mrs Agnes Copeland-Smith in a large floral hat, her ample chest swelling with pride, not only because her old but sprightly husband was much admired in the locality for devotion to his parish and for his fine mind, but because she had been awarded the OBE, quite out of the blue, for her government work. People understood about "government work" in that sleepy commuter town and were quietly mannered about the award, not making too big a thing of it. No one talked about it but everyone "knew" and that was enough for Agnes.

"Wake up Harold," she said to her husband, whose hands were clasped and his eyes closed. He turned his head and gave that quizzical little smile which irritated her. He spent all his time praying: one could take religion too far. "Say hello to Mr and Mrs Hamilton, dear. They made the donation to put the sink in the vestry. You remember dear, he is the secretary of the local Conservatives. We're coming to your cheese and wine party I hope? Shake hands Harold." She did not exactly give her husband a kick beneath his robes but touched his ankle firmly with her stout shoe.

"I think it will be a boon for the church and solve a lot of problems," said Mrs Hamilton as the blustery lead-grey sky threatened rain.

She looked identical to Agnes in many ways, but was wearing a different colour coat. People often took them for sisters. She had helped Harold with his English pronunciation when he was taking his divinity examinations, getting rid of that silly German accent he had picked up. Mrs Hamilton's shrill voice could probably be heard the other side of the churchyard.

"It will certainly stop those awful gypos from the 'site' filling their slop pails in the churchyard and walking over the new graves in their muddy boots. They just ignore the notice about no dogs, don't they Rupert? And Rupert found one of the ruffians had left a big end on his grandfather's grave. When he tried to move it, nearly doing himself a mischief in the process, the man came back and told him to leave it alone, that it was his and that he had put it there to be safe while he went to the pub. He threatened you with violence, didn't he Rupert? They did it on purpose to taunt us. And the women, dirty isn't the word. They should all be sterilized and to my mind the police should be allowed a free hand."

The man in the British Legion tie exchanged a look of fellow feeling with the vicar. There was something about him that reminded the vicar of Harry. They had never said what had happened to him. He felt it odd that here in England he had never met an Englishman quite like Harry. Often he thought he glimpsed that face in a congregation or bus queue and it sent a shiver down his spine. Where was Harry's sense of duty here? He had taken it for granted to find such qualities in Berkhamsted, but in many ways the people here were no different from those he had met in his early life. And for him to reach that conclusion was far from good.

Not that they were exactly evil, not in any planned way. He recalled his text for the sermon. "And when they were come out they (the devils) went into the herd of swine; and behold the whole herd ran violently down a steep place into the sea and perished in the waters." The vicar smiled to himself. In Paraguay if he had run with the herd Rupert might have ended up a drug smuggler and his wife a poorly paid whore.

Hertfordshire had to make do with less meaty sins.

"You will take a strong line with the gipsies vicar?" shouted Mrs Hamilton in his ear as if he were congenitally stupid or deaf.

"Oh yes," replied Agnes Copeland-Smith OBE. How he hated it when she spoke for him. "Oh yes, Harold can be firm. A little demon when he has to be be, aren't you dear? And he's had some experience of dealing with gipsies before, haven't you Harold?"

He gave a wise little nod. As his wife took his arm and they walked to the churchyard gate he whistled a snatch from *Tosca*. The Reverend Harry Copeland-Smith was looking forward to his lunch.

Brian Callison

'There can be no better adventure writer in the country today.' *Alistair MacLean*

'One of the best writers of modern sea stories.'
Daily Telegraph

A FRENZY OF MERCHANTMEN
A PLAGUE OF SAILORS
TRAPP'S PEACE
THE DAWN ATTACK
THE SEXTANT
A SHIP IS DYING
SPEARFISH
THE AURIGA MADNESS
THE BONE COLLECTORS
A FLOCK OF SHIPS
A WEB OF SALVAGE

FONTANA PAPERBACKS

Richard Sharpe

bold, professional and ruthless
is the creation of

Bernard Cornwell

A series of high adventure stories told in the grand tradition of Hornblower and set in the time of the Napoleonic wars, Bernard Cornwell's stories are firmly based on the actual events.

Sharpe's Eagle
Richard Sharpe and the Talavera Campaign, July 1809

Sharpe's Gold
Richard Sharpe and the Destruction of Almeida, 1810

Sharpe's Company
Richard Sharpe and the Siege of Badajoz, 1812

Sharpe's Sword
Richard Sharpe and the Salamanca Campaign,
June and July 1812

Sharpe's Enemy
Richard Sharpe and the Defence of Portugal,
Christmas 1812

Sharpe's Honour
Richard Sharpe and the Battle of Vitoria, 1813

'The best thing to happen to military heroes since Hornblower.' *Daily Express*

Adam Hall

'This is how the spy thriller should be written: foolproof plot, switchback-fast, every fact ringing right.'
The Times

'Adam Hall is Top Boy in the spy thriller class.'
Observer

THE TANGO BRIEFING
THE SINKIANG EXECUTIVE
THE SCORPION SIGNAL
THE MANDARIN CYPHER

FONTANA PAPERBACKS

Duncan Kyle

'One of the modern masters of the high adventure story.' *Daily Telegraph*

GREEN RIVER HIGH
BLACK CAMELOT
A CAGE OF ICE
FLIGHT INTO FEAR
TERROR'S CRADLE
A RAFT OF SWORDS
WHITEOUT!
STALKING POINT
THE SEMONOV IMPULSE

FONTANA PAPERBACKS

Patrick O'Brian

His highly praised novels of Nelson's navy follow the fortunes of Captain Jack Aubrey.

'Jack Aubrey is a worthy successor to Captain Hornblower.' *Sunday Mirror*

'Taken together the novels are a brilliant achievement. They display staggering erudition on almost all aspects of early nineteenth-century life, with impeccable period detail . . . in addition Patrick O'Brian has a gift for the comic which Forester lacks.' T. J. Binyon, *Times Literary Supplement*

MASTER AND COMMANDER
HMS *SURPRISE*
THE MAURITIUS COMMAND
THE FORTUNE OF WAR
THE SURGEON'S MATE
THE IONIAN MISSION
TREASON'S HARBOUR
DESOLATION ISLAND
POST CAPTAIN
THE FAR SIDE OF THE WORLD

FONTANA PAPERBACKS